P9-DYD-917

blue plate special

by Michelle D. Kwasney

chronicle books · san francisco

Library of Congress Cataloging-in-Publication Data
Kwasney, Michelle D., 1960–
Blue plate special / by Michelle D. Kwasney.
p. cm.
Summary: In alternating chapters, the lives of three teenage girls from three different generations are woven together as each girl learns about forgiveness, empathy, and self respect.
ISBN 978-0-8118-6780-1
[1. Forgiveness—Fiction. 2. Self-esteem—Fiction.
3. Mothers and daughters—Fiction.] I. Title.
PZ7.K9757Bl 2009
[Fic]—dc22
2009005322

Book design by Amy E. Achaibou.
Typeset in Adobe Caslon Pro.

Manufactured in China.

10 9 8 7 6 5 4 3 2

This product conforms to CPSIA 2008.

Chronicle Books LLC
680 Second Street, San Francisco, California 94107

www.chroniclekids.com

What the daughter does, the mother did. —Jewish Proverb

For all daughters

Madeline

ELMIRA, NEW YORK, 1977

"REGISTER FOUR IS NOW OPEN WITH NO WAITING," a ceiling voice booms, interrupting the Stevie Wonder tune playing over the intercom.

The light for the express lane blinks on. Mom hurries toward it, cutting off a white-haired lady in a fuzzy pink warm-up suit.

I straggle behind, trying to catch up. By the time I do, Mom's unloaded the contents of our basket onto the conveyor belt: a box of Ritz crackers, a jar of store-brand peanut butter, a six-pack of Pabst Blue Ribbon beer, and two cans of Coca-Cola. White Hair is parked behind Mom, emptying her carriage, clearly breaking the *Limit 12 Items* rule. I count ten cans of cat food, two packages of one-hundred-watt lightbulbs, a carton of Virginia Slims cigarettes, and a tube of generic hemorrhoid cream.

"Excuse me," I mumble, attempting to squeeze past her cart. But squeezing isn't a viable option when you weigh over two hundred pounds. My butt catches on a candy rack, dragging a shelf of Necco Wafers to the ground. I bend to pick them up, then straighten and smack my head on a newspaper display. President Carter's face glares at me, unforgiving.

"Excuse me," I say again, louder.

Finally, White Hair backs up to let me through and I step into line beside Mom.

Welcome to Grand Union! I'm Joyce! presses the register keys, totaling up our purchase. Joyce is as fat as I am, but she's a lot older and has large, bulgy frog eyes. The stone on her mood ring is black. "Nine dollars and sixty-two cents," she reports, staring past Mom and me.

Mom thumbs through a fistful of food stamps. Usually they're something I manage, since I do most of the shopping, but today she feels like playing grown-up.

Joyce stares at the stamps, like Mom's produced a handful of dog shit. "You can't pay for beer with *those,"* she snarls.

"I'm aware of that," Mom snarls back. She leans into my side, whispering, "Do you have four dollars I can borrow?" Her liner's painted thicker on one eye, making the two sides of her face seem mismatched.

"You already owe me twelve," I remind her.

White Hair cranes her neck to watch us. And even though I'm embarrassed, I'm pissed too. I turn to glare at her hemorrhoid cream. Her face reddens and she looks away.

"Pleeeaaassse?" Mom begs, pouting.

I hate it when she uses her whiny-little-girl voice. Huffing, I dig in my pocket.

Every month, after Mom signs her welfare check, I take it to the bank and cash it. After I pay the rent and utilities, I divide what remains between us. Mom's half covers her cigarettes and beer for the month. Or it's *supposed* to. With my half, I buy stuff like toilet paper and laundry detergent and soap—things food stamps don't cover. Whatever's left I hide in a red shoebox in the back of my closet. I've saved close to three hundred dollars that way. After I graduate, I plan to go to the community college and study to become a nurse. With the practice I've had taking care of Mom, I think I'd be good at that job. Plus, I'd get paid for it. Needless to say, Mom doesn't know about my shoebox. She'd be into it the minute she ran out of beer money.

I count out four ones for Mom, smoothing them flat on the counter.

Joyce rolls her big, bulgy frog eyes. "You still need nineteen cents."

I reach back into my pocket and pull out a dime and two nickels. Except I don't hand the coins to Joyce, I drop them on the conveyor belt, grinning as I watch her fat fingers struggle to collect them.

Mom cradles her Grand Union bag carefully—like it's a baby she's carrying—and starts for the *Exit* door.

Not bothering to wait for my penny, I follow her. Fast.

Or as fast as a fat girl can travel.

* * *

The hills along Route 17 are dabbed with early fall colors. It's over forty-five minutes to Cherry Hill Cemetery. Mom insists on driving, and I feel carsick. Then I get a headache. I reach into my pocketbook for two aspirin and swallow them down with my Coke.

By the time we reach the cemetery, the sun is low in the sky. The graveyards closer to home lock their gates at dusk, but not Cherry Hill. It's there for Mom anytime, day or night, making it her cemetery of choice for what we're about to do.

Mom passes the visitor's center, weaves through the narrow lanes, and parks her Charger in our usual spot.

As I walk to the trunk for our grocery bag, leaves crunch under my feet. I carry the bag to where we always sit—beside a white concrete angel that's a good foot taller than I am. Her wings are spread open, her back is arched, and the folds in her gown churn around her. She reminds me of the winged victory goddess I saw slides of in art history class, except this statue has a head. The inscription carved on her base says:

SOPHIE DESALVO
BELOVED DAUGHTER
MARCH 1, 1959–SEPTEMBER 15, 1961

We were born the same year, except Sophie had only two birthdays, which is completely unfair. Death should be reserved for old people like White Hair. I picture her slumped across the conveyer belt at Grand Union, grabbing her heart with one hand, clutching a tube of generic hemorrhoid cream with the other.

Next to Sophie's angel, a fountain gurgles. A breeze blows and I feel the spray on my face. Even after I blink several times, the droplets still cling to my lashes.

Before getting out of the car, Mom cranks up the radio and rolls down a window. Neil Diamond's gravelly voice leaps out, puncturing the dusky silence. Even though he's singing one of my favorite songs—the one about the misunderstood gull from the movie *Jonathan Livingston Seagull*—it doesn't stop me from thinking that it's disrespectful to play pop tunes where people are buried. But mentioning this to my mother wouldn't do any good. This is part of her ritual.

Mom joins me, unfolding the wooly blanket she keeps in the backseat. It's left over from an old boyfriend, Jake. He had a dog, and the blanket still smells just like him. The dog, that is, not Jake. She opens the blanket across the low flat stone she calls Our Rock. As if that cold gray mass is meaningful because we've claimed it. As if we've made some mark on the world by sitting here time after time—that in a hundred years, after we're both dead and gone, someone will put a plaque on the stone that reads: *Leona and Madeline Fitch Once Sat Here.*

The sky turns a deep, shimmery pink, so bright it doesn't look real.

Mom pops the top on a can of beer. She tips her head back, swallowing again and again, like she hasn't had liquid in a week. I open the peanut butter and dip crackers in the brown goo, savoring the thick, salty crunch.

By the time Mom's finished her fifth beer, and I've polished off the crackers, the last band of color has disappeared behind the black hills. I glance at the moon, which hovers over Sophie's angel, bathing the concrete in cool, silvery light.

I lick my finger, dab Ritz crumbs off the shelf my boobs make, then eat those tiny flakes too. I'm still hungry. I have a bottomless chasm in my middle. The Beast, I call it. Sometimes it's insatiable—I could peel Grand Union open like a can of SPAM and empty all the aisles down my throat, and even then the Beast would cry, *"More!"*

Mom starts on beer number six. It's the one I call the Talking Beer. Soon she'll fill the night with more words than you'd ever guess she owned.

I lean my head back, glancing up at the stars. I find one that blinks on and off and I study it, praying it's telling me something.

My mother burps, and I can smell the beer stench on her breath. Without excusing herself, she announces, "I won't be seeing Kyle anymore."

Of course, I already know this. That's why we're here at the cemetery, after all. To mourn another lost boyfriend. To add another name to the Men Who Ditched Leona Fitch list.

"I thought he was going to be the one," she continues. "He was so thoughtful."

She's right. Kyle was thoughtful. He gave me a brown bobblehead dog the first time Mom brought him home to meet me. And he earned bonus points for the fact that—in the six weeks he dated Mom—I never once caught him staring at my rolls of fat or my massive chest. But eventually Kyle bailed out, just like all the others.

There's a long silence between us.

Mom pokes me with her bony elbow. "*You* gotta boyfriend yet?"

"Dozens." I roll my eyes. "Boys know fat's where it's at."

Mom extends a finger, playfully tapping my chin—actually two chins—and I get a lump in my throat. She almost never touches me. Not that I blame her. People don't like to touch fat. "Maybe if you dressed a lil' diff'rent. . . ." she slurs. "Maybe if you showed a lil' flesh, you'd get some action."

"Right," I snap. "Welcome to Sea World. Step right up and pet a real live whale. Can't get much sexier than that."

Mom gets quiet again.

I glance over, seeing if she's still upright.

"We're quita pair," she says, forcing a smile. "I drinka lil' too much and you eata lil' too much." She lifts her Talking Beer toward a patch of stars. "Here's to whatever makes you happy."

Her head drops, landing on the giant hill my shoulder makes.

Softly, she starts to cry.

Happy is the last thing I'd call us.

Desiree

Johnson City, New York, 1993

as i try to sleep
a mouse squeals.
i picture him struggling
to unglue his tiny body
from the damn sticky paper
mam (my asshole mother)
uses to trap rodents
in our apartment.
i imagine how that
poor, dumb creature
must feel—
lying there,
unable to
move,
slowly
dying.

* * *

i wonder where
i'll be in three years
when i turn eighteen—
if i'll have some stupid job at kmart
like mam,
or if me and jeremy
will move in together and
rent matching duplex apartments
with carol ann and eric.
us girls will learn to cook
while jeremy and eric watch football.
and when we decide to have kids,
i'll be the best mom on the planet.
i'll read my little girl stories
and french braid her hair
and make her cocoa when it snows.
she'll never hear what i heard:
i'm too tired.
i've got a headache.
it's time for my soaps.
no *e*'s for effort there.
screw that.

* * *

larry is the only guy
mam's dated since i was born.
at first i thought
he must be desperate
or in a passing mood for some pork,
but he's stuck around for over a year.

two weeks before summer vacation,
he asks mam and me out to dinner.
i'm sick of studying for finals,
glad to have something else to do.

in larry's brown nissan
he chomps a toothpick
while mam rants
about her swollen feet.
i'm in the back with my walkman,
guns n' roses ripping through my brain
as i doodle jeremy's name on my jeans.

at ponderosa
we act like a family—
nice but scary too,
especially if you're not used to it.

after dessert
we window-shop at the mall.
a sappy michael bolton song
oozes through the turd-colored walls,
and mam reaches for larry's hand,
telling him she loves that song.

i roll my eyes and gag,
but i'm stopped in my tracks
by a black halter top
on a headless mannequin
i absolutely have to buy.
except all i have is twenty bucks and
the shirt costs twenty-six.

i beg mam to float me the extra.
instead she goes ballistic.
you're not going anywhere in that,
looking like a two-bit hooker!

i think i'll combust,
my face is so hot.
i bolt toward the nearest exit,
expecting mam to call, *come back!*
but she doesn't.

i pause at a candy kiosk,
turn to see if she's watching.
larry waves.
mam just stands there.
i grab an almond joy,
shove it in my pocket,
and hurry straight for the door.

* * *

home's five miles away
and i'm too chicken to hitchhike,
so i lean against larry's car,
waiting for the happy couple to return.

a half hour later
we're packed inside the nissan again.
the a/c doesn't work.
the hot vinyl burns my legs.
mam's sweat smells like fried fish.

i open my window,
lean my head out, inhaling.
on the return trip, no one speaks,
but there could be worse things in life
than icy silence on a freaking hot night.

* * *

at home
i change into a tank top and shorts.
i have to walk past mam and larry
to stick my melted almond joy
bar in the fridge.

they're parked on the sofa
between two pedestal fans,
drinking beer and channel surfing,
reminding me of a pair of trained monkeys.
mam stops at *murphy brown.*
go put some clothes on, dez.

i roll my eyes.
give me a break.
this is how people dress.
normal people, i want to add.
mam wears long sleeves year-round.

from the kitchen
i hear mam tell larry,
she dresses like a whore.
fuck you, i say, so quiet

i think she won't hear me.
except she does.
mam charges.
her palm cracks against my cheek
so hard i bite my tongue and taste blood.
she's about to take another swing
when larry grabs her from behind.
go, dez, he hollers, *get out of here!*
so i do. i get the hell out.

* * *

jeremy's parents are at a movie.
we hang out at his place,
smoke a joint,
watch a few episodes
of *the simpsons,*
make out.

i get home around midnight,
shaking from the damp night air.
mam's bedroom door is open.
she's asleep,
alone,
a gross glob of snoring flesh.

my stomach rumbles.
i head to the fridge for my almond joy.
returning through the living room,
i notice him—larry—
spread out across our sofa.

when he sees me,
he sits up quickly,
his shadow
slicing the quiet,
knifelike, precise.

his cool blue eyes singe
the gray space between us.
he pats the sofa
like his hand is saying,
come here, but i don't.
i drop down across from him,
in the chair mam sits in to watch
all my children and *general hospital,*
tv pals she prefers to me.

sinking into the crater in the cushion,
i peel back the wrapper on the almond joy.
because there are two matching halves,
i decide i should offer one to larry.
i hold the candy bar out to him.
larry swallows his half whole.
he doesn't even chew the nut.
is she still pissed? i ask.

larry stands. *she'll get over it.*
he walks toward mam's room,
pauses by the hallway night-light,
shakes his head back and forth.
then he closes her door.
slowly. quietly.

when larry returns,
i notice his shirt
is unbuttoned.
his chest hairs poke out
like one of those wiry doormats
you wipe your boots on in winter.
he catches me looking,
and my face heats up.
i stand to leave,
but larry says,
hey, not so fast.

he reaches beneath the sofa,
removing a wrinkled bag.
i know your birthday was two weeks ago,
but here—he hands it out to me—
i got you a belated gift.

i peer inside suspiciously,
in case it's a trick,
but it isn't.
holding up the halter top
mam went nuclear over,
i ignore what larry says next.
i can't wait to see it on you, dez.

Ariel

Poughkeepsie, New York, 2009

WAITING FOR MY OLD DELL TO BOOT UP, I finger-dust the shell set Dad gave me three years ago on my twelfth birthday. The shells are organized in a clear shadow box with tiny labels identifying each one. My favorite is the miniature conch—bumpy and white on the outside, smooth and pink on the inside. Mom has one just like it, except she found hers herself, on a beach near where we used to live. On the card that came with the gift Dad wrote, *Maybe these will help you remember Florida, Peaches.* Apparently, peach was my favorite baby-food flavor. I can't remember, just like I can't recall living in Florida, but I never remind Dad of that.

My monitor blinks on and I smile at the desktop photo of Dad and me, taken the morning we left the Sunshine State. My enormous diapered butt is balanced on his wide, lean shoulders, and there's something pink spilled down the front of my onesie. Dad is bare-chested and sunburned. He's wearing denim cutoffs, and his long sandy hair is held back by a red bandanna, which I'm clutching with my small, dimpled hands.

Looking at that sweet little-boy face, I'd never peg Dad as a murderer. But he is.

When the jury found him guilty and the judge sentenced him to twenty years in prison—reduced because he was a minor—Mom claims he never made a single excuse. To this day, Dad says he did what he had to after he learned the Truth. Whoever said "the truth shall set you free" didn't have him in mind. For Dad, it did just the opposite.

I don't blame him. I miss him, that's all. Sometimes I haul out his old CDs and play them on the antique boom box stored in the basement with his stuff. Or I open up the foot locker that holds his clothes, hugging a sweatshirt, inhaling his smell, imagining how his voice might've sounded when he read me a bedtime story, picturing what our first snowman might've looked like. I dream about the day he'll live with us again, but Mom tells me not to get my hopes up. That even if Dad does get paroled early, it'll take time to see if, quote, *their relationship is still intact,* unquote.

We visit Dad four times a year—near all our birthdays and again before Christmas—and he and I talk on the phone. I'd love to see him more often, but the drive is rough, over three hundred miles each way, so four trips is all Mom can manage.

I sign in to check my e-mail, glad there's a message from Olivia.

> Hey Ariel,
> Dad and Steve are having a dinner party Friday night at 7.
> They're making baked lobster, your favorite! Can you come?
> XO, Liv

Of course, I'll have to disappoint her. Friday is date night with Shane.

I hear Mom's car pull into the garage. Minutes later, the kitchen door opens abruptly, smacking the wall behind it.

"Shit!" she says, followed quickly by "Sorry! I owe a dollar!" Mom claims that when she was my age, every other word out of her mouth was a swear, so she uses a Potty Mouth Jar to keep from having a relapse.

"Hi, Mom," I call, starting for the kitchen.

Her book bag is crammed with folders and legal pads. Mom works for Aunt Lee as a research assistant, and whenever Aunt Lee's near a book deadline, Mom carts home tons of work.

I rescue the brown paper sack tucked beneath her arm. One whiff tells me it's filled with Chinese takeout. I peek inside the first of four containers. Shrimp with cashews and snow peas, my favorite. Immediately, my mouth waters.

Mom wriggles out of her coat, kicks off her shoes, and hurries down the hall. "Gotta go! Gotta go!" she calls, imitating the overactive bladder commercial. The bathroom door whips closed.

I set out place mats and plates, toss out the napkins that came with the meal, and reach for two linen ones instead. Mom grew up poor, so she insists on the real McCoy.

Mom reappears, sipping what's left of her morning tea, then collapses in a chair.

"Long day?" I ask.

She glances at her overstuffed book bag. "You know it. Aunt Lee's editor wants to see part three by the end of next week."

Sitting across from Mom, I unfold my napkin on my lap. I'd die if I got anything on my new low-rise jeans. They're Shane's favorite pair. He says I look sexy in them. *Me.* Sexy. God. I hand Mom the brown rice and keep the white for myself. "Does Aunt Lee think she'll meet her deadline?"

Mom smiles. "Remember who we're talking about."

"Right," I say, filling my plate. "I forget, Aunt Lee invented Type A behavior."

I stand, heading to the fridge for more soy sauce. The chintzy packets you get with your take-out are never enough. When I open the door, a *Hillary for President* magnet drops to the ground. I keep bugging Mom to pack up her campaign gear, but she refuses. Maybe she's waiting to see if Hillary will try again in 2012.

I restick the magnet, grab the soy sauce, and hurry back to my seat. A shrimp is gripped between my chopsticks, about to be devoured, when the phone rings.

Mom groans. "I'll bet it's a telemarketer."

I'd like to remind her that if we had a phone with caller ID, we'd know who it is. But Mom doesn't believe in replacing things before they break or die a natural death. So we've been stuck with the same antique cordless for, like, ten years. Thank God for gifts from Aunt Lee. If it weren't for her, we probably wouldn't even own a microwave.

"I'll get it." I hurry for the phone before it stops ringing, but it isn't on the charger where it should be. I sprint from room to room, hoping it's Olivia calling. In middle school we nicknamed our predinner conversations the Nightly Food Report. I'd tell Liv what Mom was making for supper and she'd tell me what her dad's partner, Steve, was cooking. Then we'd score their choices like we were judging the Olympics: Mom—chicken tetrazzini: 8.2; Steve—salmon patties with lemon-dill sauce and parmesan-herb risotto: 9.6. We never reported vegetables; they were irrelevant. In high school, the food report fizzled because we both agreed it was juvenile. But we still talk every night. Well, we did until two months ago when I started dating Shane.

I finally locate the phone under a futon pillow and press Talk. "Hello?"

A man announces he's Doctor somebody and asks to speak to Mom. I return to the kitchen and hand her the phone.

"Yes?" Mom listens intently. The color drains from her cheeks. She coughs. Excuses herself. Takes another sip of tea. "Are you sure?" she asks.

"Mom," I whisper. "Did something happen to Dad?"

She shakes her head no.

"Aunt Lee?"

Another no.

"Who then?"

Mom's chair scrapes the floor as she stands. She crosses the room and reaches in the junk drawer for a pen. I follow and look over her shoulder. On a pad she writes: *Chemung County General, River Road, Elmira.* Which is no help to me.

"Thank you for calling," she says flatly, hanging up. She holds the phone against her chest like she's cradling a small, hurt bird.

Mom says there are pivotal moments in life that divide our existence into distinct compartments. Like when she had me at sixteen, life became Before Ariel and After Ariel. She could never go back to being who she had been. As I take the phone from her, returning it to its base, I have an eerie feeling this might be one of those moments.

When I glance at her again, she's crying. "Mom," I say, "what's wrong?"

She grabs a tissue and dabs her eyes. "It's my mother."

Mom never talks about her mother. Not that I mind. As far as I'm concerned she's just a mean old woman who kicked Mom out of the house when she was fifteen and pregnant. "What about her?" I ask. It comes out sounding cold, but I don't care.

"She asked the hospital staff to try and locate me. They Googled me so her doctor could call and tell me . . ." Mom hesitates. "She has stage-three breast cancer."

"Breast cancer," I repeat matter-of-factly.

"She had a double mastectomy today. She was in surgery for eight hours."

I look down at my own breasts, which aren't big enough to draw attention, but they're there. Where they should be. Both of them. "Is she going to die?" I ask.

"I don't know," Mom answers.

My mouth is so dry, my lips stick together. I walk to the fridge for a bottle of water, press it against my hot cheeks, then take several long swallows.

I've never even met my mother's mother. And I probably wouldn't like her if I did. But, still, I feel this ache, this *loss.* And I have no idea why.

Mom walks to the window over the sink. Her mascara's running and she looks like the guys on Dad's old KISS CD. She twirls the wand on the blinds, shutting out the fading sunset. Then she starts down the hall toward her room. Once inside, she closes her door, and the sound of it echoes in the hall. A closed door means *I need time/space to think,* a message we both respect. Except it's usually me who sends it. Mom hasn't closed her door since the judge denied Dad's parole request two years ago.

When I taste my food again, it's cold. I stick my plate in the microwave and push the reheat button. I wait near the window, reverse-twirling the wand on the blinds. Bands of magenta ooze like spilled paint across the darkening sky. Second by second, they shift, growing thinner, sparser.

The microwave beeps, but I don't move. Not until the last band has vanished.

Madeline

CONSIDERING THE SHAPE MOM'S IN WHEN WE LEAVE the cemetery—and the fact that she had her license revoked after her last DWI—she doesn't balk when I ask for the car keys. And I don't argue when she tells me she wants more beer.

I pull into a 7-Eleven. Bugs circle the light above the door. A red neon lottery sign buzzes, blinking *Win Big.*

Mom reaches under her seat, wiggles her fingers inside a rip in the cushion, and produces a five-dollar bill. I don't mention the money she owes me.

She weaves toward the glass storefront. School started a few days ago so the displays are still lined with notebook paper and calculators and pencils. Inside, Mom darts past them, heading straight for the beer cooler.

A shiny blue Camaro pulls into the parking space beside me. Its windows are open, and the radio is cranked up high. I recognize the station right away—92 Rock Revue out of Binghamton. When Janis Joplin starts singing "Me and Bobby McGee," the bass pounds like a second heartbeat in my chest. I lean back, rest my neck on the headrest, and close my eyes. I mouth the words to the song. And I breathe. Deeply. Relaxing, I let go. My hands drop from the steering wheel and land with a silent thud in my lap. Nothing exists anymore. Not the car or the store or the empty can my toe crunches against when I straighten my legs. Nothing. Nada. Zip. Everything has disappeared. Dissolved. Me included. I'm not Fatty Maddie or the Fat Girl Nobody Talks To. I am bodiless. Liberated. A spirit that moves with the music.

I have a secret fantasy that somewhere there's another person who understands how I feel. Someone who knows what it's like to ache because the words to a song are so beautiful. Who feels the melody pulse through his veins, more real than his own blood. Someone whose throat tightens and eyes dampen because there's no way to contain the emotion.

When the song ends, a commercial for Tame Creme Rinse zaps me back to reality. As I open my eyes and glance sideways, a boy hops out of the Camaro. He's a few years older than me, and his hair is cut in a shag. When the dome light comes on, the girl in the passenger seat shields her eyes. "You want anything?" the boy asks her.

The girl looks away, twirling a strand of long blond hair around one finger. She reminds me of Marcia Brady.

Annoyed, the boy says, "I *asked* you a question. You want anything?"

Still, Marcia Brady doesn't answer. I wonder if she's his girlfriend. If maybe they've just had a fight.

"Frig that," he says, yanking his keys from the ignition. He slams the car door, and the dome light cuts off. And 92 Rock Revue vanishes too.

The night fills with unwelcome silence. My brain kicks into gear, reminding me that I am a body, not a spirit.

I watch the boy swing the store door open. Watch him pass Mom in the potato chip aisle then peer inside the cooler she left moments ago.

Marcia Brady reaches for a poncho. It's crocheted in citrus-colored zigzags like the afghan I want to start in home ec class. She slips it over her head and leans forward, resting her face against the dash. Her pale hair shimmers, pink in the lottery light's glow.

I wish I could be her for five minutes.

When the girl sits up again, I notice she's crying. How could someone so thin, so pretty—riding in a shiny blue Camaro with a boy who remembers to ask if she wants anything—possibly be that upset?

Abruptly, the girl turns. In my direction. Her face tightens and her sadness evaporates, replaced by sudden irritation. She scowls, yelling through her window. "What are you staring at, fat girl?"

"N—nothing," I stammer. I look away, exhale, slump down low in my seat. Crouched, I count to sixty, deciding one full minute is enough time to prove I'm sorry. But when I try to straighten up, there's a problem. One of my stomach rolls is wedged beneath the steering wheel. Frantically, I jerk from side to side, except it doesn't do any good. I'm trapped. I can't move, can't breathe.

Panicking, I grip the steering wheel to lift myself out. But the wheel is slippery and my hand slides off, smacking the horn, sounding a long, loud blast.

People inside the store turn to gawk. Marcia Brady stares too. And when her boyfriend reappears, dropping a six-pack of Budweiser in the backseat, the girl pokes his arm, pointing at me, saying, "Check out the fat girl. She's stuck!"

I look down at my pinned stomach. Then up at the boy and girl, laughing. At Mom, walking toward our car, cradling her beer like a baby again. I bite my lip to keep from crying.

Mom slides in and slurs, "Whassamatta? Yourfaceisallred."

My heart slams against my chest. "I'm stuck!" I blurt out.

Mom's eyes focus on my pinned stomach. She starts to giggle, then presses a finger to her lips, shushing herself. "Thelatchisontheside," she manages, nodding toward the floor.

Jesus, I'm so stupid.

I feel for the lever on the lower edge of my seat. Hold it in, press it back. The seat glides away from the steering wheel. Finally, I can breathe.

Elton John sings "Goodbye Yellow Brick Road" as the Camaro pulls out of the space. A space the boy won't remember parking in five days from now, or five months, or five years.

But I'll remember. Because I will always be stuck here. In this spot. In this body. I will never be a spirit. Or anything other than what I am.

As his car merges onto the main road, Marcia Brady's still laughing.

* * *

By the time I pull into our driveway, Mom is passed out cold. I wake her and help her out, steadying her as she stumbles up the steps to our apartment.

Inside, she collapses on our sofa. Within seconds, she's snoring.

I slip her shoes off and put them in her closet, careful not to disturb the pillars of playing cards stacked in one corner. A carton of Mom's cigarettes comes with a free deck, and she's saved over two hundred of them, still wrapped in their original plastic. Lord knows what she plans to do with them. Maybe build a house someday.

Returning to the couch, I open the ratty green blanket folded across the back—the one I plan to replace with a homemade afghan—and I spread it across Mom's sleeping form. "G'night," I say, even though I know she can't hear me.

Desiree

dressing for school,
i slip on a black pleather skirt
and my new halter top—
mostly to keep mam from finding it
when she snoops through my stuff,
treating me like a whore
who can't be trusted.
she has no clue
i'm still a virgin.

over the halter top
i button a denim shirt,
tie it in a knot at my waist.
i twist my long, dark hair into a coil
and clip it at the back of my head.

downstairs,
mam's at the kitchen table,
watching the morning news,

pigging out on sugar doughnuts.
as i walk to the fridge
and pour some o.j.
her eyes bore holes into my back.
skirt's kinda short, isn't it?
her version of good morning,
and a thick-tongued and slurry
one at that.
sure as hell,
she's stoned on headache pills again.

i down my juice,
turn to set my glass in the sink.
still, she's studying me,
recording my many fuckups:
skirt's too short,
hair's too long,
makeup's too heavy.
too, too, too.
why are you staring at me?

she reaches for another doughnut.
sometimes i can't believe
how much you look like
—she cuts herself off—
someone i used to know.

who?

without answering,
she reaches for the tv clicker

and ups the volume,
dismissing me.

* * *

after the last bell,
i meet jeremy and carol ann
by the bike rack.
eric used to walk home with us too,
but he lined up an after-school job
at the gas 'n' go
making five bucks an hour.
lucky shit.

the three of us stop
at farth's market,
aka the fart mart.
jeremy uses a fake i.d.
to get a bottle of cheap sangria
and a pack of newport 100s.
i don't like menthol,
but i keep my mouth shut.
jeremy's buying
and i am totally broke.

outside the fart mart, we light up,
start our usual trek
along a dirt road
littered with crap
no one ever cleans up—
beer cans, food wrappers, used condoms.

just ahead
the water tower rises
like a huge blue zit from
the pockmarked pavement below.
we lean against the turquoise blue tank,
unscrew the twist top on the wine,
pass the bottle back and forth.
the warmth goes off inside me,
a bomb that quiets everything.

carol ann tells knock-knock jokes
that aren't the least bit funny,
but i slap my knee,
pretending they are,
because laughing
feels so damn good.

when the wine is gone,
we walk into town,
mildly buzzed, wavering.
burger king smells taunt me.
i'm starving. either of you got cash?

sorry, jeremy answers,
spent all mine at the fart mart.
carol ann glances at her watch.
it's time for dinner. i should go.
me too, jeremy says.
ma's making meat loaf tonight.
aw—i scruff his hair—
her baby's favorite meal.

he slaps my hand away.
jealous?

of course i am.
carol ann's parents
are crunchy granola, and
jeremy's mom sees a shrink,
but they've still got mam beat.

we're about to go our separate ways
when larry's brown nissan
slows to the curb beside us.
my long, skinny legs are reflected
in his mirrored sunglasses
as he leans his arm on the window ledge.
hey, good lookin', wanna ride?

jeremy and carol ann exchange a look that says,
who's-that-crusty-old-perv-coming-on-to-her?
so i tell them, *it's cool.*
larry's my mother's boyfriend.
then,
because i feel lazy
and riding trumps walking,
i wave good-bye and
swing the door open.

there's a paper bag
on the front seat.
dinner, larry explains.
you can toss it in the back.

when i move it, i peek inside.
there's a six-pack of beer,
a bag of doritos,
and a grinder,
meatballs and sauce.

my stomach groans. majorly.
larry laughs. *hungry?*
i sit, buckle up. *starving.*
well, then—he turns down a side street—
let's find a place to eat.

larry parks behind the train tracks.
a salvage yard's on one side,
woods are on the other,
and the air smells like dirty socks.

we sit on the hood,
still warm from the engine,
and larry parks the bag between us.
within seconds
we're chowing down.

larry twists the tops off two buds,
passing one my way.
it's nice to be treated
like a grown-up for a change.
i clink my bottle against his. *cheers!*

how'd your day go? he asks,
a question mam never thinks of.

i shrug. *the usual.*
school's not my favorite topic.
i show up. i leave.
maybe someday
i'll graduate.

when the sandwiches are history,
larry claps crumbs off his hands,
reaches in his pocket for a smoke,
then tips the pack my way.
come on, have one.
i won't rat ya out to your ma.

as we sit there, smoking,
larry complains about mam—
how she's getting more headaches
and taking more pills
and never has energy for anything.
he emphasizes *anything.*
i read between the lines.
gross.
i don't know how you put up with her,
i say, my words all loose and slurry,
and this time it's larry who shrugs.

* * *

larry finishes three beers,
and i polish off two.
when i lie back on the hood,
the clouds spin

and my stomach feels like hell.
i sit up slowly, telling myself,
you will not be sick,
you will not be sick.
still, i lurch forward,
hurl orange dorito barf on larry's fender
and all down the front of my shirt.
damn.

tears fill my eyes.
larry reaches over. *hey, it's okay.*
you got something on underneath this?
i nod. *yeah.*

he undoes the knot
on my skanky shirt,
lifts it over my head.
i actually believe him
—that it'll be okay—
until i notice
him staring.
hey, the top
looks great on you.

i cross my arms.
cleavage appears.
i uncross them.
larry opens the last beer and tips it back.
gluggluggluggluggluggluglug.

i close one eye because
i suddenly see two of him.
i wanna go home.

no you don't, dez. trust me.

whaddaya mean?
i try to sit up straight
without lopping to the side,
but it's hard.
why don't i wanna go home?

your ma went on a royal rant.
she trashed your room today
after finding a love note
from that jerry boy.

shit! *jeremy,* i correct him.
what'd she say?

larry rubs his chin.
she said, i quote, if she's sleeping
with that loser, i'll kill her.

i roll my eyes. *bitch.*
larry nods like he agrees.
so, are you?

am i what?

sleeping with him.

jesus, that's none of your business!

we're quiet as roadkill.
clouds gobble up the sun.
a raindrop lands on my shoulder,
then another.

i slide off larry's hood,
stumble toward the passenger side,
where i trip on something.
the ground rises up to meet me.
like a plastic straw
someone dropped
on the cafeteria floor,
larry picks me up that easily.
i wait for him to let go,
but he doesn't.
the solid place
between his legs
hardens as he
presses against me.

heavy rain stings my arms.
my halter top sticks to my front.
larry inches me toward the car,
tips the passenger seat forward,
waves his hand toward the back.
why don't you climb in?
you can lay down.

you'll feel better.

no. i wanna sit in the front.
i wanna go home now. please.
i reach to push the seat in place,
but larry sticks his arm out,
blocking me.

i.
want.
to.
go.
home.

larry doesn't listen.
he takes my small hand in his giant one
and backs me through the open door.
i know what is about to happen.
it never occurs to me
that i can stop it.

again
i'm that
plastic straw.
larry is bending me,
bending me, lowering me
onto the ugly plaid blanket
i've sat on dozens of times,
doodling jeremy's name on my jeans.
his boozy breath,
hot on my neck, whispers,

dez, i've wanted you for so long.
i tell him, *no, no, no,*
but the sound can't leave my throat
because a shadow collapses my lungs—
a heavy shadow with chest hair
like a wiry floor mat
that scrubs and scrubs
at my bare breasts,
and i wonder,
where did my halter top go?

before i can ask
my skirt's hiked up to my waist
and larry's pants are unzipped.

rain pounds the windshield,
and day surrenders to night.
black birds cackle and call,
and trees fold in on the car,
enclosing us
in giant parentheses.

as the thunder rolls in,
i say good-bye.
good-bye to
the mind that was mine
and the body that was mine,
which suddenly
aren't mine
anymore.

now
i am a speck
of something microscopic
stuck to the dome
of the ceiling light,
watching a man's ass
pump up and down,
up and down,
watching a girl's hair
unravel like a skein
of dark yarn,
watching her
face go blank
as a smooth stone
someone has tossed
out to sea and
possibly,
quite
possibly,
forgotten.

MOM'S SITTING AT THE KITCHEN TABLE wearing the lavender bathrobe I bought her two Christmases ago. She's just showered and her hair hangs in long, damp waves. She looks so young. It's no wonder people confuse us for sisters.

As I walk into the kitchen, two slices of cinnamon-raisin bread pop out of the toaster. Mom glances up. "Honey, would you—?" she starts, but I've already grabbed a butter knife and plate.

I set the buttered toast beside Mom's Earl Grey tea. When I grab a Dr. Pepper from the fridge, she gives me the evil eye and gets up to pour me an OJ instead.

"Thanks," I say sarcastically.

Mom sits again, dunking her tea bag up and down.

I notice that her eyes are puffy. "Still thinking about the phone call?"

Mom nods. "I can't figure out what to do. Aunt Lee's got a book deadline coming up, and I'm not even halfway through collecting—"

"Mom, what are you talking about? What's Aunt Lee got to do with this?"

She meets my gaze. Sometimes it gives me the creeps how much we look alike: same olive skin, high cheekbones, long dark hair. Only our eyes are different. Mom's are brown as dark chocolate, and mine are blue like my father's. My biological father's, that is. Though Mom's always quick to point out that, unlike his, *my* eyes are a warm, vibrant blue—like a cloudless sky or cotton candy.

Mom's teacup comes in for a not-so-graceful landing, clunking hard against the saucer. "I need to see her."

"But you'll see her today," I say, sure she means Aunt Lee. "At work. Right?"

"I'm not talking about Aunt Lee." She swallows hard. "I need to see my mother."

I squint, as if Mom's a blur I'm trying to bring into focus. "But you told me you didn't want anything to do with her, and that's why I've never—"

Mom holds up a finger, shushing me. "She's got cancer. That changes all the rules."

* * *

It's only mid-November, but the cold weather must have put some of our neighbors in a festive mood. As I leave for school, I notice several have hung their holiday lights. I breathe into my scarf, hoping the half-mile walk will warm me.

Olivia's waiting for me in the usual spot—in front of the Starbucks a block from our school. She's hovered over the steam from her latte, marching in place to keep her feet from freezing. When she sees me walking toward her, she reaches to collect her stuff off the metal newspaper box beside her. But she's interrupted by a bleep. She flips her phone open, moving her lips as she reads. "Text from Steve," she says without looking up. "My after-school cello lesson's canceled. Hang on, I'm gonna answer. This'll only take a sec." Her thumbs fly faster than I can follow. Then she claps her cell closed and peers at me over her glasses. "God, you look terrible. What's wrong?"

"Nice greeting."

Liv grabs her things and we start to walk.

"I'm serious. If I could read auras, yours would be the color of pocket lint. Did you and Shane have a fight or something?"

I almost never talk about Shane with Liv. Her dad's a psychotherapist, which has rubbed off on her; she tends to overanalyze things. "No," I explain, "I didn't sleep well. Last night Mom got a phone call from a hospital upstate."

"Is someone sick?"

"Her mother."

Liv sips her latte and her glasses fog up. "You never mentioned having a grandmother."

"I've never met her. Mom and her haven't spoken in, like, forever."

"Then why the sudden interest?" Liv asks.

"Her mother has breast cancer."

Liv turns to face me. "Oh, Ariel, I am so sorry."

I shrug. "Thanks."

We stop at the crosswalk opposite school, waiting for the light to turn.

"My mom, um," I start. "She wants to see her."

"Ouch. Family Dysfunction One-oh-One. Are you going too?"

The light turns and we cross.

Nervously, I laugh. "I have no clue."

"Well, when would you leave if you did?" Without waiting for my answer, Liv adds, all dramatic, "*Please* don't say this weekend. The dinner party is Friday."

I don't tell her that I wouldn't have been able to make it anyway—like I said, Friday night is date night with Shane. I just frown and say, "Yeah, I know."

On the steps up to the school a band geek carrying a trombone case cuts ahead to hold the door open for us. "Hey, Liv," he says, smiling widely.

"Hey, Derek," Liv says back. "See you at practice tomorrow."

When he's out of range, she rolls her eyes.

"A secret crush?"

"Not too terribly secret. But so not going anywhere."

We start down the hall toward the junior homerooms. In the distance, I see Shane, waiting at my locker for me. I feel the same rush I felt the day he appeared in my study hall after transferring in from California. His eyes were so dark they looked black, his lips were full and inviting, and his thick, just-below-the-ears hair fell in shaggy waves I found myself wanting to run my fingers through. And when he stood to leave, I couldn't help noticing how his 501 jeans hugged his lean but lovely backside.

Today he's wearing his biker jacket, a Ludacris T-shirt, faded jeans, and the black Harley boots I put a dent in my savings account to buy him last month. Mom had a fit when she found out I'd spent close to two hundred dollars on a gift for someone I'd only been dating four weeks. Even Aunt Lee, who's usually the queen of diplomacy, agreed my gift was "excessive." But I'm sorry—they didn't see Shane's face light up the day he tried those boots on at the mall. Or watch his expression gray as he slipped them off. When Shane mentioned his birthday was coming up, and that his mom never gets him anything except a card—if she remembers that—I knew I'd be back for those boots.

When Shane spots me, his chin lifts.

"Doesn't that bug you?" Liv asks. "Shane, like, having your

locker open before you get there, and knowing everything you've got inside?"

My skin tingles as I slip into his orbit. "Why should it? He's doing something nice for me." Without taking my eyes off Shane, I elbow her side. "You're just jealous."

She shrugs. "Maybe. Look, want to do something after school? You know, since my cello lesson's canceled? We are soooo overdue for some girl time."

She's right. We are. But I'll want to check with Shane first—to see if he's made plans for us—so I try to sound hopeful without promising anything. "We'll talk after school, okay?"

"Sounds good." Liv turns toward her locker. "Buh-bye."

Approaching Shane, I try to put on a sexy smile, but I can tell my lips aren't cooperating. They're grinning. I probably look twelve. I'm already self-conscious enough about being the youngest junior in my class—thanks to Miss Blandford who convinced Mom I should skip third grade because my standardized test scores were so high. When you add that to the fact that I have a parent in prison for murder, it's easy to see why I haven't exactly been a friend magnet. But now, I'm somebody. Half of a couple. Part of an us. I belong somewhere.

"Hey, there." Shane's eyes travel up and down and—gulp!—they're like fingers, caressing me. "You look appetizing today."

I'm wearing a velour shirt with a pair of low-rise jeans I ordered online because they reminded me of Shane's favorite pair. "Thanks," I say, glad he noticed.

Shane leans in to kiss me. His breath is minty, and his lips are waxy and soft. When our lip-lock ends, I catch my breath and hang up my coat. Reaching for my books, I panic, remembering I have an advanced algebra and trig quiz I forgot to study for. After the phone call last night, I could barely think, so I vegged out on the futon watching *Friends* reruns until I fell asleep. I woke up at three in the morning—still waiting for Shane to call. Which he always does. Every night. Sometimes three or four times.

"I was surprised not to hear from you last night," I say, trying not to sound like I'm pressuring him.

Shane flashes his shy smile—the one where a corner of his delicious mouth turns up, making a cute little dimple in his cheek while the other corner barely moves. "I couldn't call," he says. "I decided I need some cash flow to help keep my hottie girlfriend happy. So I got a job."

I feel myself blush. I am so not a hottie. "A job? Where?"

"Pizza King."

Shane claims he can't toast a bagel without burning it, which is why he never eats breakfast. *"You?"* I joke. "Will that be good for business?"

He snags a belt loop on my jeans, pulling me to him. "Smarty, I'm a driver . . ." I turn and he draws me closer. ". . . and we *deliver.*"

Oh. My. God. I seriously want to put my hands on him. I glance around to see if any teachers are watching.

"We've got any topping you want." He licks his lips, and a bolt of white heat zips through me. "Hamburger, pepperoni, sausage . . ."

I reach my foot back and close my locker with my heel. Leaning into his shoulder, I say softly, "But I don't eat meat, remember?"

"Soy chips, then . . . tofu . . ." Shane's lips tickle my ear. "Bean curd . . ."

I giggle as he backs me against my locker. "Tofu *is* bean curd," I whisper.

The bell for first period rings. The stragglers hurry past, ducking into their classrooms, which is what I should be doing.

"Shane Miller!" a voice booms. Ms. Delphi, the vice principal, is poised beside us in her I-mean-business stance.

My spine straightens. I expect Shane to step back. To put space between our bodies. To apologize. But he doesn't.

"Mr. Miller?" Ms. Delphi repeats.

I throw her a look that says: *I know we shouldn't be doing this and we're late for class, but I can't move until Shane does.* She isn't focusing on me, though.

Shane turns slightly to smile at her. A smile that isn't shy. One that's almost, well, *smug*. I've never seen it before. "Yes, Ms. Delphi?"

I squirm a little, but I'm basically pinned—something that might be kind of exciting under other circumstances, but not while the VP is watching.

Ms. Delphi glances from Shane to me, then back at Shane again. "It appears the young lady would like her mobility back, Mr. Miller."

How is it that I've gone to school here since ninth grade and Ms. Delphi doesn't know my name, but Shane's been here two months, and she knows his?

"Oh!" Shane fakes a look of surprise. "*Would* she?"

My cheeks are burning and my heart beats double time. "Um, yeah."

"Pardon me, then." Shane steps to the side and blood rushes back into my limbs. "How could I be so . . . so *thoughtless* not to notice?"

Ms. Delphi studies me. "Are you all right, Miss—?"

Shane drapes an arm across my shoulder. "Of course she's—"

"I wasn't speaking to you," Ms. Delphi interrupts, and Shane glares at her.

I'm so embarrassed, I could die. "I—I'm fine, but I'm supposed to be taking a quiz. Excuse me." I clutch my books and hurry down the hall toward class.

When I arrive, Mr. Hollenbeck has already chalked ten binomials on the board. "Late pass?" he whispers, so as not to disturb the communal scratch of pencil lead.

An unexcused tardy will cost me. And since I'm only carrying a ninety-two, my lowest grade this term, it's not like I can afford it. "Sorry," I whisper back.

I open my notebook and copy the problems off the board. But I can't wrap my mind around all those *x*'s and *y*'s. Tapping my pencil, I glance over at Jenna Peters, who's already solving problem number four.

She shields her paper, shooting me a *do-you-mind?* look.

A flood of thoughts force their way into my mind. Thoughts like, *Why was Shane so disrespectful to Ms. Delphi? Why didn't he call last night to say he had a job?* I could've phoned Olivia if I'd known we weren't going to talk.

When I glance up again, Shane's parked outside the classroom door, holding a detention ticket.

How many? I mouth.

Five, he mouths back, grinning. It's so obvious he doesn't care he's in trouble. I wish I had a fraction of his gumption, his confidence.

As Mr. Hollenbeck stands to collect the quizzes I notice Jenna's finished all ten problems, and I haven't solved even one. When he reaches for mine, he stops and leans in, so close I can smell his coffee breath. "Would you like to schedule a makeup, Ariel?"

I've always read people well—even when I was a baby, according to Mom. The one time I met my biological father, I threw a fit and cried myself blue. Now I'm reading Mr. Hollenbeck, and his face is filled with major concern. But I can't embarrass myself by sucking up in front of Shane. Especially after his bad-boy act with

Ms. Delphi. I mean, how would that look—he shows off for me, and I turn around and act all vanilla?

I throw a quick glance at Shane and bite my lip to keep from buckling. "No, thanks," I say, loud enough for him to hear, then I redirect my gaze to the floor. I don't lift my head until Mr. Hollenbeck has moved on, collecting the rest of the quizzes.

Madeline

It's after midnight. Mom's snoring on the couch while I play a Beatles album in my room. Not much wakes her when she's loaded. When Elmira flooded during Hurricane Agnes five years ago, emergency workers pounded on our door, evacuating us. They had to physically *carry* Mom downstairs and into their van. She woke in the shelter the next morning and whispered to me, "How'd I get here?" It's no wonder she never could pinpoint who my father was.

Yawning, I click on my box fan and stretch out across my bedspread. But when my eyes start to drift closed, Marcia Brady is there with her perfect hair, pointing a finger at me and laughing. The cavern in my middle rages, threatening to implode and swallow me whole. *Feed me!* the Beast demands. *FEED ME!*

I have to quiet it, of course. I head to the kitchen, polish off three peanut-butter-and-banana sandwiches, a tall stack of Oreos, a jumbo glass of milk with several spoons of Quik stirred in, and a freezer-burned Fudgesicle.

The Beast coos, contented.

When I return to my room, everything inside me feels pleasantly numb. And calm. The Beatles album has ended. The record player arm bobs back and forth, a soothing sound. I crawl into bed, curl into a large, round ball, and draw my arms around my middle. Hugging my stomach is almost like hugging another person. A person who's happy with me.

This time, when I close my eyes, Marcia Brady is gone.

* * *

When I start for school in the morning, it's barely light out and the air is cool. I like fall. I don't sweat as much, or feel self-conscious wearing long sleeves. I cross the street to avoid a group of girls clustered together, waiting for the school bus.

My last school-bus ride was in third grade. Kids mooed as I started down the aisle wearing an ugly plaid dress. I was inches from an empty seat when a foot shot out, tripping me. Fat Girl flies. Fat Girl lands with a splat. I could hear the stitches on my dress pop, exposing my slip underneath. A boy with Coke-bottle glasses grabbed my lunchbox, flinging what I'd packed in separate directions: two fluffernutter sandwiches, a package of Raspberry Zingers, a bag of Fritos, a Mallo Bar. The bus driver hit the brakes and whirled around. *Finally,* I thought, *someone's going to make the kids stop being mean to me.* You still have faith in adults when you're that age. But it doesn't take long to smarten up.

"Hey, you!" she yelled. "The girl in the aisle! No getting out of your seat till I come to a complete stop. Those are the rules. What's your name?"

Eyes on the floor, I mumbled, "Madeline."

"I can't hear you!" she snapped. "Speak up!"

"Fatty Maddie!" the boy who'd trashed my lunch hollered.

Everyone howled as I hurried toward an open seat, and the driver jammed the bus into gear. At school I went straight to the nurse, who used several safety pins to hold my dress together. I begged her to let me go home to change, but we lived over two miles from school, so she told me to call Mom for a ride. The phone rang seventeen times before I gave up. Like I said, my mother can sleep through anything.

By the time I arrive at the high school, the streetlights have flickered off. I move through the day in the usual way. Show up for classes, turn in homework, eat my free lunch, draw stares. Still, I dread the three o'clock dismissal bell. School isn't my idea of a good time, but it beats the hell out of what's waiting for me at home. Usually I prolong leaving by hanging out in a wooden lean-to dubbed the Smoking Lounge because it's the only place on school grounds kids are allowed to light up. Not that I smoke, but there's a bench inside and a view of the athletic field so I can watch whoever has practice.

Today, it's the varsity cheerleaders. As I park myself on the bench the coach organizes a pyramid. Jeannette Landeau kneels, then Sharon Ranson and Debbie Carter, and so on, until it's time to start the second row. Muralee Blawjen waits. She's the head cheerleader, so she's usually on the very top. Except this time, as she climbs to her spot her foot slips, and the row-two girls tumble, collapsing on top of row one. Sharon Ranson goes into hysterics when one of her contacts falls out. But as everyone crouches, helping her look for her lens, they're laughing the entire time. Even though it's 100 percent Muralee's fault the pyramid crumbled and Sharon lost her contact, no one's mad at her. Everyone loves Muralee—even me, who has a thousand reasons to despise her. There's no way she could ever screw up.

When practice is over, the coach blows her whistle. The cheerleaders hurry toward the school, and I walk to McDonald's for a snack.

As I'm finishing off a hot cherry pie and a chocolate milk shake, Muralee, Jeannette, and Sharon bound through the side door and start toward the counter—my cue to leave.

But as I collect my stuff, a boy in a McDonald's uniform sits down across from me. He has blond flyaway hair and John Denver glasses, and there's a ketchup stain on his collar. When he pokes a straw through the lid on his soda, it scrapes the slit and makes a farting noise. "Mind if I sit here on my break?"

I glance around, making sure he's talking to me. There's no one else even close.

"Okay," I mumble, but I'm not sure a sound comes out, so I nod too.

He sips his soda. "I'm Tad. What's your name?"

I clear my throat, hoping my voice will work. "Madeline."

"Pretty name."

I feel myself blush.

He—Tad—reaches in his shirt pocket for a pack of cigarettes. He taps one free and lights it. I notice that his nails need cutting. And they have breading or French fry paste or something packed underneath them. He tips the pack toward me. "Want one?"

"Um, no. But, thanks."

Tad turns his head to exhale so he won't blow smoke in my face. "You go to school?"

I can't believe this is happening. That someone is talking to me. I pinch myself under the table, relieved when I feel pain. "Yeah. Eastside High. You?"

"Not anymore. I quit when I turned sixteen."

I nod like I understand, thinking: *What would I do if I wasn't in school all day?* The thought depresses me.

Tad studies me. Intently.

"What?" I say, blushing again.

He taps his cigarette in a small, tin ashtray. "*What* what?"

I whisper, "How come you're sitting with me?"

He looks around. There are plenty of empty booths. "Want me to leave?"

"No. It's just that I, um, I wondered, you know . . . why."

He shrugs. "I've seen you here before. You seem like a nice person."

"Nice?" I repeat.

He flashes a crooked grin. There's a gap between his two front teeth. "Yeah. Someone who won't bust my balls."

I bite the insides of my cheeks to keep from smiling. "Oh."

The cheerleaders pass by, carrying trays. I notice Muralee has fries and a soda. The ends of her auburn hair are damp, and I can smell her fruity shampoo. She sits two booths over, and Jeannette and Sharon drop down across from her. Sharon glances my way. "Wow," she says, loud enough for everyone in the smoking section to hear, "that guy's into serious pork." Jeannette laughs, but Muralee doesn't. Her eyes connect with mine, and I get this feeling she's sorry Sharon made fun of me.

"You know those girls?" Tad asks.

"No way. They're cheerleaders."

He stamps out his cigarette. "So?"

"*So?* They're pretty and popular and"—it's hard to say the word—"skinny."

"*You're* pretty," Tad says. But before I can bask in the moment, he glances at his watch and adds, "Oops, sorry. Break's over."

I try to hide my disappointment. When Tad stands, I notice he's tall. Not skinny but not fat, either.

"Maybe I'll see you tomorrow," he says. "I always take my break at the same time."

I'm not sure if he's asking me to meet him or not. If I tell him

I'll be here and he's only being polite, I'll look like a jerk. "Uh, I . . ." I fumble, trying to decide what to say.

Tad lifts his hands like he's caught in a TV holdup. "Hey, no one's forcing you."

As he turns to leave I manage to free up my words. "See you tomorrow!" I call.

Two booths over, Sharon huffs and rolls her eyes.

But for the first time ever, I don't give a rat's ass.

Desiree

we're here, larry calls. *you awake?*
i'm in the backseat,
curled into a ball.
i don't answer.

i had a nice time tonight, dez.
i can't wait to see you again.
things'll be tricky with your ma and all,
but if we're careful, she'll never find out.

i uncurl,
open the car door,
move slowly toward the porch.
it feels like i'm watching someone else
put one foot in front of the other.
i'm not sure where i've gone,
but i'm not here.

the apartment is dark,
so i let myself in with my key.
i tiptoe up the stairs
and pause outside
mam's room.
i wish she'd wake up
and notice something is wrong,
that she'd pull me
into her thick arms,
tuck my head beneath her
flabby chins, and say,
there, there, it'll be okay,
like all the tv moms do.

breath held,
i inch open the door to my room.
sure enough, mam's trashed it.
drawers are tipped upside down.
clothes cover the floor.
jeremy's notes are
strewn everywhere.
it's a strange comfort,
seeing the room match
how i feel inside.

in the bathroom
i strip for a shower.
my shirt reeks of puke,
and my panties are bloody.
i bury them in the bottom of the trash,

duck beneath the pelting spray,
adjust the water so hot that
welts rise up on my skin.
i scrub my sticky thighs
with the pumice soap
mam uses on her feet.
my skin turns red
as cherry pop-tart filling,
but i can't wash larry off.
his weight still crushes my chest,
and his smell won't leave my hair—
even after i've shampooed
once, twice, three times.
when the water runs cold,
i sink to the shower floor,
shivering.

* * *

the next morning,
the body that claims to be mine
zones out in front of *x-men*,
eating cocoa puffs straight from the box.

someone knocks at the door,
and mam hurries to answer it.
two sets of footsteps
climb the stairs.
i run to the bathroom,
close the lid on the toilet,

and sit, rocking,
waiting to find out who's there,
even though i already know.

where's dez hiding? larry asks.
mam snorts. *who the hell knows?*
the teakettle whistles.
the lid swirls off the
jar of instant coffee.
spoons clink against
the sides of mam's ugly mugs.

shaking,
i hurry into the hall,
steal two of mam's smokes,
grab my denim jacket off a hook.
i'm halfway through the door when
larry says, *whoa, somebody's pants are on fire!*
and mam just laughs and laughs.

* * *

jeremy's dad works
at the jiffy lube on saturdays
while his mom does grocery shopping
and picks up her heebie-jeebie meds,
so jeremy's the only one home.

i file past the annuals
that line the front walk,

color-coded to match the house,
and signal with my usual knock.

jeremy answers,
wearing levi's with no shirt,
his hair wet from a shower.
normally, i'd smile and say,
you look sweet enough to eat.
but today i'm silent.

upstairs
jeremy loads
a steppenwolf cd
in his boom box
and "born to be wild"
rattles the speakers.
he's such a '70s retro junkie.

while jeremy moves to the beat,
i stretch out on his bed,
staring up at his
glow-in-the-dark ceiling stars,
inhaling the scent of his pillow—
a little-boy smell i love.

jeremy crosses the room,
bending to plug in his blow-dryer.
sometimes he kids around
and calls it a blow-*job* dryer,
saying if he could

invent something
that looks like a regular dryer
but secretly gives head instead,
he'd be rich in two seconds flat.

jeremy flips the on switch,
pointing the gun at his head.
his hair lifts up and out,
wild as a lion's mane.
when he's done,
he lies beside me,
rolling closer for a kiss.
tears fill my eyes,
barreling down both cheeks
like niagara freaking falls.

jeremy loops his arm behind my neck.
hey, what's wrong?
when i don't answer,
he pulls a blanket over us
and strokes my hair.
we lie side by side,
staring up at his ceiling,
at those goddamn sticky stars,
like maybe they're real or something.

jeremy's lids drop closed.
i turn to study his face.
other than a few stray zits,
his skin is perfectly smooth,

and he barely has enough fuzz to shave.
i know we're the same age,
but he looks so much
younger to me now.
or maybe
i'm suddenly older.

i hate to disturb him,
but there's something
i have to ask.
jeremy?

his eyes open,
but only halfway,
like he's not ready
to let the world in yet.
um, i start, licking my lips,
which are suddenly dry as burned toast,
what would you do if someone hurt me?
i'm not saying anyone did—
i shrug, trying to look casual—
i'm just curious . . .

he scratches an itch on his ear. *who?*

anyone, i mean, no one.
well, let's say it's a guy.
what would you do if he,
you know, messed with me?

jeremy's eyes are open wide now.
his gaze locks with mine.
messed with you how?
my palms are sweating.
i wipe them on my jeans,
tempted to say, *oh, never mind,*
but an invisible force won't let me.
so i struggle to get the words out:
by making me have sex.

jeremy leaps off the bed
as if someone's threatened
him instead of me.
what would i do?
he lifts his arms
like he plans to pluck
the answer from the sticky stars
then he slaps his hands
on his thighs, hard.
the sound echoes
like a shotgun being fired.
he shouts, *i'd fucking kill the guy!*
words i find hard to believe.

jeremy couldn't kill anyone.
not with those little-boy looks
and that little-boy smell
and that little-boy fuzz on his chin.
no way. not jeremy.

except when he lies down beside me again,
holding me tighter than before,
i have to admit—
i really do like his answer.

Ariel

By the time school's out, it's turned into one of those gorgeous fall afternoons you really appreciate because you've said good-bye to summer and didn't expect to feel the sun's warmth again until spring. I stick my scarf in my backpack and revel in walking with my coat unbuttoned, making mental plans along the way. As soon as I get in, I'll call Olivia. Since her cello lesson was canceled and Shane has detention, she and I will be able to hang out. She's right, it really *has* been too long. Filled with anticipation, I feel my steps grow lighter.

But when I get home Shane's motorcycle is parked in our driveway and he's sitting on the front steps. This probably sounds terrible, but I'm actually kind of disappointed. "I thought you had to stay late," I say, starting up the sidewalk toward him.

Shane reaches down, picks an aster that survived the first frost, and holds it out for me. "Now what kind of greeting is that?"

"Sorry." I take the flower and bend to kiss him. "How'd you get out of detention?"

"Work excuse." He grins. "I just left out the fact that I don't go in until seven."

"Aren't you sneaky." I sit beside him. "Can you believe how warm it is?"

He loops an arm around me. "That's why I'm here. Wanna go for a ride?"

I notice the second helmet on Shane's seat. "Sure. Just let me stick my stuff inside and make a superquick call to Liv." I dig through my book bag for my keys, which, after searching every corner, I realize I don't have. "I must have locked my keys inside," I tell Shane. "Wait here. I'll be back in a few."

I duck into the garage and feel under the container of Ice Melt, where Mom hides the spare for the kitchen door. When I turn, Shane's behind me, so close I plow into him. "Oh, I wasn't expecting—"

"Anything wrong?"

Mom wouldn't be happy if she knew Shane saw where the spare is kept. "No, I just—um, no."

He glances at Mom's empty parking spot. "Mind if I wait inside?"

Shane hasn't seen much of our house. Everything's been handled at the front door. Probably because Mom's always been here. Having to remind him about the no-boys-allowed-inside-unless-Mom's-home rule makes me feel like such a baby, so I tell a lie instead. "Shane, um, on second thought, can I have a rain check on the bike ride? I started to get a headache on the way home. I think I'll take some Tylenol and chill."

Shane studies me. Does he know I'm lying? "It's probably tension," he says. "You worry a lot about grades."

"I *have* to worry about grades. The SATs and ACTs are coming up, and if I'm going to get into a decent college, then—"

"*Shhhh.*" He steps behind me, rests his hands on my shoulders, and gently works the muscles. As his thumbs glide up and down my neck, rubbing with just the right amount of pressure, my eyelids drop closed and a sigh escapes from my throat. "Show me to your room," he says, faking a French accent. Shane does amazing impersonations. "Monsieur Miller will give you a massage, *chérie.*"

What he's doing feels so good, I actually consider his offer. But when he reaches to take the key from my hand, I come to my senses. "Shane"—I step away—"I, I can't."

Hooking a finger through my belt loop, he pulls me close again. "Come oooooon. Live a little." He kisses my neck. I'm melting.

"Shane . . . please . . ." I say, out of options. "You know my mom's rule." I can imagine how juvenile that sounds to someone brave enough to stare down the Veep.

His lips nibble their way toward my ear. "But Momster's not here to enforce it. Besides"—he stops, mid-nibble, rests his chin on my shoulder—"you don't need a rule like that with me. I'm the one who's gonna take care of you, remember?"

That's what Shane told me on our first date. The Weather Channel had predicted thunderstorms, so he'd borrowed his mom's car. On our way back from New Paltz, where we'd seen a movie and had dinner, it got foggy and started to pour. Sheets of rain blew sideways across the highway, jerking us back and forth, and traffic slowed to a crawl. Cars pulled off the road, their lights glowing ominously; I could barely make out the vehicles they belonged to. Just outside Poughkeepsie, thunder split the sky—which had taken on a bizarre greenish cast—and chunks of ice started to ping off the windshield. Then the chunks grew larger, the size of golf balls, pounding like an army of boots charging over our heads, slamming the windshield with such force I worried the glass would shatter. Finally, I couldn't help it. I was so freaked out I whispered, "Shane, I'm scared." One hand still on the wheel, he reached over, touching me. "You're shaking," he said, and flipped his signal on. He pulled to the side of the road, reached into the backseat for a blanket, and opened it over me. Then he drew me as close as he could without either of us getting impaled on the emergency brake. His jacket smelled garlicky from the restaurant we'd eaten at. I nestled my face in his sleeve so I couldn't see the windshield anymore. "Relax," he said. "I'll take care of you. I won't let anything bad happen." Those were his exact words. God, I felt so safe. So protected. Shane lifted my chin, kissing me. His lips were full and smooth and moist, tasting of basil from the bruschetta we'd shared. I didn't sleep a wink that night—I was too busy replaying that kiss. My first.

Remembering, I blink back tears. I want to let Shane in. I want to hear him talk to me that way again. But Mom will be so pissed at me. "Shane," I blurt, before I chicken out, "I'm sorry, but I can't let you in."

Shane just stands there, watching me. It's as if he's dropped an emotional blank screen in front of his face, a screen I can't see past or penetrate.

"Shane. Please. Say something."

Silence.

Suddenly the garage feels claustrophobic. My forehead is damp, my stomach queasy. I glance outside, toward the driveway. Air. Sun. Open space. Just what I need. Except when I start toward it Shane takes my arm and whirls me around. We're face-to-face. The blank screen has vanished. He's smiling his sweet, shy smile.

"Wanna see what I brought you?" he asks me.

I'm reeling, attempting to adjust to the shift in his mood. But I'm a sucker for surprises, so I say, "Yeah, okay."

Shane reaches into his jeans pocket, then sticks both hands behind his back.

If it's that small, it might be jewelry. What if it's a ring? My heart speeds up.

"Which hand?" he says, shoving his closed fists forward.

I tap a knuckle on his left hand.

Shane uncurls his fingers. His palm is empty. *"Ahhhhhnnnnnt!* Try again."

Excited, I tap the other hand. He doesn't open it, though. "Shane, come on."

I wait. Shane doesn't budge.

Standing there, staring at his balled-up fist, I'm beginning to feel like a jerk. Sure, I want my surprise, but I do have *some* pride. I turn toward the steps, pretending I'm not bummed. "Never mind, Shane."

He shrugs, walks toward his bike. "Suit yourself. You would've liked it a lot."

Shane's halfway down our driveway when I call, "Okay. I give. Show me."

He stops, but he doesn't face me. It looks like he's talking to our mailbox when he says, "You can ask nicer than *that,* can't you?" There's a sexy tease in his voice.

I start toward him. "Would you *please* show me what the surprise is?"

Shane turns, holding his clenched fist forward.

I peel his fingers back. One at a time. Just to draw out the moment.

Except Shane's palm is totally empty. My face burns. "What the—?"

He flashes me the same smile he flashed Ms. Delphi. Then he drops that damn blank screen again. I bite the insides of my cheeks to keep from crying as he heads down the driveway toward his bike.

* * *

I toss my book bag on the kitchen counter, right beside my missing keys, and dial Olivia's number. I need to hear a familiar voice—a voice belonging to someone who won't confuse the hell out of me.

Steve answers. *La Bohème* is playing in the background.

"Steve, it's Ariel," I rush out. "Is Liv there?"

"Sorry, love. She said to tell you she phoned a few times, and when she couldn't reach you she went to the Galleria."

I glance down at the answering machine. Sure enough, there are two new beeps.

"Want me to give her a message?" Steve asks. I hear sizzling noises in the background and realize he's making dinner. I think of the Nightly Food Report, and miss Olivia even more.

"No, thanks," I say, and hang up.

I change into my Nikes, grab my keys, tuck the emergency spare back below the Ice Melt, and head for the university where Mom works. I timed it once—if I jog instead of walk, I can be there in eighteen minutes.

The whole way there my brain OD's on one question: *Why would Shane play such a mean joke on the person he supposedly wants to take care of?* As I step off the elevator for the English department, mentally exhausted, I still haven't found an answer.

Inside the office a work-study girl is on the phone, and it's obviously a personal call. I notice her nose piercing is infected. I clear my throat, but she ignores me.

I glance through the window of the conference room. Aunt Lee's laptop is open on the table, and she's explaining something to Mom. When Aunt Lee sees me, she smiles and signals me in.

Mom looks totally spent, like a weak sneeze could knock her over.

Aunt Lee kisses my cheek. "Want a Diet Coke? Mindy can fetch it for you."

I wouldn't have pegged Nose Ring for a Mindy. "No, thanks," I answer.

There's a long moment of awkward silence. Then Aunt Lee says, "You look upset, sweetie. Your mom told me about the phone call from the doctor last night." She glances at Mom, then back at me. "Is that what's bothering you?"

I trace the stitches on the arm of the chair, realizing I shouldn't have come. I mean, Mom's mother has cancer, and I'm upset over a stupid joke that's so inconsequential in the bigger scheme of things. Still I mumble, "Well, not entirely."

Mom's eyebrows arch. "Ariel, is it Shane?"

Sometimes I feel like she's waiting 24/7 for the moment he screws up. According to her, Shane's possessive, calls too often, and doesn't give me enough space. Then there's, quote, *something she just can't put her finger on,* unquote, which doesn't stop her from trying. Still, I really need to vent. So I shrug. "Maybe."

Aunt Lee glances at the clock. "I've got a class in ten minutes. But you two stay and talk." On the way out, she pats Mom's shoulder. "Take all the time you need."

Mom watches the door close. "Honey, what's going on?"

I feel my eyes fill. It's ridiculous, the way I'm overreacting to Shane's joke, but I know I have to talk about it. So I tell Mom what happened. Except I pretend he and I were at school. I don't want Mom worrying about Shane hanging around our house when she's not there.

Afterward, I study Mom's face, waiting for her to laugh, to inform me that Shane's prank, although insensitive, is typical of how teenage boys act. Hell, maybe Dad used to play jokes like that on her.

Instead Mom's forehead wrinkles. Creases collect at the corners of her eyes.

"Mom, what?"

She reaches for my hand. "Honey, I know you like Shane a lot. But what he did to you, well, it was genuinely mean-spirited."

I pull my fingers away. "Mom, it was a joke."

"Ariel, when someone needs to embarrass another person to make himself—"

"Time out! You've been watching too many Lifetime movies. You asked what was bugging me and I told you. I'm *over* it," I lie. "Okay?"

Mom stares at a container of freshly sharpened pencils, and I realize I've hurt her feelings. "Look," I say, "I've got homework I should start."

Mom forces a smile. "I'll be home around seven. I'll take you to the Purple Planet if you don't mind eating that late."

The Purple Planet is my favorite vegetarian restaurant. Their baked risotto is to die for. "Sure," I say, starting for the door.

I'm almost through it when Mom calls, "I thought we'd go this weekend."

I turn. "Go where?"

"To see my mother. The trip should take about four hours. We could leave early on Friday if you don't mind missing school. We'll spend the day at the hospital, stay overnight, visit again on Saturday, then take off. That way I'll have Sunday to work. How's that sound?"

Shane and I haven't missed a Friday night together since we started dating. "Give me some time to think about it," I tell her.

Mom could pull rank, but it's not her style. She nods. "See you at seven."

By the time I get home, the sun is setting. When I check the answering machine, there are two new messages, both from Shane, but I don't feel like talking yet. I hit Delete so Mom won't find them, nuke a bag of popcorn, and search for the remote control. Aunt Lee bought us a really nice hi-def TV for Christmas last year. Mom argued that we couldn't accept such an expensive gift. But, I'm happy to say, Aunt Lee won in the end.

I surf the channels and stop at a *Simpsons* rerun, which makes me think of Dad. Mom says when they were teenagers, they used to watch the new episode together every Tuesday.

Just as I'm getting comfortable, the phone rings. I pray it's Olivia, back from the Galleria. Still, I let the machine screen the call.

There's a short silence, then a man's voice says, "Peaches? You there?"

I hurry toward the phone and pick up. "Dad! You're psychic."

"Hey, who you calling psycho?"

I laugh. "I said psychic. I was just thinking of you." I drop down backward onto the futon. "It's so good to hear your voice. How are you doing?"

"Same shit, different day," he answers. Mom gets mad when Dad swears while he's talking with me, but I don't mind. I think it's kind of cool.

"Yeah," I say back, "same here."

I hear yelling in the background.

"Everything okay?" I ask him.

"Yeah. I'm on the phone near the TV room. Some bonehead got a hold of the remote and flipped to *Nancy Grace.*"

"I'd yell too," I say.

We both laugh.

"So how's your mom doing?" I hear Dad light a cigarette.

"Busy. Aunt Lee's got a deadline coming up so she's putting in a lot of overtime."

"And how about you? How's school? You keeping those grades up? Still seeing that guy? Sean, is that his name?"

I don't point out the fact that he shot me five questions at once. "It's *Shane,*" I say. "We've been dating almost two months."

"Wow. Getting serious." He exhales loudly—blowing smoke out, probably—then he lowers his voice. "Has your mom, uh, has she had the Talk with you?"

"Oh, God, Dad. Please don't tell me you're asking what I think you're asking."

"Come, on, Peaches. Listen to me. We ain't living back in the dark ages. If you're planning to get serious with this Shane fella, make sure you're taking precautions."

Someone makes a catcall in the background.

Dad yells, "Get outta here! I'm trying to have a private talk with my daughter!" To me he says more quietly, "You're young, Ariel. You got your whole life ahead of you. If you two decide to get, you know, intimate—"

Another catcall.

I'm sure my face is bright red. "I've got it"—I cut him off—"I'll be careful."

"Okay. Good." Dad's words land heavy and hard. He pauses then adds, "Look, Peaches, it's really hard, being in here, but I think about you every day, and I want you to have the life you deserve. With all the opportunities and choices you're entitled to." His voice catches. He coughs to cover over it. "I love you."

"I know, Dad. I love you too."

There's a long silence. "So, uh, is your mom around?"

"No. Sorry. She's working."

"Well, um, I'm almost outta time anyway. Tell her I called. And Peaches—?"

"Yeah, Dad?"

"Just remember, you only get to be a teenager once. Don't grow up too fast."

A lump crowds my throat. I'm close to the age Dad was when he was forced to *grow up too fast.* But I want our call to end on an up note, so I say, "Care to leave me with a Homerism?"

"Operator!" Dad shouts, sounding exactly like Homer Simpson. "Quick! Give me the number for nine-one-one!" Then, in his own voice, he says, "Look, Peaches, I've gotta run. I'll talk to you again just as soon as I can."

The phone clicks. The silence that follows is deafening.

I press the receiver to my cheek like I always do after Dad hangs up, holding onto those final few seconds, slowing the disconnect.

"I miss you," I say out loud, even though he's already gone.

Madeline

When I arrive at McDonald's after school, Tad's at the same booth we shared the day before. He looks up from his orange soda and smiles as I walk toward him. An ache floods my heart when I realize no one's ever looked glad to see me before.

"Hi," he says, lighting a cigarette. The smoke swirls around his head. He looks like the mysterious Wizard of Oz.

"Hi," I say back, sitting across from him. The waistline on my pants digs into my stomach. I shift, trying to get comfortable.

I wait for Tad to say something. Instead he blows smoke rings, watching me. I mean, really watching me. And he's smiling while he's doing it.

In no time at all, liquid trickles down the inside of my shirt, and I'm hosting my own personal Sweat-a-Thon. Maybe this is a mistake, I tell myself. Maybe Tad's helping the cheerleaders play a practical joke, and in ten seconds the entire squad is going to spring out of hiding, laughing at me.

Tad's voice zaps me back to reality. "You wanna cheeseburger?"

Of course I want a cheeseburger. I want five or six of them, inhaled in rapid succession. My hands shake beneath the table. "Yes," I mumble, as if I'm ashamed to admit I like food.

I reach inside my pocketbook for my wallet. The electric bill was higher than usual this month, so I'm glad I thought to slip a five out of my shoebox before school.

Tad stands, holding his hand up. "My treat. You want fries?"

I stare at a Happy Meal ad. I'm so nervous, I could eat the paper it's printed on. "Okay. Thanks."

"Small, medium, or large?"

Even large isn't large enough. "Small."

"And to drink?"

"Orange soda, please."

Tad starts toward the counter.

A little boy two booths away turns in his booster seat to look at me. Tapping the woman next to him, he says, "Mommy, that lady has two chins."

I stare at my lap, embarrassed.

When Tad reappears and sets a tray on the table, he tips his head toward the boy who insulted me. "Cute kid"—he smiles—"I wanna have a ton of them someday. How about you?"

Kids seem like a lot of work. But I don't want to sound disagreeable, so I shrug and say, "Sure. Why not?"

Tad passes me a cheeseburger, and my mouth waters. Peeling back the wrapper, I remember something I heard once on a TV show—that if you focus on each bite of food and chew every mouthful twenty times, you'll fool your stomach into feeling full faster. I decide to give it a try. The chewing sound echoes in my ears. On the count of twenty, I swallow.

Trying to think of something to say, I remember another bit of TV advice: If you don't like talking about yourself, ask questions instead. "So, um," I start, "where did you go to school before you—?" I stop myself. *Damn! I've screwed up already.*

"Quit?"

"Uh, yeah, but I mean, if you don't want to talk about it, I understand, I . . ."

"That's okay. I don't mind. My dad and I moved here about a year ago. But before that I went to school in Johnson City, this skanky town outside—"

"Binghamton."

Tad smiles. "Been there, huh?"

I nod, not bothering to volunteer more.

"Ever seen Cherry Hill Academy?"

"Near the entrance to the cemetery." I pray he doesn't ask me how I know.

"Right again." Tad's glance lingers, and warmth flutters through my middle.

When he looks away, the temperature plummets.

Tad unwraps his cherry pie. I could suck down the entire thing in the time it takes him to open the end flaps. "I didn't plan to quit high school," he says. "I was getting by with straight Cs. Well, except for a D in American studies. But I was in it for the long haul. Cap and gown, diploma, the whole crop of crap. Then Benny Aldridge—he's my best friend, well, was—he changed all that the day he stole a car."

"He stole a *car?*"

"Yeah. Except Benny wasn't the brightest crayon in the box. He drove it to school the next day. Parked it in the teacher's lot."

"Really?"

"Cross my heart. Third period, me and Benny are watching this dumb-ass movie in science when Mr. Myers, the principal, buzzes in on the intercom, calling us both to the office. Man, Benny was freaking. And I can't figure what I've done. But Myers's face is all puffed up and red when he tells us to take a seat. Myers has these animal heads mounted on the wall behind his desk, and I keep picturing our heads up there too. Myers turns to Benny and says, 'Mr. Aldridge, I understand you drove to school this morning.' Benny says, 'Yes, sir. Is there a problem?' And Myers says, 'There are two problems, son. First, you parked in the teachers' lot. Secondly, you're required to provide a copy of your vehicle registration to the main office in order to access our facilities.' Benny's face screws up—like I said, not the brightest crayon—so Myers translates for him. He says, 'In order to *park* here, Mr. Aldridge.' Then the light goes on inside Benny's thick skull, and he says, 'Ohhhhhh.' Myers sits forward in his big leather chair and tells him, 'I'll excuse you for a moment to retrieve it.' Benny gulps, looking like he's gonna piss himself. 'You mean now?' he says, and Myers nods his little bald head."

I can't stand the suspense. I look up from my French fries. "What did Benny do?"

"Only thing he could. He leaves to get it. I try to go with him, but Myers tells me to stay put. He asks me, 'Did you have anything to do with this, son?' and I answer, 'No, sir, Mr. Myers.' He nods. Pauses. Then he says, 'Perhaps if you could find a way to sever your connection with Mr. Aldridge, you'd have more time and energy for your studies, Thaddeus. I think you're capable of far better work than you're producing. In fact, your English teacher, Mrs. Dunbar, tells me you've got quite a knack for words.' And even though most of what he said stinks, I concentrate on that last part. *'You've got quite a knack for words.'* Best compliment anyone had ever given me."

Tad sits back, silent.

"What's wrong?" I ask. "Why'd you stop?"

"I just realized how I must sound. I'm telling you my friggin' life story here."

"But it's fascinating. I want to hear more."

"Really?" Tad squints. "You're not shittin' me?"

Little does he know how conversation-starved I am. "Not a chance. I swear."

"Well, okay then. Where was I?"

"Your principal complimented you on having a knack for words . . ."

"Right." Tad licks pie goo off his thumb. "But I don't get to gloat long 'cause now Benny's back, flattening out this piece of paper he found in the glove compartment. Myers takes it from him, reading out loud, 'Marsden Williams, 45A Hamilton Court, Johnson City.' He gives Benny the evil eye and says, 'I'm sure you can explain this.' Benny's looking kinda green. He says, 'Uh. Sure. He's my uncle, sir. He let me borrow the car.' Well, Myers gets on the horn and phones up Uncle Marsden and, of course, he doesn't exactly agree with Benny's explanation."

My cheeseburger sits on its wrapper, half-eaten. I'm so caught up in Tad's story, I'm not even hungry anymore. "What happened next?"

Tad reaches for one of my French fries, whirling it through a ketchup blob. When he places it on his tongue, I get a chill. Not a cold chill, though. A nice, pleasurable chill. One I wouldn't mind feeling again.

"Benny got sent to juvie hall." Tad sighs. "School wasn't the same after that. These two nimrods on the wrestling team started badgering me. When they decided to make me their human punching bag and broke my nose, well, I got sick of it and quit. I'm kind of sorry I did, though. I woulda been the first person in my family to finish high school."

"You could get your GED," I say.

"I'd like to"—Tad shrugs—"but it's a lotta work, what with a job and all."

I force my voice to stay calm so I won't sound as excited as I am. "I could help you study."

Tad stares at his hands. I notice his nails are clean, trimmed close to his fingers. He doesn't say anything back. Not one single word.

I panic when I realize what I've done: I've forced myself on him and ruined everything. When Tad glances at me, I know what he's thinking: *Sure, I'm nice to the fat girl and look what happens.*

My stomach grumbles, waking the Beast. Suddenly I need to eat. A lot.

I stand quickly, before Tad can hand me any lame excuses about why he doesn't want my help studying. It's obvious why he wouldn't want *my* help. *My* company. *My* anything. Just look at me.

Collecting my assignments, I hold them close, burying my heart beneath a fortress of books and binders. I plan my next stop: Belle's Soda Shop. There's a triple-hot-fudge sundae there with my name on it. I'm about to leave when Tad clears his throat and says, "Change your mind?"

I turn to study his face, trying to understand what's going on. "What . . . ?"

"About helping me study. Seems like you're bailing out on me."

"N—no," I stammer. "When you didn't answer, I—I thought—"

"I have to warn you. I really stink in history. I only got a—"

"—D in American studies," I finish for him.

"Yeah." Tad smiles. And as he does, he looks right at me. I mean, into my eyes, which I don't remember anyone doing before. Ever.

The Beast relaxes. My whole body—all two hundred plus pounds of it—breaks out in goose bumps. I smile back, which feels strange—working this muscle I'm not used to using, stretching it so far I feel the corners of my mouth start to quiver.

Just then, the side door bursts open. As the cheerleaders start toward the counter to order, Muralee glances my way. Maybe she notices me smiling. Maybe she thinks it's directed at her. But she does the most incredible thing. She smiles back. A small, quick smile clearly intended for me.

Tad checks his watch. "Break's over. See you tomorrow?"

"I think I'm free," I tell him. And perhaps, for the first time, I am.

* * *

Mom's passed out on the couch and there are a dozen or so empty beer bottles on the floor. One's tipped sideways on the coffee table, and the daily paper's soaked from the spill. She's circled three help-wanted ads. I peer inside the soggy red ovals, curious to see what she plans to pretend to be qualified for this week. Receptionist. Accounting assistant. Teacher's aide.

I toss the newspaper and bottles in the trash then sop the beer off the table. I can tell from the temperature of the spill that the puddle's been there a while.

When I notice the spent cigarette clenched between her fingers, a familiar ache grips my middle. The "accident," as she calls it, happened the day after my tenth birthday. Mom was drinking beer and watching TV, and I was in the kitchen, polishing off the last of the cake her boyfriend at the time had bought me. I smelled smoke—except it wasn't the usual chalky smell of cigarette smoke—so I started for the living room. Mom must've fallen asleep and dropped a lit cigarette because flames were coming from the blanket crumpled near her feet. I reached to grab an unlit corner and pull it away from her, but the hot red tongues leaped up, setting my nightgown sleeve on fire too. I screamed so loud Mom came to, shoved me to the floor, and rolled me across the rug. I howled in pain as she drove me to the ER, wavering all over the road, offering slurry promises she'd never smoke when she was "tired" again. But promises wouldn't undo that night, wouldn't unburn the scaly lizard arm that, thanks to her, became mine for life.

I grab a soda from the fridge and turn on the TV, waiting for the set to warm up. The picture tube's shot, so everything's either shades of red or shades of green, depending on how you adjust the color dial. Things have been green for so long, I decide to give red a try. I flip the TV dial, stopping at *Gilligan's Island.* The channel's fuzzy so I play with the antenna, then collapse on our ugly stuffed chair. When I open my soda, the tab goes *psssssssst,* and Mom's eyes flutter open. It figures—that a can top popping would wake her.

She rubs her eyes, groaning. "What time is it?" she half-slurs, half-asks.

"Six o'clock."

"How can it be that late already?"

"I don't know," I snap. "It just is." I glance at her. She looks like hell. She probably hasn't eaten all day. Jesus, I get so sick of taking care of her. But if I don't do it, who will?

In the kitchen, I scrounge through the cupboards.

I have no explanation for what happens next, no idea why I pick this moment to start dieting. Except I know it has to do with Tad—the first person to really look at me. Suddenly I care what he sees.

I return to the living room with a SPAM sandwich and an instant coffee for Mom, plus a tossed salad and tap water for me.

Mom bites into her sandwich. "Mmm, good. Where's yours?"

"All I want is a salad," I say, piercing a tomato with my fork. "I'm not hungry."

"Not *hungry?"* Mom opens her mouth and laughs. Bread crumbs are smashed against her teeth.

Grossed out, I look away. At the TV. At Mr. Howell, who's got an idea for getting his shipmates off the island.

"That's like *me* saying I'm not thirsty," Mom continues. She sips her coffee, to which I've added three spoons of sugar, hoping to make it more appealing. If I can eat a salad for dinner, Mom can drink coffee with hers, right? People are capable of change.

Mom makes a face and spits the coffee back in the mug. She stands, leans into the wall to steady herself, and stumbles toward the kitchen, mumbling, "I could go for a beer."

Desiree

my report card comes in the mail
the week after school's out.
my grades are just above passing,
enough to keep me out
of summer school,
which is good,
because i must have
some kind of stomach bug.
i've ralphed, like, a dozen times.
my appetite's fine, though.
when jeremy bought me
breakfast at the geronimo,
i scarfed down my three-egg omelet
before he could butter his toast.

jeremy and i pass our days
doing a whole lot of nothing.
mostly we hang out

at the water tower.
if the weather sucks,
we play nintendo
or watch tv or make out.

i think about us going all the way,
but i worry: will jeremy know
i'm not a virgin?
in the meantime,
i pretend like i am.
when he tries to unzip my jeans,
i nudge his hand away and
concentrate on him instead.
he doesn't seem to mind,
but i feel like such a liar.

* * *

one night,
when i get home from jeremy's,
i smell food cooking.
not some bogus crap like
hamburger helper or
kraft mac and cheese.
homemade food,
which i haven't tasted in ages.
i head to the kitchen to see what's up.

mam's radio is set
on the '70s station she joneses on.
singing along to a sappy love song

by some vanilla motown wannabe,
she waltzes around
in a flowered muumuu,
shaking a spatula to the beat.

i clear my throat
so she'll know i'm there.
she turns, actually smiles at me.
don't you just love that song?
i shrug. *yeah, it's okay.*

her face is honest and soft.
the words to that song are so pretty.
they make me think of your father.

my father?—i turn—
you never talk about him.
my heart fills with a million questions.

mam reaches into the cupboard
for the old red shoebox
she adds five bucks to every week
after cashing her kmart check.
moving the bills aside,
she holds up a wicker tube—
some cheesy carnival prize
the size of a tampon.

your father gave this to me.
he won it at the arcade
the day i decided what

i wanted my life to be like.
there was a family, picnicking,
that i knew was meant to be us.
and we were supposed to eat
hot dogs grilled on a hibachi
and hold hands when we said grace.
she turns the wicker tube
round and round in her hand.
but when your dad died—
her face grays—*that family*
died right along with him.

what's that make us?
i want to ask.
a table with one
of its legs sawed off?
but a timer dings and mam
returns the tube to the shoebox,
closing the lid,
closing down the conversation too.

she slides a casserole out of the oven.
cheese bubbles on top,
and my mouth waters.
looks good, i mumble.

i'm glad—mam turns to face me—
'cause larry's coming for dinner.
it'll be nice to have the three
of us together again.

i glance down at the third plate
set in front of larry's sometimes spot,
and reality hits me.
i bolt toward the door, calling,
sorry, got other plans!

* * *

carol ann's mom and dad
insist i call them pete and joan.
they let me hang out
whenever i want,
for as long as i want,
no questions asked.

bill clinton smiles at me
from a poster over their disposal.
before he got elected president
their kitchen was like a
freaking museum.
even the dish towels had
vote clinton! pins
stuck through them.

i arrive just in time for dinner.
joan sets an extra plate,
loading it with tofu kabobs
and curried tempeh strips,
which i pretend to enjoy.
after dessert—
tofutti with carob chips—

me and carol ann wash dishes
while pete and joan slip out back
to smoke pot on the porch.
i glance out the window,
noticing how their hands touch
as they pass the joint back and forth,
how pete winks at joan and
she leans in to kiss his lips—
a deep, smoky kiss that
lasts until the joint burns down
to pete's fingernail and he says, *ow!*
and joan lifts his finger to her mouth,
sweetly kissing that next.

tears fill my eyes.
i've gotta pee, i mumble.
i hurry to the bathroom,
sit on the edge of the tub.
i want what pete and joan have,
those small things bodies do—
like kissing a burned finger—
which say i love you
more than sex ever will.

* * *

upstairs, carol ann
fishes two hard candies out of
the drawer of her wicker nightstand.
i chew mine instead of sucking it and
my mouth fills with hot minty slivers.

how rude! carol ann snaps,
imitating stephanie on *full house.*
she loads a cd and
whitney houston's voice
fills the room. i moan.
give me pearl jam, nirvana, metallica—
music to take me away from my feelings,
not draw me closer to them.

carol ann sits beside me
on the bed. *check this out.*
she pulls her long hair back,
showing me a hickey on her neck.
i make a face. gross.
hickeys look like what
they are—skin sucked blue.
there's nothing sexy about them.

me and eric are probably
gonna do it soon, she tells me,
leaning backward across her spread.
her hair is a huge amber fan,
encircling her zit-free face.
when she stretches, her shirt rides up,
showing off the navel piercing
pete and joan signed for.

for our first time, she continues,
eric and i are going to rent a motel room.
you know, so it feels more real.
and i want a bottle of red wine—

one with a cork, not a twist top.
oh, and candles.
loads and loads of them.
she raises up on one elbow.
how about you?
what do you want
your first time to be like?

i used to wonder that all the time—
where jeremy and i would be
when it would happen,
how it would feel,
if it would hurt.

carol ann sits up.
wellllll? i'm waiting for an answer here.
a voice inside nudges: *tell her!*
my tongue wraps
around the words:
something happened . . .
but when i open my mouth to speak,
the phone rings,
and joan calls up the stairs,
carol ann, it's eric!
and i swallow
the words down fast.

* * *

five minutes after i get home
jeremy phones to say

his parents are leaving
for the weekend
and he's having a party.
i change into faded jeans and
my favorite nine inch nails tank top.
on my way through the door,
mam calls my name.

i follow her voice
to her tv chair,
where she's watching *unsolved mysteries,*
pigging out on double stuf oreos.
desiree, she starts,
all serious,
like she plans to take a stab
at maternal concern.
that or she's constipated.
you and that jerry boy
aren't having sex, are you?

i stand in front of the tv.
it's jeremy.
and why would
i tell you if we were?

she stares through me
like i'm invisible.
her x-ray vision freaks me out.
i step aside.

mam's pupils light into mine.
he sounds so horny
in those notes he wrote you.
all he thinks about is getting in your pants.
i'm worried about you, desiree.

i fold my arms across my front.
well, if you hadn't snooped,
you wouldn't have to worry.
besides—i grab my denim jacket
off a hook—*jeremy's a really sweet guy.*
i'd appreciate it if you'd cut him some slack.

mam reaches for another oreo.
you could treat larry better too.
he's been like a father to you,
including you in everything we do.
lately all you do is ignore him.

my stomach is a lava pit.
i want to scream:
you have no idea what
your precious larry did to me!
but i don't.
i watch mam walk to the fridge
for a coke, and before
her fat ass is planted
back in her chair,
i'm gone.

* * *

i stop at the fart mart
on my way to jeremy's.
a counter kid with a
million greasy pimples
talks on a cordless phone,
going, *yes, sir, no, sir,*
probably kissing ass with the boss,
mister mega-fart himself.
i waltz up and down the aisles,
lift a pack of marlboros,
a box of ritz crackers,
a can of spray cheese.
when i turn to leave,
the kid calls, *have a nice day!*
i wave and holler back, *you too!*

* * *

i can tell jeremy's buzzed
as he weaves toward me
and hands me a beer.
the party's small,
and everyone's watching mtv—
"creep" by radiohead.
munchies! carol ann squeals
as i unload the crackers and cheese.

a few hours later,
when the food and beer are gone,
everyone's paired off, making out.
i follow jeremy to his room,

amazed by how neat it is.
his clothes are picked up
and his bed is made,
decked out in a new green comforter—
an emerald island, floating
in a sea of blue carpet.
with the sticky stars glowing on the ceiling,
it's almost like being at the beach.

a light clicks on in my brain.
if we have sex while jeremy's buzzed,
he'll probably never guess
i'm not a virgin.
for a moment
i'm me again.
pre-larry me.
i lie across jeremy's bed,
patting the empty spot.

jeremy inches toward me,
blurry-eyed from drinking.
but there's something else
in his gaze—
like maybe he's drunk on me too.

his lips move slowly,
soft and sweet as butter
melting across warm toast.
he unbuttons my shirt
then starts for my jeans.
when i don't stop him

like usual,
he looks at me,
grinning, expectant. *dez . . . ?*

i nod,
grin back.
except before jeremy continues,
he asks, *are you sure you're okay with this?*
are.
you.
sure.
you're.
okay.
with.
this.
seven words
i should have heard before
but didn't.
seven words that make me
want to cry.

yeah, i whisper,
fighting tears,
because suddenly i realize
i'm not just covering larry's tracks,
i'm clearing a new path for jeremy.

as his fingers glide across
my breasts, my stomach,
and down, down to a
place that is damp

and waiting,
i imagine i am new again.

i don't float out of my body
or watch from the ceiling
like i did with larry.
i'm in my body
feeling every kiss,
every touch,
every quake.
jeremy is safe,
my heart tells me.

* * *

afterward,
jeremy's arm is
looped behind my neck,
nestled in just the right spot.
the other, sleep-laden and heavy,
is draped across my chest.
my boobs are smooshed,
but i don't move.
i memorize every detail:
jeremy's sweet, soapy smell
mixing with something
musky and mysterious,
the street light squeezing
through the mini blinds,
covering him in thin white stripes,
the smile teasing his lips.

if i were an artist,
i'd paint a picture of him.
but i suck at art
like i suck at everything in school.
so remembering will have to do.

* * *

when i get home,
i reach in my underwear drawer
for the tiny calendar i use
to keep track of my periods.
carol ann says
i'm lucky to be so regular,
that i'll never be caught
like she was last june,
bleeding through a pair of white jeans
in the middle of a history final.

she's right.
i'm never early. or late.
every month's exactly the same—
four days, x'ed in red,
twenty-six days apart.

since larry did what he did,
i have a new calendar ritual.
just before i crawl into bed
i x away the day that just passed.
it's like i'm saying to myself,
you survived another twenty-four hours

without killing someone or screaming.
except i mark my surviving larry x's
with a black sharpie
so when i *do* get my period
and switch back to red,
i won't screw up the system.

i'm still waiting though,
still watching those black x's
march their asses across four rows,
moving in on the fifth.

after my first time with jeremy,
i mark black x number thirty.

Ariel

AFTER TALKING WITH DAD, I START ON MY HOMEWORK. When the phone rings again, I let the machine screen the call.

"Hey, Ariel." Shane sighs. "Look, I know you're home 'cause your voice mail kicked in, which means you were on the phone. I need to talk to you. Pick up, okay?"

I hurry toward it. "I'm here," I answer. "I just got off the phone with my dad."

Shane's one of the few people I told about having a dad in prison who didn't get all weirded out. "Have a nice talk?" he asks me.

"Yeah, we did."

"How's your headache?"

I'd forgotten about my lie. "Better."

"I left you two messages," Shane says. "How come you didn't call me back?"

"Oh, um, I wanted to take a shower and wash my hair first," I lie again.

Shane clears his throat. "When I didn't hear from you, I got worried you were still upset with me about the joke. Ariel, I shouldn't have done that. I was playing around with you because

I was bummed you wouldn't let me in. But it was a mean and stupid thing to do, and I'm really sorry. Forgive me?"

Even if I was still upset, the awkward softness in Shane's voice could easily melt it away. "Yeah, I forgive you."

"Good. Thanks." Shane pauses. "Are you alone?"

"Yeah. Mom's working late. We're going out to dinner when she gets home."

"Cool. Look, um, I still have an hour before work. Can I stop there on my way? Maybe we can sit at the kitchen table and talk. I'll wear my Boy Scout badge."

Not again. "Shane," I start, trying to sound upbeat, "some night when you don't have work—when my mom's home—I'll show you the house and we'll hang out in the rec room where it's private and watch a DVD or something." I shove my hair behind my ear. Again and again. After about the eighth time, I stop myself. "How does that sound?"

There's a long silence. I'm starting to get the headache I lied about.

"How old are you?" Shane asks.

I laugh nervously. "You know I'm almost sixteen. Why are you asking me that?"

"Because. The sixteen-year-old girls I knew at my old school passed the I-can't-make-Mommy-mad-at-me stage at, like, twelve."

His words hit me like a slap in the face. In fact, a slap would have probably hurt less.

"Shane, stop. You're hurting my feelings."

"And you think you're not hurting mine, Ariel? More than anything, I want to take care of you, and you're guarding the door and clinging to your mother's rule like I'm a friggin' predator or something. How do you think that makes me feel?"

Tears well up in my eyes.

"Look, Ariel, I care more about you than I've ever cared about anyone."

"You . . . do?"

"Yeah, I do. That's why this is eating me up inside. I just want to see you. To sit in the same room with you and look at you and talk with you and, and"—his voice cracks—"and keep you safe from the *real* pricks of the world."

Steadying the remote, I point it at Bart Simpson's face. When the screen goes black, I get a sudden chill. Why do I feel like I've shut down something bigger than a TV show? I take a deep breath. Let it out. "Okay. Park near the shrubs so the neighbors can't rat me out. And don't come to the front door—cut through the garage instead."

"Be there in fifteen minutes," he says. "Can't wait to see you."

"Me too," I say back, but Shane's already hung up.

I hurry to the bathroom for a quick shower so Shane won't find out I've lied. I wet my hair but don't wash it. There's not enough time for that.

Eleven minutes later, I hear knocking at the kitchen door. I rush to my room and glance out the window. Sure enough, Shane's black Yamaha is parked beside our long row of hedges. "Just a second!" I call, grabbing my robe, reminding myself that if I really had showered when I said I did, I'd be completely dressed by now.

When I turn, I stub my toe on the corner of my computer desk and fall, face-first, cracking my forehead on my nightstand. I touch my left eyebrow, which is throbbing. Already there's a goose egg forming.

I hear Shane trying the kitchen door, which, of course, I locked when I came in. "Ariel?" he calls. "Where are you?"

I throw open my closet, searching for something easy to slip on.

Shane's knocking morphs into pounding, and I'm nervous the neighbors will hear. "Ariel, are you okay?"

"Be there in a minute!" I grab a black hoodie, faded Levi's, a pair of bikini panties, and a sports bra. Then, remembering what Shane says about sports bras—that they, quote, *take two wonderful breasts and transform them into a uniboob,* unquote—I trade it for a satiny white one.

After I slip on my panties and bra, the pounding stops. Still in rush mode, I whirl back around, reaching for my shirt and jeans. But when I glance into the mirror over my dresser, I gasp.

In the glass, there's a second reflection—Shane's. He's leaning against the doorframe to my room. Shane and I have unbuttoned and unzipped our clothing while we've made out, but the garments pretty much stayed put. Now, I feel exposed. "I told you I'd be there in a minute," I say, grabbing my bathrobe and tying it around me. "How did you get in?"

Shane holds up the emergency key.

Shit. I completely forgot about the spare.

My pulse pounds in my neck. I'm usually so calm and rational. Most Likely to be Picked for Team Captain in the Event of a Natural Disaster—that could be my moniker. But now I feel something shift in my brain, the synapses firing differently.

I'm mad, I realize. I push past him and start through the door.

Shane grabs my arm and whirls me around. When he lets go, his eyes lock with mine. Even though he's not touching me, I still feel pinned in place by that gaze.

"Don't be upset," he says, reaching for my chin, turning it toward him. "When you didn't answer, I was scared something had happened to you. That you were hurt."

I walk to my dresser and grab my hairbrush, tugging on a tangle. Mentally, I recap what just happened, looking at it from *Shane's* point of view. Finally, I decide I can't blame him. I might have done the same thing if I was that concerned.

Shane steps behind me and takes the brush. He glides the bristles down my scalp, clear to the end. "I worship every inch of you," he says, gathering the tips of my hair into a clump, which he brings to his lips, kissing it. "Right down to your split ends."

I elbow him. "I don't have split ends."

"Do too," he teases. He rests his chin on my shoulder, studying our reflections in the mirror. When he lifts my bangs away from my forehead, the lump from my fall leaps into view. He touches the bruise. "Hey, how'd this happen?"

"I tripped and hit it on my nightstand."

"Ouch." He smoothes my bangs back. "I hope no one thinks *I* did that to you."

Confused, I watch his face in the glass. "Shane, why would they?"

He laughs and I jump, which makes him laugh even harder. "Hah! Right! Why would they?"

He loops his arms around my waist, undoing the tie on my robe. The bow on my bra appears, a rectangle of stomach, a sliver of panties. Self-conscious, I reach to close it.

Shane moves my hand aside. "You're beautiful," he whispers. Then he leans in, kissing my neck. I watch him in the mirror as his dark hair falls across his face, as his lips creep slowly toward my ear, then tenderly nibble the lobe. His tongue inches inside, exploring the innermost folds. Shane's kisses ignite something that's never been on fire before. And if we were making out somewhere else—in a movie or at a concert—I'd be fine with what's going on. But this is not happening somewhere else.

Shane moves closer, pressing his full weight against me. His hand reaches through the opening in my robe. His fingers ease beneath my bra.

I glance at my clock. "Shane," I whisper, "I should get dressed. It's six thirty. You have to go to work. And my mother will be home soon."

"I'm not afraid of the Momster," he breathes, moving against me. The bones that stick out on either side of my hips grind against the edge of my dresser. When a sudden sharp pain rages there, I say, "Ow!"

Shane takes my hand. Turns me around. Lowers me onto my bed.

"I want you." His lips graze my neck again. But now the good feeling's gone.

"Please, Shane. I think we should stop. I don't think I—"

Shane's mouth covers mine, silencing me. He reaches to unzip his jeans.

My pulse races. I pray for Mom to show up. I don't care that I'll have to confess it was my fault Shane came over. Or how it looks that I have my bathrobe on. I just want to hear the familiar sound of her car pulling into the garage.

My heart wallops my throat so hard, I'm scared my neck might explode. "I'm not *ready!"* I blurt out. Except I can't tell if the words make a sound, or if I only *think* them.

But they must. Make a sound, that is. Because Shane rises up from my bed. Avoiding my eyes, he zips his pants. Adjusts his T-shirt. Takes a step back. Then he starts down the hall, past Mom's room, the bathroom, the guest room.

Suddenly I feel guilty. I'm not sure why, but I do. Big time. "Shane"—tying my robe closed, I follow him—"don't go. You said we could talk. Remember?"

I step between him and the kitchen door.

There's a raw, unfamiliar pain in Shane's eyes I've never seen before. He looks so vulnerable. Could he really be the same confident person who took on the Veep? All traces of that person are erased now.

I reach to touch his face, but he pushes my hand away. That's when I realize he's crying. "Shane," I whisper, "what's wrong?"

Hard, wrenching sobs shake his body. It's almost too private to watch. He gulps air, like someone trying to stay afloat. "I—I care—way too—much about—you."

Our eyes meet. Then lock. Something deep in our centers connects. I couldn't look away if I wanted to. We're joined. Perhaps permanently.

Shane doesn't look away, either. "Y—you're my whole fucking universe," he chokes out. "You're all I think about, Ariel, the only person I want to b—be with. Ever."

Oh. My. God. Ever. As in *forever.* He cares that much about me.

When Shane blinks, our gaze is interrupted, and I feel like my lifeline's been cut. I clasp his waist, holding tight, so I won't drown without him.

Shane doesn't reach back, though. He removes my arms, placing them at my sides like he's posing a mannequin. Then he reaches for the doorknob.

"Wait!" I shout, surprising myself.

Shane turns. "Wait for what, Ariel?" He flips up the blank screen again. Studies me with the same cool look you'd use to examine a specimen in chem lab.

The detachment undoes me. I can't take it. I want him back. I untie my robe, let it part. "I've changed my mind. I *am* ready."

Shane reaches down, touching the bruise that's forming on my hip. "I didn't mean to do that," he says, and his eyes fill again. He gathers the ties on my robe, knotting them across my front. "You're not ready, Ariel. Not for someone who loves you the way I do."

I open my mouth to speak, but Shane presses a finger to my lips.

Turning, wordlessly, he leaves.

As I watch him cross our garage, then start outside, activating the motion light, I make a silent promise to myself. I will be ready next time. Maybe after Mom and I return from our trip to Elmira.

Yes, I decide.

That's when.

Madeline

I AM OFFICIALLY DIETING, something I never dreamed I'd do. Food is the only thing that's ever mattered to me. But now I have Tad. Tad, who thinks I'm pretty and smart and nice. I would like to add thin to that list. Looking good for him is my number one priority. And I love having a priority. I feel like I'm doing something normal people might do. People who don't avoid everyone they come into contact with. People who don't shut themselves in their room at night with a two-thousand-calorie "snack" because that's the only thing they have to look forward to. I'm glad to leave that club. As long as I have Tad, I'll never go back. Ever.

On Saturday morning, I wash Mom's and my clothes at the laundromat, same as I do every weekend. Except, instead of coming straight home afterward, I park the laundry basket inside the door to Franklin's Five and Dime. Wandering the aisles, I search for AYDS Appetite Suppressant Candy, which I saw advertised on a TV commercial. When I find it, I buy two boxes—one chocolate and one butterscotch.

Each morning that next week, I eat a bowl of Total cereal with skim milk then pack my lunch: a single sandwich—lettuce, tomato, and

Velveeta cheese with Miracle Whip—a bag of carrot sticks, an apple, and a Tab cola. And every day after school, I meet Tad at McDonald's and drink a diet soda while I help him study for his GED.

The second Friday after Tad and I start meeting, I'm wearing a pair of size eighteen pants and a pink cardigan I bought at the thrift store. Coming through the door, I feel like Donna Fargo when she sang "The Happiest Girl in the Whole USA."

But once I'm inside, all those good feelings vanish. Tad isn't sitting in our usual booth, waiting for me. I case out the non-smoking section. The counter area. The hallway outside the bathrooms. No Tad.

My heart pounds so hard, I'm scared I'll go into cardiac arrest. I hurry back outside, hyperventilating.

A voice calls my name. When I whirl around, my tote bag butts me in the rear. It's heavy—loaded with books and binders for every subject, so I'll be prepared for whatever Tad's in the mood to learn about.

"Madeline!" I hear a second time.

I scan the parking lot. Tad's head pokes out the window of a navy blue pickup truck. It's rusted in spots, and there's a dent on the passenger side.

I hurry to him, out of breath. "W—why aren't you working?"

"They changed my hours," he tells me. "I'm off at three."

My heart sinks. I don't get out of school until three, and then I have a fifteen-minute walk. I'll never get to McDonald's in time to see Tad. Suddenly I want a Big Mac. Three Big Macs. Five. I could kill for them. I reach into my pocketbook, unwrap an AYDS candy, and pop it in my mouth, chewing furiously. I'm not following the directions on the package—I'm supposed to chew two before a meal—but I have to quell the storm churning in my middle. I have to quiet the Beast.

"Hey," Tad says, smiling, "don't look so glum. It's good news."

I'm suspicious. What's good for everyone else usually stinks for me. I narrow my eyes. "Like what?"

"They made me the new assistant manager for the seven-to-three shift."

I glance at my watch. It's three thirty. "So . . ." I start.

"So I'm off work," Tad finishes.

"So . . ." I repeat. Like I'm an imbecile who only knows one word.

"Sooooooo, where do you want to go?"

"Go?" Now I'm turning into a parrot.

"Yeah. For a drive." He hops out, motioning to me. "You've gotta get in on the driver's side. The door on your side doesn't work."

Tad said *my* side. I stare at the open door.

"Don't worry," he says, watching me. "The dent wasn't my fault. Honest. I was inside the 7-Eleven when it happened. Hit-and-run."

My mouth won't move. Nodding is all I can manage. I step up onto the running board. My thighs just barely clear the steering wheel as I slide across the seat. But I make it to the other side.

My side.

Tad clears his throat. "I was wondering . . ." His thumbs do a nervous dance on the steering wheel. "If maybe you'd like to see a movie."

"A movie?" I fasten my seat belt to keep from leaping into the air. "Uh, sure."

"Good." He smiles. "*Airport '77* is playing at the Royale Theater." He glances at the clock on his dashboard. "The next show's in forty-five minutes."

Tad parks near the recreation area that runs along the river. On the walk to the theater, I grow excited. I've never been inside a movie house before.

At the concession stand Tad asks for popcorn and Raisinets, and I get a Tab. Inside the theater, we sit near the back. I'm amazed by the size of the screen—a hundred times bigger than a TV. When the projector starts and the previews come on, the sound is everywhere. Above me, below me, around me, filling me up when I breathe.

In the darkness, Tad reaches for my hand, sending a million shock waves surging through me. My God, I'm actually being touched. I'm feeling what girls like Muralee Blawjen get to feel all the time. For a moment, I block out the giant screen and the amazing sound, and I focus on this one thing, attempting to memorize every detail. Tad's damp palm, shielding my hand like a pup tent. The tickle of knuckle fuzz when he weaves his fingers through mine. And the amazing warmth. Warmth like I've never felt before but suddenly can't live without.

When the film ends, the downtown stores are closed. As we amble past them Tad slips his arm around my waist. I never want the moment to end. I want to walk up and down Main Street a billion times, Tad's arm drawn around me as the stores open and close, as the window displays change from fall to winter to spring to summer and back to fall again. By then, I'll be thinner than Muralee Blawjen. I'll be finished with high school, and maybe Tad will ask me to marry him.

Tad stops in front of a poster gallery, studying a Salvador Dali print—the one with the melting clocks. "That's so cool," he says.

"It's called *The Persistence of Memory,*" I tell him.

He looks at me, surprised. "Hey, how'd you know that?"

"Art history class."

Tad turns to face me. He takes my hands in his. "Mind if I kiss you?"

"Yes," I whisper, blushing. "I mean, no. No, I don't mind. Yes, you can kiss me."

Gently, Tad's lips meet mine. I taste the lingering saltiness of his popcorn, the sweetness of his candy. But mostly, I taste life—which I'm discovering is quite delicious.

* * *

All that next week, I meet Tad at McDonald's to help him study. Then we go for a drive and park along a country road and kiss some more. When it's time for Tad to take me home, a part of me always dies. I never want to let go.

On Friday, he invites me to have dinner and see another movie. Other than having fried chicken at the bowling alley snack bar where one of Mom's boyfriends used to take us, I'm not used to eating out. I have no idea how dressed up to get. So I play it safe and wear my new size sixteen bell bottoms and a frilly peasant blouse with elastic at the wrists so the sleeves won't accidentally ride up and show off my ugly lizard arm. And because it's late October, and the night air is getting chilly, I bring along a blazer too.

Tad parks in front of a diner called the Second Chance, just before the exit to the highway. I've driven by it dozens of times, on the way to Cherry Hill Cemetery, but I've never been inside. I feel like I'm on the stage set for *The Wild Wild West.* Saddles and wagon wheels and old shotguns hang from the ceiling beams. Movie posters from Westerns like *Rooster Cogburn* and *The Magnificent Seven* and *High Plains Drifter* line the dark, paneled walls. Tad leads the way toward a deserted back corner. He slides into a booth, and I sit across from him.

"You look really nice," he tells me. "You're wearing makeup, aren't you?"

I panic, worried I didn't put it on right. "Yeah. Does it look okay?"

"Sure. It makes your eyes stand out." He squints. "There's something else too."

"I've lost weight," I volunteer.

"That must be it." He fishes in his pocket for a coin and drops it in the miniature jukebox mounted to the wall beside our booth. He punches a number and I recognize the song right away—"If You Leave Me Now" by Chicago. In it, a man is begging a woman not to go away. He says he'll die inside if she does. I know exactly how he feels. That's how I'd be without Tad. I wouldn't have anything to live for.

A waitress arrives, wearing a Western shirt, blue jeans, and a cowboy hat. "Evenin', kids," she drawls, slapping two menus on the table. "Start ya off with a drink?"

Tad smiles. "Two beers, please."

The waitress grins. "You got IDs saying you're eighteen?"

Tad's toe taps mine under the table. "Okay, make that two Pepsis."

"Diet for me please," I add, reaching in my purse for two AYDS candies.

When the waitress returns with our drinks I order a chef salad and Tad asks for the Blue Plate Special, which—that day—is fried fish, a baked potato, and a side of lima beans.

After she drops our food off, Tad's lip curls. "I hate lima beans."

I laugh. "Then why'd you order them?"

"Well, I didn't order lima beans, per se, I ordered the Blue Plate Special."

Tad must read my confusion. He reaches into his wallet, pulling out a flattened stack of tickets. He passes them over to me.

"Good for one daily Blue Plate Special," I read aloud.

"You used to be able to buy those tickets in advance, and you'd save fifty cents on the meal." Tad draws a breath and scratches his ear. "My mom gave me those two weeks before I started first grade. I asked her why she was doing that when we usually paid by the day. And she looked away, playing with her clip-on earring, telling me, 'Well, you're a big boy now, you won't want your mama tagging along with you all the time. You might want to come here on your own. Or bring your dad or a friend from school.' She forced a smile, and my stomach felt queasy, but I couldn't pinpoint why. I said back, 'Why would I wanna come here without you?' but she just stared off again."

"And then what happened?" I ask him.

"She left two days later. Up and moved to New Mexico to shack up with some asshole lawyer. Haven't seen her since."

A dark, aching silence crowds the space between us. I reach for Tad's hand and ask him, "Did you ever use any of those tickets?" because that's all I can think to say.

"Nope. Haven't stepped foot inside the front door since my mom was with me." Tad swallows hard, and his Adam's apple bobs up and down. "It's funny, but when you're a kid, your brain gets a hold of these strange notions and acts like maybe they're true or something. And I think a part of my little pea brain told me that if I ever used one of those tickets and ate a Blue Plate Special without my mom, that would prove she wasn't coming back."

"You're here now, though."

"Yeah." He buries the tickets in my palm and squeezes my fingers closed around them. "Because you are."

* * *

The next morning, I wake with a terrible headache. I swallow two aspirin, but a half hour later, I'm still hurting. Tiny lightning bolts zip back and forth behind my eye sockets. When I perk Mom's coffee, the sound magnifies, hammering away at my temples, and the smell makes me want to puke. But I've heard coffee helps a headache, so when the brewing's done I pour myself some. I add three spoons of sugar and an ice cube, then gulp it down before I can taste it.

After two mugs, the pain lets up. I gather our laundry and start for the laundromat.

I'm on a bench inside reading a *True Story* magazine when the bell jangles and Mom waltzes through the door. I always do our laundry alone, so her presence puts me on alert. "What's up?" I ask, flipping a page.

As she sits next to me, the scent of V05 hair spray settles down alongside her. "Madeline, I met this guy . . ."

Jesus, here we go again. "Where'd you meet him?"

"At Domenic's." Domenic's is a newsstand where she occasionally picks up a paper and glances at the classifieds so she can report to the welfare office that she's looking for work.

"What's his name?" I ask flatly. Not because I care. I'm just passing time.

"He was buying vanilla pipe tobacco. I hope I get to smell it sometime."

I stare past her—at our sheets, twirling in erratic circles in the dryer. "His name?"

She looks away, which I take to mean she either doesn't know or can't remember.

The dryer buzzes. I give the sheets a quick feel and drop another quarter in the slot. "So where's Mystery Man taking you?"

Her cheeks look sunken, and there's this weird blue cast to her face. "Huh?"

I roll my eyes. "On your date. Where's he taking you?"

"Oh, well, we don't exactly have a date yet. We talked is all. He works at the hardware store." She giggles. "Never know when I might run out of nails."

"Or screws," I mumble, standing to buy a Tab from the soda machine. When I return and pop the tab Mom licks her lips like one of Pavlov's dogs. She feels in her pocket and pulls out several wrinkled bills. Her hands shake as she presses them flat on her knee. "I need to stop at the store. My redheaded aunt's in town."

"I've got a box of pads in my room," I say, testing her. "Take some of mine."

Mom holds the bills tightly, like a kid trying not to lose track of her allowance. "That's okay"—she stands and starts toward the exit—"I don't want to short you."

* * *

A sound startles me, and I jump up from the couch. When I realize it's Mom coming in, I glance at the clock. It's past mid-night. I think of the announcement that comes on just before the late news, saying, "Parents, it's 10 P.M.—do you know where your children are?" When I was little, I used to wonder why they didn't have one for *kids,* asking if they knew where their *parents* were.

The TV test pattern is on, which means I fell asleep and missed the ending to *Carrie.* Damn. I was really looking forward to seeing her use her telekinetic powers to get revenge on her classmates at the prom.

I listen for the sound of Mom's shoes hitting the floor near the door. I can tell a lot by the lapse between clumps. But I have to factor in the foot gear. Mom wore shoes with laces to the laundromat, not slip-ons. They take longer to remove.

Clump!

I wait. Count. Five-Mississippi. Six-Mississippi. Seven-Mississippi.

Clump!

Eight. Not bad. The record is twenty-nine. But that was in the winter, when she was wearing boots with zippers and buttons, and she fell after the first clump.

"Mad'line?" she calls. "Mad'line, honey?"

"In the living room," I answer, monotone.

She weaves toward me, one hand on the wall to steady herself, then drops down beside me on the couch. When she props her feet on the coffee table, I notice that her socks don't match. She lights a cigarette, inhaling. Her head rocks back, her mouth opens in a yawn, and smoke wafts out in sooty tufts, like it's rising from a smoldering brushfire.

I wait for a commercial to ask, "Where are your Kotex?"

When she doesn't answer, I glance at her. She's passed out already. A paper pokes out of her breast pocket. I take it out. A phone number's written on the back of a vanilla pipe tobacco label. Jesus, she doesn't waste any time.

"I met someone too," I tell her, even though she doesn't hear me. "Why don't you ask me what *his* name is? Why don't you ask where I met *him?"* I turn to glare at her. "Oh, wait, I forgot. You don't give a shit because everything's all about *you."*

Gray ash balances on the tip of her cigarette. Watching the red tip burn slowly downward, I feel anger bubbling inside me. "Tell me what I'm supposed to do"—my voice grows louder as my heart speeds up—"if *my* boyfriend ever wants to touch me the way *your* boyfriends touch you." I shove my sleeve up and thrust my scaly lizard arm forward. "Tell me!"

She doesn't answer, of course.

As I grab her cigarette and mash it out—so hard I burn my fingertips—my brain registers a smell I'll never forget. I rush to my room, slam the door, and put Janis Joplin on my turntable.

Tears cool my hot cheeks as I crank up the volume as high as it will go.

Desiree

one tuesday night,
about a month after
jeremy and i start having sex,
i decide to take a shortcut home.
walking down railroad avenue
behind the tire store,
i watch for my cue to turn off—
an old dead-end sign
sprouting like a rusted tulip
from a sea of knee-deep weeds.

a car slows down behind me.
a voice calls my name.
a man's voice.
i keep walking.
but the car speeds up
then turns in front of me,
so abruptly i plow into the hood
and fall backward.

larry steps out,
hurrying toward me.
you all right, desiree?
he holds his hand out to help me up,
but i stare a hole in it. *you hit me!*
don't be so dramatic,
he says, all calm,
you walked into my car.

i start to run.
at first i'm faster,
and larry has trouble keeping up.
but when i reach the dead-end sign,
he gains on me,
moving closer.

the mouth of the woods opens.
shadows gobble up the trees.
larry grabs my arm,
whirls me around.
what the hell's the matter with you?

i try to pull away.
let me go or i'll scream!
larry shakes me.
why are you ignoring me?
why can't i ever see you?
jesus, we made love and now—

made love? i shout.
are you crazy?
you raped me!
larry reels back like i've slapped him.
that's not the way
i remember it,
sweetheart.

i rush forward and take a swing.
larry catches my fist midair, twisting it.
i'm a pretzel, bent backward and down
till my knees touch the ground
and pain rages in my shoulder,
sending a message to my brain.
my lips can't help it,
they cry, *owwww!*

larry lets go
except he doesn't offer
to help me up this time.
standing on my own, i yell,
i'm telling on you!
i'm telling my mother what you did!

his face fills with concern.
i think he might apologize,
admit everything was his fault.
but his expression changes
as suddenly as rain evaporating

from a hot summer sidewalk.
a cold, hard stare takes its place.
your ma knows you're sleeping
with your boyfriend, desiree.
she tells me what a slut you are.
who do you think she'll believe?

* * *

i've missed two periods.
still, i pretend i have one.
i figure out where the
red x's *should* go,
and when jeremy
asks me to do it,
i tell him i'm riding
the cotton pony,
moan about killer cramps,
say, *let's watch the simpsons instead.*

* * *

on labor day weekend,
the last weekend
before school starts,
jeremy's parents take off
to visit friends in the poconos,
and jeremy throws another party.
dan, his friend from the wrestling team,
pops a porn video in the vcr,

except the tracking is totally screwed up
and the dialogue doesn't match
the mouth movements.

on my way to the bathroom to pee,
i bump into carol ann and eric,
just coming in from outside.
i can tell from their eyes
they got stoned.
plus carol ann's top is on inside out
and eric's fly is unzipped.
as eric starts toward the keg
carol ann leans into my side.
what's up?

i want to tell her,
i'm three months late
for my period.
instead i say,
nothing. what's up with you?
she laughs, then blurts out,
me and eric just did it
in his brother's truck.

so much for motels
and candles and wine.
when i reach to touch her arm,
she slides past me,
calling eric's name in a
strange high-pitched voice—

eeeeeh-rrrrrric—like he's a toddler
she's lost track of at the mall.

* * *

when school starts again,
i'm actually psyched because
i'm bored out of my freaking mind.
even hanging out and partying gets old.
the second monday
after classes begin,
carol ann sits on the sink in the lav
watching me stroke on mascara.
soon my lashes look like spiders,
legs blinking opened and closed.
the eyes they encircle stare back at me,
dull as a pair of scuffed marbles.

carol ann fluffs her hair in the mirror.
has jeremy asked you yet?

asked me what?
it comes out sounding bitchy,
but i can't help it.
i'm not in a carol ann mood.
lately i'm not in an anybody mood.

you know, carol ann coos.
to the harvest ball.

i grab my handbag off the sink.
there's a wet stain on the fake suede.
yeah, jeremy asked me.

carol ann grabs my hands,
jumping up and down
like a windup toy.
i pull away before i hurl.
all manic, she rushes out,
the four of us can double-date!
eric's brother'll let him borrow his truck.
me and you can shop for dresses together!
how's this weekend? huh?

i break thc bad news: that i can
barely afford to buy cigarettes,
let alone a dress for a dance.
no problem, she says,
my parents'll loan you the money.

i picture saturday on my calendar—
black x number 97.
sure, i say,
forcing a smile.

* * *

on saturday,
carol ann and i
meet at burger king

before dress shopping.
i order a bk big fish value meal
and dive at it when we get to our seats.
carol ann shakes her head. *ew. what's up*
with the stinky fish, whopper girl?
i shrug, talk with my mouth full.
just in the mood for something new.

she rolls her eyes,
squeezes sauce on her chicken tenders.
so did you and jeremy do it yet?

um—i sip my soda,
chew on my straw—*yeah.*

no way! she slaps my arm.
and you didn't tell your best friend?

it was jeremy's idea not to tell, i lie.
he wanted to keep it between us.
he said it would be more—i search
for the right word—*sacred.*

i wait for carol ann to laugh, but,
judging by the look on her face,
she's creaming her jeans instead.
wow, i didn't know guys
could be so romantic.

within minutes,
she's inhaled her meal.

she jumps up, tugging my arm.
come on, we've got shopping to do!

* * *

i've never been inside
randolph's department store.
i thought it was strictly
for the blue hairs.
a saleslady with
apple red lipstick that bleeds
into the cracks around her mouth
eyes us as we come through the door.
may i help you? she asks,
curling her lip like she smells
fresh dog shit on our shoes.

carol ann flashes a phony smile.
we're looking for junior party dresses.

red lips leads us
into a large pink room
filled with dresses the colors of
lucky charms marshmallows.
i feel like i'm trapped inside
a barbie doll case.

carol ann gathers
an armload of dresses,
and i find one i can semi-tolerate.
as i start for a fitting room

tucked behind a handbag display,
carol ann draws the curtain
on a extra-wide room in the corner.
pssst!—she waves me over—
c'mon in here with me.

just what i need.

inside
i hang my dress on a hook,
turn away to unsnap my jeans,
wrestling them off, they're so tight.
so is the size 7 dress i picked out.
damn, i can't even zip it.
try a 9, carol ann tells me,
that'll work.
and it does.
but will it still work
a month from now?

Ariel

I COMB MY BANGS FLAT and give them a hefty blast of freeze spray. Still, Mom notices my bruise during dinner. "How did that happen, Ariel?"

I explain to her about tripping and cracking my forehead on my nightstand, leaving out one important detail—that I was rushing around like a maniac because Shane was pounding on our door. Fortunately, Mom's so preoccupied with our upcoming trip to Elmira, his name doesn't come up once. He's there with me, though. All through dinner, I remember how fragile he looked crying in our kitchen.

The next morning, I wear Shane's favorite outfit—an Old Navy hoodie that clings after it shrunk in the dryer, and my low-rise Riders. Except I have some serious PMS bloating going on, and the jeans fit tighter than usual. I check my backside in the mirror to make sure I don't have VPL.

When I meet Olivia at Starbucks, there are two beverages on the newspaper box instead of one. "For you," she says, handing me the taller one. "Chai tea. I figured you could use the caffeine since you looked like crap yesterday."

"Thanks. I think." I take the cup as we start to walk.

"So," she says, "what happened after school yesterday? I thought we were going to try to do something together."

"Sorry. Shane was there waiting for me when I got home."

"Oh."

"Don't be mad, Liv."

"I'm not mad." She sips her latte. Looks away. "We just haven't hung out in, like, a really long time."

A gust of wind whips past, lifting my sprayed-down bangs.

Liv stares at my forehead bruise. "Ariel, what happened?"

I reach to smooth my bangs back, except my glove creates major static and my hair boings out in every direction. "Nothing. I fell."

I start walking again, but Liv doesn't follow along. I turn. *"What?"*

Liv beams a look of concern. "Ariel, is there anything you want to tell me?"

She's channeling Dad the Psychotherapist again. "No, Liv, there's nothing *to* tell. But I am freezing, so let's go."

Liv catches up to me, touches my sleeve, whispers, "Ariel, did Shane hit you?"

I think of what Shane said when he saw the bruise. *I hope no one thinks I did that to you.* This creeps me out, but I try to act normal. "No, Liv. God. Why would you say such a terrible thing?"

"I don't know, I just—" She forces a frown away. "Never mind. Sorry."

When we start walking again, Liv's phone bleeps, and I'm relieved to have the focus off me. She flips it open, reads a text, rolls her eyes. "Puh-*lease.*"

I try to peek at the message, but her scarf is blocking the screen. "What is it?"

"Dad wants to friend me on Facebook. Isn't that covered in a parenting manual somewhere? 'Do not stalk your sons and daughters on social networking sites.' She claps her phone closed. "Speaking of Facebook, you really should sign up." She flashes a phony smile. "*Virtual* visits are better than nothing."

"Come on, Liv. You know I'm too private to report my status to the world every day. *Ariel is happy because she talked to her dad in prison. Emoticon: smiley face.*"

Olivia laughs.

"I could see my profile page now," I continue. "I'd have, like, two friends. You and Shane."

"My dad'll friend you."

"Okay. Three. Except, wait, Shane thinks Facebook is for losers."

"Excuse me? *Maya Angelou* accepted my friend request." Liv shakes her head and turns. "And FYI, you wouldn't have to worry about a shortage of friends. No one knows all the people in their network. I'm friends with orchestra nerds and band geeks from schools all over the country I'll never meet."

We stop at the walk opposite school, wait for a bus to pass, then cross.

"Well, in my book," I tell Liv, "a friend is someone like you—a real live person I can hang out with and have an actual conversations with."

"Yeah? And when's the last time that happened for more than ten minutes?"

"Offering free guilt trips today?"

She smiles. "Speaking of which, you are coming to the dinner party, right?"

We start up the stairs to the school. "Sorry, Liv, I can't."

"Ariel, come on. It won't kill Shane to give up one Friday night with you. Didn't anyone ever teach him to share?"

At the top of the steps I hold the door open for her. "It's not Shane's fault. My mom and I are leaving for Elmira on Friday morning."

"Oh my God. To see your grandmother?"

I nod.

"Are you nervous?"

"Big time."

She loops her arm through mine and bumps my hip. "See, this is why we need some time together. Rent a few chick flicks, ingest mass quantities of sweet and salty foods, commit a few random acts of insanity—" She crosses her eyes and sticks out her tongue.

"Stop"—I elbow her side—"you're making me laugh, and I've gotta pee."

She elbows me back. "Don't let Shane hug you then. Things could get ugly."

We pause outside the media center.

"Well"—Liv tips her latte toward my locker, where Shane's waiting—"I should let you go."

"Yeah. Probably."

"Call me after my cello lesson. Or stop by."

"Yeah. I'll try."

Her tentative smile says, *Bullshit, you will.* "Buh-bye."

I turn, approaching Shane, expecting him to look at least a *little* upset after what happened the night before. Instead he flashes a wide smile. How can he be the same person who cried his eyes out in our kitchen just over twelve hours ago? Studying him, I slip my jacket off and hang it on the hook. "Are you . . . *okay?*"

"Fine. But you're finer. Look at you. *Grrr.*" He wrap his arms around my middle, pulling me closer.

My nether regions ignite. But the flame's snuffed out when Shane pinches me, once on each side of my waist. Which hurts. "Hey"—I pull away—"why did you do that?"

He smiles again. "Just checking out your little muffin top."

I'm so embarrassed, I could die. "It's not a muffin top, I—oh, never mind." When I reach for my books, I notice a gift bag on the top shelf.

"For you," Shane says.

"Really? Why?"

"To make up for not having a real gift the other day. And"—he leans in to kiss me—"today's our anniversary."

I had no idea I was supposed to buy a present for our two-month anniversary, but I should've at least thought of a card. "Shane," I confess, "I don't have a gift for you."

Thank God he doesn't seem disappointed. He hands me the bag. "Open it."

I wiggle my fingers beneath the tissue paper, gasping as I lift out a cell phone. It's the same one I've been begging Mom to buy me at the mall. I flip it open. A photo of Shane appears on my wallpaper. He's peering from behind a dark curtain of bangs, smiling that shy smile I love.

"I already programmed it for you." Shane reaches over and pushes a button. A number I don't recognize appears.

"Whose number is this?" I ask.

"Try it and see."

I press the Talk button. "Only U" by Ashanti plays—Shane calls it our song. He reaches in his pocket and flips open a phone that matches mine. "Helllllooooo?" he answers, all sexy.

"I can't believe you," I say, talking into my cell. "This is so cool. Thank you."

"You're welcome," he says into his.

It seems weird to be on the phone with each other when we're only a few inches apart, so I clap mine closed.

Shane holds his out, clicking a picture of me.

I blink at the unexpected flash. "God, thanks for the warning. Let me see."

Shane shows me the picture.

"Delete it," I beg. *"Please.* My eyes are closed and my mouth is open."

"I know." He licks his lips. "Hot."

I try to grab his phone away, so I can get rid of it myself, but Shane tucks it back in his pocket. "Now we have our own private love connection," he says, imitating Arnold Schwarzenegger. Then, in his own voice, he adds, "Seriously, now we can be there for each other twenty-four-seven."

This creeps me out just a little. I mean, I love having a boyfriend and feeling on the inside of some club everyone else signed up for, like, years ago. But promising every minute of every day seems kind of over the top.

"You want that too, don't you?" Shane tips his eyebrows and frowns. And even though it's obviously a put-on face, it makes me think of him crying in our kitchen, showing me a side of himself he's possibly never shown to anyone. Yes, it really did happen. Just like I remember. Despite how Shane looks or acts today, it was real. And you can't mess with a person's trust after he's let you in that deeply, that completely. It would be cruel. "Of course," I say, losing myself in his eyes. "Of course, I want that, too."

* * *

On my way home, I get a craving for a Diet Coke. Mom never buys soda unless Aunt Lee's visiting, and then we'll have Dr. Pepper on hand.

I duck into Quik Pay, grab a can from the cooler, and get in line. When "Only U" plays, I feel in my jacket pockets for my phone, but it's not there. Then I remember I zipped it in my backpack, which I totally trash before I find it. "Hi," I rush out.

"Hey, what took you so long?" Shane asks.

"I couldn't find the phone," I admit, holding it to my ear with one hand, digging for change with the other. I slide five quarters toward Counter Guy—a tall kid with blond dreadlocks and a pierced eyebrow.

"It's a dollar twenty-nine," he informs me.

"Just a second," I tell Shane. I set my cell on the counter and search for more change. But I come up empty. "Shoot," I mumble, "I'm short."

"Gotcha covered," Counter Guys says. He reaches into a penny jar parked next to the *TV Guide*s, removes four coins, and drops them in the register drawer. "You don't recognize me, do you?"

"Um, no," I say. "Sorry."

"Music theory class last year. You sat two seats ahead of me."

"Oh, yeah," I say, even though I really don't remember. "Thanks for the pennies."

"Sure thing."

I head toward the exit, trying to cradle the phone between my chin and shoulder, open the door, and pull the tab on my Diet Coke, all at the same time. No wonder Mom complains about people talking on the phone while they're driving. Multitasking with a cell attached to your ear isn't as easy as it looks.

"I'm back," I tell Shane.

"Who was that?" Shane's words are sharp and tight.

"A guy at the Quik Pay."

"What's his name?"

"I—I don't know, Shane. He was behind the counter. I mean, he works there. And he claims he was in class with me. But I don't remember seeing him before, I—"

"Why were you talking to him then?"

He's scaring me. "Shane, I—I wasn't, really, I just, well, I didn't have enough money for my soda and—"

"Let me guess. Mr. Wonderful helped you out."

My deodorant ups the Threat Level to orange, but I try to sound calm. "Shane, all he did was give me four cents. From a jar. They weren't even his pennies."

"Why didn't you ask me? I would've come right over and given you the money."

A nervous laugh escapes my throat.

"What the fuck is so funny?" Shane snaps. "That I care so fucking much about you that I'd drive a fucking mile to give you four cents so you won't have to owe some fucking loser something for—"

"Shane, *stop!*" I shout, surprising myself. Then I add quietly, "It was four pennies. That's all. Now let's forget about it, okay?"

There's a long silence.

My throat is dry. When I sip my soda, my hand shakes.

"Look," Shane says, "I'm sorry. The minute I got in the door Ma started riding me about all this crap she needs done this weekend. Stuff my *father* should be doing."

Shane never wants to talk about his past. All I know is that he and his mom moved here because his dad abandoned them to live with his twenty-one-year-old secretary. Shane has a lot of extra responsibility now. That would make anyone jumpy. "It's okay," I say. "I'm sorry too."

Outside Quik Pay, our connection gets fuzzy.

"You're breaking up," Shane tells me. "Call me when you get home."

"Okay. Talk to you then." I stuff my phone in my backpack, take a swallow of Diet Coke, and decide to take the long way home.

* * *

Mom's car is in the driveway. She's almost never home before I am.

As I open the door, she calls, "Hi, honey, how was your day?"

I follow her voice. "Good."

Two suitcases—the kind on wheels with collapsible handles—are parked in the hall between our bedrooms. One's sky blue tweed, the other is black faux suede.

"What's with the new bags?" I ask, tossing my backpack on my bed. It slides off my slippery comforter, does a double roll over onto my rug, and lands with a thump against my nightstand. I say a silent prayer that my phone's okay.

"The bags in the basement smelled musty. No surprise. We've had them since we left Florida. These were on sale at Target. You pick, blue or black."

I'm about to say blue since it's my favorite color and the fabric matches my eyes. But then I think of Shane's eyes, so brown they're almost black, and point to the darker one.

Mom rolls it toward me. As I sit at my desk to unlace my Nikes, I notice she's still standing in the doorway. Her look says, *I need to talk.*

Aunt Lee claims there are two kinds of people in the world: the Slow Easers, who remove a Band-Aid bit by bit in slo-mo, feeling every hair pull loose, and the Quick Rippers, who endure a sudden, sharp pain but have that baby off in no time.

"Wanna sit down?" I ask, in my typical Slow Easer style.

Mom, the Quick Ripper, says, "I'm mad at her."

"Who?"

"My mother."

"Why?" I know why *I* would be. I'd have a hundred reasons.

"For getting sick." Mom swipes a tear—roughly, like she's mad about crying too. "For making *me* be the one to come to *her.*"

"She really sucked as a mother, didn't she?"

Mom reaches for my Kleenex box and dabs her nose with a tissue. "On a scale of zero to ten, I'd give her a two."

I stare at the black travel bag. "Why do we have to go see her? Why can't we just send flowers? Or call?"

"Because, she made a point to locate me. That tells me she wants me there. That she needs me."

"God, Mom, look at the times you needed her, like when she found out you were pregnant with me and—"

"Ariel," Mom interrupts, something she almost never does, "I promised myself I'd never be the kind of person she was—so consumed by my own pain that I wouldn't have anything to give."

"And you've kept your promise, Mom. This is different."

She crosses the room to drop her tissue in my pail. "Maybe not as different as you think."

"Mom," I start, "what's that supposed to—?" My phone rings, and I freeze.

"Ariel, is that a cell phone?"

"Um, yeah." I bend for my backpack, digging through the pockets.

Mom reaches below my bed. The phone must have fallen out of my pack when it slipped off the comforter. She holds it out asking, "Is this what you're looking for?" It's obvious she's waiting for an explanation.

"Can I explain after I take this call? Please, Mom?"

She hands me the phone, then leaves, closing my bedroom door behind her.

I flip the cell open. "Hi, Shane."

"Decided to take the scenic route, huh?"

"The . . . what?"

"Your walk home. You went the back way—past the landfill and across the Meadows instead of going through town."

I'm freaked out. "Were you *following* me?"

"Didn't have to."

"Then how . . . ?" My voice fades, and the question hangs there.

He hums the *Twilight Zone* theme song. "Want some company?"

I tap the black bag with my toe. "My mom's here."

"Plan B then. Want to go somewhere? I don't have to be at work till six."

"Actually, Mom and I are kind of in the middle of talking."

"About what? You sound worried."

If I'm worried about anything at the moment, it's telling Shane I'm going away for the weekend. Which is precisely why I haven't mentioned the phone call to him yet. Like I said, we've never missed a Friday night date.

"Come on, Ariel. No secrets. Is this about the guy at Quik Pay?"

I almost laugh but think twice. "No, it's not about him."

"Then what?"

I walk to my window. Specks of half-rain, half-snow are falling, and it's just starting to get dark. "My mom got a call from a hospital upstate. Her mother has cancer."

"Bummer," Shane says.

"Yeah." Before I can chicken out, I add, "This weekend we're driving to Elmira to see her. We're leaving on, um . . . Friday."

"Oh."

A long silence follows. My shoulders clench.

"Well," Shane says finally, "at least we've got our cell phones."

I'm so relieved he's not upset. "That won't make it any easier to leave you."

"You really mean that?" I can almost hear the smile in his voice.

I feel myself smiling too. "Of course, I do."

Madeline

THE NEXT MORNING, I walk to Franklin's Five and Dime for more AYDS diet candy. On my way to the register with two boxes, I see her. Muralee Blawjen. She's wearing a peach jumpsuit and a navy blue blazer, hunched over a small package, her body bent forward like a question mark. I'm embarrassed for her when I realize where she's standing—in the aisle where the condoms are kept. Rumor has it Mr. Franklin is the only store owner in the area who doesn't hide the rubbers behind the pharmacy counter.

Muralee looks over her shoulder at Mr. Franklin, who's on the phone with a customer, then back at the box she's holding.

Ducking behind a display of Epsom salts, it occurs to me that I'm the only person in the galaxy who knows what Muralee Blawjen is doing at this moment. But I don't get to gloat for long, because what I see next takes me by surprise.

Muralee opens her blazer and tucks the small box inside. Then she whirls on one heel and darts down the aisle in my direction.

I don't move fast enough to get out of her way. She runs right into me. Literally. Stunned, she glances at her hand—the one hidden inside her blazer—then up at me. Her eyes are green as summer grass. Softly, she says, "You saw me."

"B—but it was an accident. I didn't mean to. I—"

She glances toward the pharmacy again, where Mr. Franklin's still on the phone, then leans in so close I feel her breath on my ear. "Please don't tell. This'll be our secret." And then she kisses my cheek. Not Sharon Ranson's or Jeannette Landeau's or Nancy Topek's cheek. My cheek.

The bell over the door jingles as she slips through it.

Something pulls me back to the spot where Muralee had been standing. I study the space on the shelf left by the package she stole. Then I glance at the box beside it. A home pregnancy kit.

"May I help you?" a stern voice asks. Mr. Franklin is beside me with his stout belly and wiry eyebrows and clean, talcum-powder smell.

"N—no," I stammer and turn on my heel, rush to the register to pay for my diet candy.

When I get home, my mother's at the kitchen table, drinking coffee and smoking. The classifieds are open in front of her, and I notice she's circled two ads. As I reach in the fridge for some orange juice, I feel her staring at me. "Did you lose weight?" she asks.

I pour the juice. Half a glass. The rest I fill with tap water. It's important to cut calories wherever you can. "Twenty-two pounds," I answer.

"Wow." She stamps out her cigarette. "You look good. And pretty. I never noticed that before. That you're pretty, I mean."

I consider telling her there's a lot she's never noticed. But that would make it sound like I want something from her. Which I don't. I've let go of needing anything from her because I have Tad now. "Thanks," I say politely, setting my empty juice glass in the sink.

In my bedroom I begin my weekend homework, starting with English, my best subject. Mr. Bryant said to choose an object and write a narrative from the object's point of view. I choose an egg because that's the first thing that comes to me. An egg with tiny cracks in its surface and a hint of something inside, tenderly tapping its way out.

* * *

I do a juice fast over the weekend and drop another three pounds. On the way to McDonalds on Monday, a construction worker leans over a beam and whistles. I look around to see who it's for, and he waves. At me. My God.

I arrive at McDonald's at the same time Tad does. Inside, we drink sodas and study. Then we head for his truck, parked between a Dumpster and a row of trees. He holds the door open for me, and I slide in. When Tad turns the key, the radio comes on. One of my favorite songs, "Baby I'm-a Want You" by Bread is playing. Before he shifts into reverse, I ask, "Can we leave after this song?"

"Sure." He closes his eyes, listening too.

The guitar strums low and sweet, moving from chord to chord, pulling me away from myself. I let go. Give in. Disappear inside the sounds. Velvety voices chime in. The lyrics describe my feelings for Tad exactly.

I *do* want him.

I *do* need him.

I *do* pray he'll stay with me always.

When the song ends, I bite my bottom lip to keep from crying. I stare straight ahead and tell Tad something I've never told anyone. "Sometimes, when I listen to music," I start, "my heart kind of, well, it swells, expanding like it's connecting to something outside me.

Something *holy* almost." I want to say more. To tell Tad the song made me think of him, but I can't seem to take that step.

"What that guy said about someone being the one he cares enough about to hurt over?" Tad swallows hard. "That's how I feel about you."

"And that's how I feel about you!"

I slide closer and we kiss. Our mouths part and Tad's tongue finds mine, inviting it into a strange, wet dance. Then his lips nibble their way across my cheek.

As his tongue probes my ear, my heart beats harder and my breath quickens. I feel something I've never felt before. Yearning.

But when Tad slides a hand beneath my shirt, I think of my lizard arm and panic. I went on my diet so I could look good for Tad, but I never decided what I would do if he wanted to touch me. Or maybe I just found it hard to believe that would ever happen. I mean, touching is what other people do. I'm not other people.

Tad's fingers inch upward toward my bra.

I have to find a way to make him stop. "Tad, wait"—I pull back—"we're in a parking lot." As if on cue, a crowd of kids races past.

Tad blinks several times, like he's coming out of a trance. "Oh, yeah . . . I forgot." Reversing out of our parking space, he says, "Guess next time we'll have to go somewhere private."

Next time. What do I do? I can make my fat disappear, but my scarred arm is here to stay. I say the first thing that comes to me. "How about someplace dark?"

Tad nods. "Dark it is."

After we've driven several miles, he says, "I told my dad about you."

"Yeah? What'd you tell him?"

"That there's this girl I like. And it's getting serious. He wants to meet you."

On the edge of town, Tad pulls onto Commercial Drive—a road we've never been down before. As he weaves through the industrial park, my stomach does a nervous double flip. "Tad, um, where are you taking me?"

He crosses the railroad tracks, turning near a bus garage. "I told you. My dad wants to meet you."

I grip the dashboard. "You mean today? *Now?*"

"Yeah"—he glances at me—"unless today's not good."

I can't disappoint Tad again. I take a deep breath. Let it out. Check my hair and makeup in the mirror. "Today's fine," I tell him.

A rusty sign announces Valley View Rentals. Tad hangs a sharp left and we wind down a one lane road lined with mobile homes. He parks beside an oatmeal-colored trailer, and an old brown dog appears, half-running, half-limping toward the truck.

"Millie!" Tad calls, stepping out, scratching the dog's scruffy head. He glances back inside the cab. "Ready, Madeline?"

"Not really," I mumble to myself.

Tattered throw rugs are tossed across a soggy walk, their edges just shy of touching, like connect-the-dots that missed the mark.

I hop from one to the next and then follow Tad up a set of narrow stairs.

"Hey, Dad," he calls. "I'm home."

We enter through a small, dim kitchen. The linoleum is dingy, the color of an old person's teeth. The living room is next, paneled in plasticky wood, its shelves lined with bowling trophies.

"Have a seat," Tad says, starting down a skinny, dark hallway. "I'll be back in a minute."

I sit on a plaid couch, staring at the TV in the corner. A ball of tinfoil is shaped around its antennae. Even though the picture's fuzzy, I still recognize the program. *To Tell the Truth.* I like that show. I can always spot the phonies.

A man appears, dressed in jeans and a flannel shirt. His hair is blond like Tad's except his is thinning on top. "You must be Madeline," he says, reaching to shake my hand.

"Um, yeah. Nice to meet you, Mr.—"

"I ain't the mister type," he interrupts, laughing. "Call me Ed. And make yourself comfortable. My son'll get you a soda pop or whatever you like. Now, if you'll excuse me"—he turns toward the kitchen—"I'm gonna fix you kids dinner."

Ed ties on an apron, the same kind I've seen on ladies in magazines. Then he opens three cans of Chef Boyardee spaghetti and two cans of mixed vegetables.

When Tad returns, I notice he's combed his hair and changed his shirt. He walks to the fridge, opens two bottles of root beer, and sits beside me.

"Cheers," he says, and we clink our glass bottles together. Even though the soda's not diet, I sip it, just to be polite.

I glance at Ed, warming the food on the stove, and get a sudden, sharp pain in my chest—the one that taunts me when I feel sad about not having a family. A normal family. For a moment, I wonder what it would be like to live with Tad and his father. I could bake them casseroles and clean—the place could use it.

"Your dad's really nice," I say.

Tad nods. "He's a good guy. It's been just him and me for a long time."

I smile nervously. Did Tad just read my mind?

After several minutes, Ed calls, "Come and get it."

There are three plates on the kitchen table, already filled with food. In the center is a loaf of bread, a tub of oleo, and a pitcher of milk. I'm looking at way more calories than my diet allows, but I don't want to be rude. I decide I'll eat less the next day to make up for it.

Tad holds a chair out for me.

Ed says, "Pardon the bachelor food, Madeline."

Little does he know that it's been years since I've eaten a meal at a kitchen table with another living, breathing person. "Don't apologize," I say, sitting. "It looks great."

I open my napkin, which is a paper towel folded in two. I'm about to reach for my fork when Ed extends both hands, palm up. At first, I think he wants us to pass him something. But when Tad clasps one of his dad's hands, and he offers the other one to me, I get it. We're supposed to join hands.

My fingers are the happiest they've ever been, nestled in those two warm palms.

Tad bows his head. Softly, he says, "Bless us, O Lord, and these Thy gifts, which we are about to receive from Thy bounty through Christ, our Lord. Amen."

"Amen," Ed echoes.

"Amen," I say too.

Ed passes me the Parmesan cheese. "You got any brothers or sisters, Madeline?"

I shake the cheese on my spaghetti. "No, I'm an only child."

"Me too," Tad says. "It's lonely, isn't it?"

I want to say: *You think not having a sibling is lonely? Try not having a functioning parent.* Instead, I shrug and say, "I guess."

Tad says, "That's why I want to have a ton of kids someday."

Ed points his fork at him. "Better find yourself a good job, kiddo. They'll cost you." He turns to me and asks, "What kinda work's your old man do, Madeline?"

My stomach clenches. "I don't live with my dad," I say, not bothering to add that I don't even know who he is. "My mom's raising me."

"Tough lot for a lady alone," he says. "What's she do for a living?"

"Oh, uh"—I fiddle with the paper towel—"she's between jobs."

Ed nods. "What's she do when she is working?"

I think fast. "She's an entrepreneur."

"Shoot!" Ed laughs, slapping the table. "I've known a few of them in my day."

Desiree

three weeks
after trying on dresses
but still a week before the dance,
me and jeremy are in his room,
watching *beavis and butt-head*,
a little caesars box open between us.
usually when we share a pizza
we have leftovers, but
i did some major
chowing down.

jeremy leans close for a kiss.
within seconds we're making out.
when he goes to lift my shirt
over my head,
it's hard to get off.
struggling, he says,
there's a little more
of you to love lately.

what the hell's that
supposed to mean? i snap.

you put some weight on, that's all.
but i'm not complaining.
he glances at my chest.
your boobs are bigger.

jeremy gives me one
of those little-boy looks
that melt my heart every time.
even though my breasts
are tender
i let him unhook my bra
and have himself a field day
with my bigger 'n' better boobs.

after we make love
jeremy turns to me and says,
dez, i was thinking, maybe you
should go on the pill or something.
you know, so that . . .
his voice trails off.

i rest my hand on my stomach,
touch the extra layer of flesh
that covers me like insulation.
you're right. i should.
we wouldn't want anything to happen.

* * *

three days later,
i take the city bus to ten center street.
inside i walk to the end of the hall,
past ashtrays spilling over with butts,
push on the door marked
planned parenthood.

a lady in a gray linen suit
leads me into an office.
she closes the door behind us
and invites me to sit, so i do.

cat calendar pictures
line one wall,
displayed in cheap plastic frames.
i stare at the october kitty,
clutching a trick-or-treat bag,
popping out of a pumpkin.
i hate seeing animals posed.
they look so exploited.
i hope the cat scratched
the photographer.
i hope he took the candy and ran.

i glance back at the lady
who reminds me of oprah winfrey.
she tells me her name, which i forget,
then she asks me mine.
desiree, she repeats,
that's pretty.

she asks me other things too,
personal questions that
i answer like a robot,
my voice flat, barely there.
i study a display below a sign
that says *birth control*—
a round pink case filled with pills,
a funny-shaped wire thing,
a brown dome that could be a
barbie umbrella except
it's missing a handle.

that's a diaphragm, oprah explains.
you fill it with spermicidal cream and
insert it into your vagina
before intercourse.
i imagine shoving that ugly
rubber thing inside me
and i can't help it, i laugh.

all straight-faced
oprah says,
desiree, before we discuss
your contraceptive options,
we need to do a pregnancy test.
come with me, okay?
i follow her down a hall
that smells of refried beans.
she stops outside a bathroom,
hands me a cup to pee in.

i close the door, fill the cup,
leave it on the shelf beside the toilet.

in the waiting room,
i play with my belt,
which barely closes around me.
a woman sits across from me.
she's maybe nineteen or twenty.
a little girl with a load in her pants
pulls on the woman's arm,
crying *mommy, mommy!*
while a younger boy
lies on the floor,
kicking his feet,
eating snot.

oprah reappears,
inviting me back to her office.
she stares at her hands like
what she has to say is etched
in the creases of her palms.
your test came back
positive, desiree.
you're pregnant.
she reaches to touch my arm,
which is nice to do,
except it makes me cry.
she backs off,
sliding a box of tissue forward.
since you're only fifteen,

i imagine this presents a challenge,
but i can help you sort through your options.
one choice, of course, is to carry
your baby to term . . .

i tune oprah out,
study the august kitten,
who is pretending to watch tv,
a clicker poised beneath one paw.

. . . *or you might want to consider an abortion* . . .

pregnant.

baby.

abortion.

those words belong
to someone else.
they have nothing
to do with me.
nothing.
nothing.
nothing.
i jump up fast,
bolt through the door,
and run like hell.

* * *

that night
as i'm changing for bed,
i glance in my mirror,
turn sideways,
touch the small swell
rising from my middle.

pregnant,
i whisper softly
so the walls
won't hear me.
baby.

then
i mouth
the darkest,
scariest word:
abortion.
three syllables,
eight letters,
but so much
more than that.

a part of me
steps aside,
tells me,
get rid of the baby, desiree.
maybe you'll get rid of larry too
and the memory of what he did to you.
you can go back to being who you were.
before.

but when i think of what that
dark, scary word *really* means—
that something,
someone,
will
—shit!—
die

i crawl into bed,
clench my pillow tight,
bury my face in the foam
and cry.

* * *

the night of the harvest dance
i can barely squeeze into my dress.
the straps cut my shoulders,
the zipper gouges my back,
and my cups runneth over,
big time.

eric's older brother lets eric
borrow his truck for the night.
the four of us squeeze in
and eric shifts into gear.
carol ann tickles his side.
let's have some fun!

* * *

the band sucks,
no one was bright enough
to spike the punch,
and there are chaperones everywhere,
thick as a swarm of summer gnats.
we head back outside to the truck
to dump our punch
and refill our cups with the wine
jeremy bought with fake i.d.

it's warm for october,
like indian summer.
just off school grounds a bonfire roars,
and the smoke-filled air stings my eyes.

as the rah-rahs strut back and forth,
showing off their size 0 dresses,
i think of something mam told me
in one of her rare talkative moods.
she said she hated the
cheerleaders at her school.
they were skinny and pretty and
popular—everything she wasn't—
except this one girl she liked a lot.
mam would watch her during practice.
jesus, i said. *did you have a crush on her?*
and mam looked at me, all serious,
and said, *no, i wanted to* be *her.*

we wander out past
the baseball diamond.

a field spills over with pumpkins.
eric twists one off its stem and
chucks it at a telephone pole.
the pumpkin hits,
splits apart,
spattering orange barf everywhere.
jeremy and eric and carol ann laugh,
so i do too, even though
i don't think it's funny.

as i turn
to head back
to the truck
for more wine
the moonlight glides
across my belly swell
and i feel carol ann's stare.
i look up, meet her gaze. *what?*
she opens her mouth, closes it,
follows me back to the truck.

* * *

at one in the morning,
the parking lot is empty.
a chalky cloud hangs
over the smoldering bonfire.
eric drives along the pot-holed road
that snakes behind the school,
parks beside a dried-up cornfield.

he pulls two blankets from the back,
opens them both across the ground.

eric leads carol ann
in the direction of one blanket,
and jeremy motions me toward the second,
a few yards away.
the smell of burned wood
and old corn mix together
as we do it,
right there
below the night sky.
and this time the stars are real.

* * *

afterward
a mist hides the moon,
and the air is chilly.
when i shiver,
jeremy takes off his
suit jacket and drapes
it across my shoulders.
his warmth surrounds me,
his smell,
his jeremyness.
gazing at me,
he lifts a strand of hair
from in front of my face,
and for the first time ever
he says, *i love you, dez.*

i never thought about
whether or not i love jeremy.
but then i remember the day
in his bedroom
when he said he'd kill
anyone who hurt me,
and i whisper back, *i love you, too.*

* * *

everyone wants breakfast.
so i suggest the geronimo,
two blocks from jeremy's house,
but eric says, *i know someplace better.*
they make a killer omelet.

eric drives us clear to elmira,
to a diner called the second chance.
the walls are paneled dark brown
and decorated with movie posters
of old farts in cowboy hats.
we grab a booth in the
smoking section and light up.
as i study the menu
jeremy reaches behind
my head, smiling.
hang on, dezzie lou,
you got a piece of corn in your hair.
i elbow his side and shoot back,
how do you think it got there, cowboy?

* * *

it's four in the morning
when we get back to johnson city.
i can't wait to peel off my dress,
drop into bed,
and sleep.

jeremy kisses me good night on our porch.
i hand him his jacket and let myself in.
inside it's dark, but
i get this creepy sensation
i'm not alone,
that someone is watching me.

as my eyes adjust
a face moves toward me
and a hoarse whisper
shatters the silence:
i've missed you, sweet stuff.

Ariel

Mom hauls out the last of our stuff, cramming it into the trunk. By the way she's packed, you'd think we were leaving for two weeks instead of two days.

I set the directions on the dash between a bottle of Apple & Eve and a bag of Soy Crisps. I'd planned on getting the directions off Mapquest, but Aunt Lee, who grew up in Elmira, insisted on writing them out herself. Across the bottom she added, *Be safe, ladies! Say hello to my high school alma mater! xo, Lee.*

"Okay," Mom says, "mental check. The doors are locked. The stove's off. I put a light on a timer. The heat's set at sixty." She turns to face me. "Is that high enough? Will the plants be all right?"

"They'll be fine." I hop into the front seat, motioning for her to do the same.

Mom peers inside the car like it's an alien spacecraft instead of a Subaru wagon with a gazillion miles on it.

"Come on," I say. "Let's go. Marge is waiting." Marge is what Mom calls her car, named after Homer Simpson's wife.

Mom wrings her hands. "I didn't cancel today's newspaper. Maybe I should have. It'll be sitting in the driveway until tomorrow night when we—"

"Mom"—I pat the driver's seat—"let's go."

Hesitantly, Mom slides in. Fastens her seat belt. Adjusts her rearview mirror. Pats Marge's dusty dashboard.

Finally, we take off. As we cross the Mid-Hudson Bridge out of Poughkeepsie, my phone rings. I'd managed to glide through the whole why-Shane-gave-me-a-cell-and-why-I-accepted-it issue by inventing a little white lie. I told Mom that Shane was worried about us traveling, and that's why he bought me a phone—so I can call for help if we have any problems.

I peel back the flap on my pack, feeling inside for my cell. Then I dig through the side pockets. Next, I dump it upside down on my lap, cradling an avalanche of CDs, makeup, and breath mints. Meanwhile, "Only U" plays and I'm cursing under my breath, getting more and more upset.

"Hey, calm down." Mom moves a magazine off the seat between us, and there's my phone, underneath it. Except the ringing stops the minute I flip it open. 1 MISSED CALL. I push View. Shane's name appears. Quickly I phone him back.

He answers in less than a millisecond. "Where were you?"

"Here. I mean, on the road. We're driving. Well, Mom's driving. You know." I sound like a total spaz. "I couldn't find the phone."

"Oh," Shane says. One word. One short, single-syllable word. But it tells me all I need to know. He's upset about something.

I lean into my door, like that might give me some privacy. "Shane," I whisper, "what's wrong?"

"Nothing." Two syllables this time. Sometimes I'm so busy trying to figure out what *Shane's* feeling I barely have a clue what kind of mood *I'm* in anymore.

"I'm sorry," I say softly, even though I really don't have anything to apologize for. Other than being a moron who can't keep track of her phone.

Shane sighs a slow, easy breath. "Okay." Two syllables again. But these are smooth and round, even as well-worn stones.

I exhale too. "So, what are you doing?"

"Missing you."

"Me too."

We talk effortlessly for several minutes. I'm smiling again, and I even laugh a few times—once so hard that I snort, then hiccup, which makes my mom laugh too.

Before we hang up, Shane says, "Call me when you get there, okay?"

"Okay."

* * *

Four hours later, Mom and I are parking Marge in the hospital lot. Inside, we stop at the visitor's desk. An old woman in a turquoise dress smiles up at us. Her pin says *Frieda: Volunteer.* A halo of white hair surrounds her head, transitioning to black a few inches from her scalp. I feel sorry for her, that she doesn't know how ridiculous it looks. "Name of the person you're here to see?" she asks.

"Murdock," Mom mumbles.

Frieda scans her list. "Are you family?"

The word must throw Mom for a loop. Her face goes completely white.

"Yes," I answer for her.

Frieda holds out two visitor stickers. "She's in room seven-twelve, bed B. Take the second set of elevators."

On the way, we pass a gift shop. There's a candy kiosk next to the register. Mom almost never eats sweets, so I have no idea why she stops. Or why she has this bizarre expression on her face—like one of those glassy-eyed people on the psychic channel who claim they can talk to dead people.

Mom holds up an Almond Joy bar. "When I was your age, I practically lived on these things."

"You?"

"Yep." Mom grins. "I used to shoplift them."

The woman at the register turns to watch us.

"She's kidding," I tell her.

"No, I'm not," Mom says, deadpan.

I take the candy bar and put it back before Register Woman decides to call security. Then I nudge her toward the elevator.

I push the up arrow. We wait.

"Do you feel ready for this?" Mom asks me.

"No." I laugh. A choppy, nervous laugh. "You?"

"Hell, no."

Mom doesn't say anything about owing her jar a dollar, so I let it go.

The door glides open with a bing. We step on, and I push the button marked seven. I always hate it when elevators stop on every floor, picking up more and more people until you're so crowded your face is mashed in someone's armpit. But, today, I wouldn't mind. I'd welcome anything to put off what's ahead.

The door opens on the seventh floor. We walk slowly, checking the numbers.

Room 712 is across from the nurses' station. The tag outside reads:

M. Murdock / Dr. Bishop
DOB: 12-11-59

From where Mom and I stand in the hallway, I can see her: M. Murdock, clad in a kelly-green hospital grown with a long-sleeved sweater overtop. Occupying the entire bed, her large form rises and falls with each breath. A big green mountain.

Seconds later, she stirs. She grabs the rails that line both sides of her bed, straining to sit up, which—judging from the look on her face—must hurt. She leans forward. Coughs. Sips from a Styrofoam cup. Points a remote at her TV. Melodramatic music fills the hallway.

Mom rolls her eyes. "*All My Children*. The theme song's imbedded in my brain."

We watch her watch TV. It feels weird—knowing who *she* is when she doesn't have a clue who we are. Or that we're standing here, studying her.

"She looks the same," Mom says. "Except older. Older and"—her eyes fill—"vulnerable." She reaches in her pocket for a tissue. When she blows her nose, it makes a honking noise.

The green mountain that is allegedly my grandmother looks up. Into the hall. Right at us. She points the remote at the TV again. The sound vanishes and a hoarse voice penetrates the sudden silence. "Is that you?" she asks Mom.

Starting through the door, Mom reaches behind her for my hand, squeezing so tightly I think she might bust a knuckle. She stops at the empty bed closest to the door. Its smooth white sheets look ready to welcome someone new. Even though we're only a few yards away, it feels more like a hundred miles.

Mom pumps my hand like it's a heart she has to keep beating. And I just stand there thinking, *This is the woman who made my mother's life hell.*

"I used to share the room with Ella Parker," she informs us, tipping her chin toward the empty bed. "Except she died yesterday.

Liver cancer." She points to the chairs that flank the dead lady's bed. "Grab those and pull 'em over."

We do as we're told. Sitting, I mentally case out the room. There's a yellow carnation in a plastic vase on the sill. A single "get well" card sits next to it. When Mom was home sick with pneumonia two years ago, she got dozens of cards. They filled the kitchen counter. And her mother has a single card. A gaudy one with too much glitter.

She reaches behind her, wrestling a pillow loose. Her face takes on the same pained expression. As she holds the pillow in front of her chest, I try to imagine what it must be like to have parts of your body removed. To look down and see scars where your breasts used to be.

The green mountain that is my grandmother wiggles her legs out from under the covers. She turns, struggling to swing them over the edge of the bed so she's facing us. Her feet are swollen and bluish.

"Fluid retention," she says, reading my thoughts. "Diabetes."

I nod. "Oh," is all I can think to say.

I glance at Mom, who's clawing a loose vinyl strip on the arm of her chair, looking shell-shocked.

"What's your name?" Green Mountain asks me.

I clear my throat. "Um, Ariel."

Her eyes narrow. "Like *The Little Mermaid?*"

Mom finally speaks. "Ariel's named after a collection of poetry by Sylvia Plath."

Mom's mother harrumphs. "Never would've pegged you as the literary type." She turns to face me again. "So, Ariel. Did your mom tell you what a shitty mother I was?"

I start to choke. Then cough.

She points toward the corner of the room. "Open that door."

I have no idea how opening a closet is going to help me stop coughing, but I do it anyway. There's an insulated tote on the top shelf, the kind I used to carry my lunch in when I was in elementary school. Mom would pack me the same thing every day—a sandwich on whole wheat bread, a bag of Sun Chips, a piece of fruit, and a container of Juicy Juice. It's funny, the things you remember.

I unzip the lid. Inside are six cans of Coke and an ice pack.

"My bingo buddy, Thelma, smuggled those in for me this morning," Mom's mother informs us. "I'm not supposed to have sugar on account of—" She glances at her feet.

"Your diabetes," I finish.

She winks at me and smiles.

I feel myself start to smile back. But a smile would betray my mom, so I pin the corners of my mouth in place and sit. Peel back the tab on my Coke. Sip.

A nurse breezes into the room. She replaces Green Mountain's water pitcher and hands her several small pills. "Nice to see you've got yourself some company," she says. Turning to Mom and me, she adds, "Just to let you know, Mrs. Murdock has four drainage tubes from her surgery, and she has to be careful with her movements. No organized sporting events during your visit, you hear?" She smiles and glides toward the door, leaving a long, uneasy silence in her wake.

"Well, if the cat's got everybody's tongue . . ." Green Mountain says, powering the TV back on.

Mom drums her fingers on the chair.

Green Mountain nods at the TV. "He's a looker, isn't he?

Mom raises her voice over the sound. "We didn't drive four hours to watch *All My Children.*"

Her mother directs the clicker at the TV. The picture fades to a black dot, and the sound in the room empties out. Now it's even quieter than before.

"So"—Mom clears her throat—"how are you feeling?"

Green Mountain's eyebrows knit together. "They cut my breasts off three days ago. How the hell do you *think* I feel?"

Madeline

THE NEXT DAY, the cheerleaders are huddled together outside English class. When I pass them, Muralee steps forward. "Um, hi," she says, clearing her throat.

I can't believe Muralee Blawjen is talking to me. In public. I feel my face go red. "Hi," I say back, and keep walking.

As she follows me to my seat Sharon and Jeannette crane their necks to watch.

"I like what you wrote," Muralee says. "You know, the essay Mr. Bryant read to the class about the egg? Nice symbolism. Convincing point of view."

I can't believe she was listening to my words. "Thanks," I say, hoping I look calmer than I am.

Muralee sits next to me, tucking a strand of hair behind her ear. Her earrings are star sapphires, and they match the blue on her cheerleading uniform. "It's amazing if you think about it," she goes on, "that the shell—the only home the creature inside has ever known—has to be completely *destroyed* in order for the new life to thrive."

I know Muralee's smart because she always makes first honor

roll, but I had no idea she was deep too. I don't know what to say back, so I just smile.

Muralee leans closer. "About what you saw me doing in the drugstore," she whispers. "You haven't, um . . . ?"

"Told anyone?" I whisper back.

She nods.

"God, no, I never would. Not in a million years. I swear."

The bell for the start of class rings.

Muralee stands. "That's great. Thanks." She crosses the room to her desk.

Jeannette grabs Muralee's arm. Loud enough for everyone to hear, she says, "What do you want with her?"

Muralee sits and opens her English book. "None of your business, Jeannette."

* * *

After school, I stop at the thrift store and buy two pairs of size fourteen slacks. They're a little tight when I try them on, but they'll fit soon enough.

As I walk in the door to our apartment, the phone rings. I sprint up the stairs, hoping it's Tad. We didn't make after-school plans because it's his day off, and he had to work on his truck. I knew there was a chance I wouldn't see him.

When I answer, Tad says, "Hi, beautiful."

I always blush when he calls me that. "Hi, yourself," I say. "How's your truck?"

"In great shape. I changed the oil and the spark plugs and fixed a bad hose that was"—he stops himself—"hell, why am I boring you with that?"

"Because I asked. And because it's interesting. Everything you say is interesting."

"And everything you say is nice. Whatcha got planned for tonight?"

"I'll probably watch *Laugh-In*. I never get to 'cause Mom hates it, but she's out."

"Oh, *really?* Care for some company?"

Tad has yet to see inside our apartment. Once I let him pull into the driveway instead of dropping me off at the curb, but that's the closest he's been. And now's not the time to test that. Sure, Mom might be out all night. But if her latest date's a disaster, she could be home in an hour. "Our place is a mess," I lie.

"Okay. Let's go out then. We can hang out at the amusement park for a while. And after it gets *dark*"—he draws out the word—"we can catch a movie at the drive-in."

I imagine us someplace dark, where I can let in the feeling of Tad's touch instead of panicking, worrying he'll see my scars. "Sure," I say, excited, "it's a date."

* * *

We cut across the picnic area behind the amusement park. Someone's grilling hot dogs on a hibachi and the smell makes my mouth water.

I notice a family at an end table. A boy and girl—a brother and sister, I'm guessing—are sharing a game of checkers. A transistor radio sits beside them, playing a song by the Jackson 5. A woman in a sundress, the mom probably, is lifting plates from a woven basket, and the man, the dad, is reaching into a cooler for a beer.

A familiar pain stabs me in the heart, reminding me: *You never got to be that little girl.* But when I remember what Tad said about wanting kids, I feel a glimmer of hope. Maybe someday I will have a shot at a family like that. Except I'll be the woman, the mom. And Tad will be the dad, and the kids will be ours. Not that I really like kids much—it depresses me, seeing them do things I never got to—but Tad likes them. And I want to make him happy.

Tad takes my hand, steering us into an arcade. Games flash and buzz and bing. Shuffleboard. Pinball. Batter Up. He pulls me toward a photo booth in the corner, then inside it where he draws the curtain and drops two quarters in the slot. He sits on the bench and tugs my arm so I'm sitting beside him. A red light blinks several times and I stare at it. Then a second light—a bright white one—floods the booth and I jump.

Tad laughs as I hop up and down on the seat, giggling.

He puts his hand on my knee, steadying me. "Let's look serious in this one." Tad raises one eyebrow, staring straight ahead.

"Serious," I repeat, sucking my cheeks in to keep from laughing.

The red light blinks. Then the white light floods the booth again.

We both bust up—sidesplitting laughter that feels so good I never want it to stop. But the third flash pops and Tad tips my chin toward him, kissing me. My eyes drift closed as his tongue finds mine, and mine finds his and—

Flash!

Minutes or hours or days later—it's hard to tell, I'm so lost in his kiss—Tad pulls away, whispering, "Pictures should be ready."

He reaches into a drop slot, holding up a strip of black-and-white photographs.

Tad looks like he always looks. But the girl sitting next to him surprises me. She's so pretty. And thin. And *happy*. Truly, completely, unquestionably happy.

"Is that how I look?" I ask him.

He turns to study me. "Of course. Why?"

"No reason." I smile. "I love the photos."

Tad hands them to me. "Keep 'em in a safe place. Someday when we're old farts we'll show 'em to our grandchildren."

Our *grandchildren*. Oh my God. Did he really say that?

"Thanks," I say, tucking them carefully in my macramé handbag.

Tad holds the curtain open for me. He crosses the arcade and stops in front of a game called Skee Roll. He drops a coin in the slot and balls glide down a long ramp toward him. "You ever play?"

I shake my head no.

"It's a lot like bowling. You wanna roll the ball into one of the rings. Fifty points a pop is the best you can do. You get nine turns. The higher your score at the end, the more tickets the machine cranks out. And the more tickets you get, the better your prize."

He lifts his chin toward the shelves that line one wall.

I notice a shiny four-slice toaster. Maybe Tad and I will get an apartment together, and that toaster will sit on our kitchen counter. I'll bet the woman at the picnic table has one just like it.

Tad cups a ball in his hand. He releases it. It whips up the ramp, bounces against a net, lands in the ring marked fifty.

He scores three hundred points in all. The machine spits out a long row of tickets.

On the next game, I attempt a few shots, but I stink. Which means Tad doesn't win as many tickets, so I tell him I'm happier watching.

Ten minutes later, he's out of change. "Let's pick a prize," he says.

The lowest shelf is lined with chintzy toys—troll dolls and Frisbees and Silly Putty eggs. The prizes on the middle shelf, like board games and G.I. Joe dolls, are better. But the best are on the top shelf. That's where my four-slice toaster sits, between a Sno-Kone maker and an Easy-Bake Oven.

"How many tickets did you win?" I ask, excited.

Tad counts them. "Sixty-two."

I notice the prizes have numbers beside them. They must tell you how many tickets you need to win them. I check the number next to the toaster. Twelve hundred. My heart sinks.

"Fifty'll buy us matching hula hoops," Tad says, looping his arm around my waist. "Or his and her cap guns."

But I don't want those prizes. I want the toaster. And the life that goes with it. "I think you should hang on to the tickets," I tell him. "And get something nice when you've saved enough."

Tad shrugs. When we reach the parking lot, he says, "Wait here. I'll be right back," and he disappears from my sight.

I lean against his truck, waiting for him. It's dusky now. The sun sits on a distant hill. The midway lights twinkle and blink.

When Tad returns he says, "Close your eyes and hold out your hand."

I do. Something clasps my index finger. I open my eyes, curious to see what it is—a long cigar-shaped tube made from pink and blue wicker strips woven together. My finger's stuck inside a hole on one end, and Tad's is in the opposite. He pulls back, tightening the grip. "Chinese handcuffs," he says. "They're for you." When he leans in, the tube relaxes, releasing me. "Better get going," he says, reaching to open the truck door. "It's almost dark."

* * *

I've driven by the Valley-View Drive-In lots of times, but I've never been beyond the front gate. Tad pays our admission and parks in a spot in the back, far from any other cars. He steps out, lifts a gray metal box off a stand, hooks it over my window, and then does the same thing on his side.

The movie, *Star Wars,* begins, music bursts from the speakers, and Tad reaches for my hand.

About an hour later, the air starts to grow chilly so Tad flips the heat on low and slides close, looping an arm around my shoulder. "Don't want my girl getting cold," he says, and soon his lips find mine. They travel down my neck, moving lower, lower, inside the V of my blouse. He glides his hands underneath the fabric, then beneath my bra, cupping a breast in each hand.

I'm on fire. I need to touch Tad, to know how *he* feels too. I untuck his shirt. My hands move across his warm chest, drinking him in through my fingers, binding us. When Tad sighs—or maybe he moans—every inch of me tingles.

Tad fumbles for the volume button, quieting the sounds on the screen. Then he reaches to unbutton my blouse. His breath is hot in my ear when he whispers, "You're so beautiful, Madeline. I want you."

My shirt falls open and it's like I'm seeing my body for the first time—my nearly flat stomach, my full breasts, cradled by the silky bra I bought for this very moment.

But then I freeze—I can see myself *too* clearly.

As Tad slips a sleeve off my shoulder, I push his hand away and draw the shirt around me again. "Stop! We need to move. To someplace darker. Over there." I point toward a spot near the woods.

"But it's crowded over there, Madeline. We won't have any privacy. Besides"—Tad strokes my cheek—"a little bit of light is good."

I try to find a way to argue his decision, but I come up empty. This is the end of the road for me.

As Tad eases my shirt off, I draw my bottom lip in, biting it to keep from crying. Seconds later, there it is. In plain view. My mottled lizard arm, silvery blue in the moonlight. I can tell from the path of Tad's eyes that he sees the scars. First, he can't stop staring. Then he looks away. At the silent screen. He exhales. Completely. Till every bit of air is forced out of his lungs.

And I inhale, just as deeply. Tad's spent breath is all I have to hold on to. I wait.

Finally, Tad asks, "What happened?"

"Um, when I was ten"—I hesitate—"my mom fell asleep smoking and, uh, she set a blanket on fire. I tried to get it away from her, but the sleeve of my nightgown caught too."

For a long moment, he's silent. When Tad faces me again, he looks more serious than I've ever seen him. He places his hand on the shoulder of my lizard arm. His fingers inch downward, a slow, careful journey. "Madeline," he whispers, "I'm so sorry for what happened to you, but it doesn't change the way I feel. I love everything about you. Everything." When Tad's fingers reach my wrist, where the scars give way to normal skin, he's erased my fear with his touch. He lifts the hand that belongs to the lizard arm, tenderly kissing the palm. Then he closes my fingers around the kiss, like he's telling me it's mine to keep.

I reach out, pulling him to me wildly, like I'm drowning, and only he can save me. We kiss as if our lives depend upon it. Like we'll die if either of us stops.

Tad's hand edges up the thigh of my jeans, slipping between my legs. My head whirs. Air floods my lungs. My heart swims. Wanting. Wanting.

I rest my hand between Tad's legs too. He moans again and whispers, "I love you."

No one's ever told me that before. Maybe my mother did once, when I was little, but I can't remember. "I love you too," I say back.

When Tad undoes his belt, I remember Muralee stealing the pregnancy test. "Tad," I ask, "do you, uh, have anything for us to use so that, you know . . ."

He feels above his visor, removing a small square package. He tears the wrapper with his teeth and unrolls a brown rubbery thing. He unzips his pants, shaping it over his privates. Which I can't believe I'm looking at. But I am. And it's very clear Tad wants me. In the same way Glenn must have wanted Muralee.

The word *Intermission* flashes across the drive-in screen. Cartoon hot dogs dance below the large red letters. Dome lights blink on. People flock toward the concessions.

Tad clicks on the radio, drowning out the blurry buzz. He leans me backward, onto his truck seat. I kick my shoes to the floor, and Tad slides my jeans off. Then I feel him on top of me and, moments later, inside me, sweetly whispering my name.

Desiree

larry's form fills the stairway.
i can smell his breath: nuts and beer.
he glances at my chest
so i look down too.
my nipples are standing
at attention from the cold.
i feel exposed,
fold my arms,
attempt to slip past.
but larry leans in,
smoothing my hair.
you look pretty.
how was the dance?

i pull away. *let me go!*
again, i try to step around him.
again, larry blocks my path.

i'm so scared
i think i might throw up.
let me go or i'll scream!

your ma won't hear you.
she had a headache.
he taps his skull.
you know percs knock her out.

he presses his lips against mine.
razor stubble scrapes my face.
i jerk my head from side to side,
trying to avoid his mouth, his breath.

stop!
louder.

as larry grinds against
my belly swell
i feel fluttering—
like a small bird moving
in some secret language
only i can understand.

tears well up in my eyes,
and for the first time,
i really, truly
get it:
i
am

pregnant.
it's *my* word now.
i've got a baby inside me,
a baby that's counting on me,
and this asshole is mashing up
against it like it's not a living thing,
like it doesn't have any feelings.

larry gathers my fingers in one hand,
pinning them to the wall above my head.
when he hikes my dress up,
the crunch of the satin
fabric is deafening—
hard, sharp sounds, like boots
cracking through frozen snow.

i feel the fluttering again.
tiny wings flap and flap
below the swell of fat
that's not just fat anymore.
no.
fat = baby now.
my baby. my daughter.
i don't know how i know
she's a girl, i just do,
and i'm not going to let
larry hurt her.

i scream—
loud enough to

wake mam from a coma.
larry covers my mouth,
and i bite his finger hard.
he jerks his hand away
and i holler,
no! no! no!

still larry thrusts against me.
the fluttering inside
turns into spasms,
and i know my baby is crying.
i'm crying too.
my tears are the lifeline
i throw out to her.
i'm trying to make him stop!
you have to believe me, baby girl!

her flutters are hurried now,
a bird gone wild inside her cage,
beating frightened wings against the bars
as her fragile bird bones are crushed,
as her small, small breath is hushed.

is this her first impression of me—
a mother who can't protect her own daughter?

it sounds so freaking familiar.

* * *

i shower so long my skin prunes up.
i don't implode with pain this time.
no. i don't feel a thing.
but my baby does.
and, someday,
larry will
pay for that.

* * *

when i wake around noon,
i hear larry in the kitchen,
using that fake, bullshit voice
people use when they're trying to sound
all sincere and sensitive, but really
they're pulling something
straight out of their ass.

i press my ear against the wall,
catching bits of what he says.
. . . don't be too hard on her . . .
tough for a girl without a father . . .
my sister . . . that way too . . .
screwed anything with balls.

a raging bull,
i storm into the kitchen.
what are you saying about me?
he looks like mister fucking rogers
the way he's combed his hair and

shaved and put on a brand-new shirt.
he clasps mam's hand, glancing
my way with a hangdog expression.
desiree, i told your ma what happened
between you and me. i told her everything.

dark prickles whirl before my eyes.
i grip the counter,
afraid i'll pass out.
you—you what?

larry repeats: *everything.*
but i told her not to be mad at you.
i'll take the bulk of the blame.
after all, i'm a grown-up and you're fifteen.
of course, you're fifteen going on twenty-one,
if you catch my drift, but—

what are you talking about? i yell.

larry glances from mam to me
then back to mam again.
well, you're what guys
in my generation called a c.t.

what the hell's a c.t.? i snap.
larry answers, *a cock tease.*

i lunge at him, landing so hard
i knock his chair over backward.
mam's stupid knickknacks

clatter off a shelf as
larry's head slams the oven door.

mam leaps up.
my god, larry, you're bleeding!

i watch the rescue
efforts in slow motion:
mam helping larry stand,
mam setting his chair upright,
mam rolling ice inside a dishcloth,
mam holding it against larry's head.
mam turning to me, spitting out,
are you happy now, desiree?
after all these years,
i finally find
someone who matters,
and you've gotta strut your stuff
right underneath his nose.

my eyes fill.
i try to blink back tears, but i can't.
your someone who matters *raped me!*
four months ago by the train tracks,
and then again last night—
right here in this apartment.
i was in the foyer, yelling.
i was crying for you, mom!

she reels, like i've slapped her.
i haven't called her *mom* in years,

but i need her to be one for me now.
a real mom. because,
at this moment,
she's all i have.
mom, i say again, *please! larry's*
trying to save his ass—and—and—
i choke on snot i'm crying so hard
—and he's using me to do it.
don't you see that?
i didn't want this to happen!
if you weren't so stoned
on your goddamn pills,
you would've heard me screaming.
mam drops the dishcloth.
ice cubes glide across the floor.

now she's crying too.
her eyes meet mine.
maybe she's heard what i've said,
i think, maybe she's going to take my side.
i'm so filled with hope
i take a sudden step toward her.

but larry stands,
stepping into my path.
dez, let's be honest.
we both screwed up. period.
i should've walked away from temptation,
but you didn't make it easy on me.

you're a liar! i shout. *i was raped!*
and i've got a baby
inside me to prove it!

mam gasps,
freezes in place.
larry touches my arm
like he's consoling me,
but i pull away.
dez, i doubt i'm the one
who got you pregnant.
don't you remember?
we used a rubber both times.
he reaches in his wallet
and holds up a trojan.
i always keep one right here,
and i put one on both nights.
you were kind of hot to trot,
but i said, whoa, dez, not so fast.
we wouldn't want anything to happen.

that—that's not true! i tell mam.
my eyes beg her to believe me.

she folds her arms and looks away.
larry always wears a condom.
i insist, 'cause that's how
i got pregnant with you.
one time your father and i didn't
use protection—and bam!

nine months later,
there you were.

but that's you! i yell. *this is me!*
you have a say with larry. i didn't!

mam yells back,
larry said you got
in his car with him, desiree.
you went for a ride together.
how do you think that looks?
she glares at me, waiting for my answer.
the veins in her temples pop out so far
it looks like her head might explode.

i—i—was hungry, i stammer, *and he had food.*

and he had beer too, mam snaps, *which you drank.*

so what? i plead. *that doesn't prove—*

and—mam interrupts me—*you were wearing*
that slutty halter top i said you couldn't have.

she's trapped me.
i'm like one of the mice
glued to her sticky paper.
except i don't squeal and beg for life.
it wouldn't do any good.
it's over for me.

mam's forehead veins relax.
she reaches for a tissue.
look, whatever happened
between the two of you,
at least larry's apologized for it.
that's more than i can say for you.
an ice cube melts near my toe.
the kitchen clock ticks like a time bomb.
and seeing as larry wore a condom, she adds,
the baby must be your boyfriend's.

i glare at her. *what makes you think*
me and jeremy are having sex?

she blows her nose, tosses her tissue.
larry went for a drive last night.
he saw you and jerry
and those other two kids
you hang out with having sex
in the middle of a cornfield
like you haven't got
a bit of modesty.

i turn to larry, fists clenched.
you followed me?
you watched?
that's sick!
i lunge at him again but
mam's big body blocks me.

jaw tight, eyes narrowed, she hisses,
if you don't mind,
larry and i would like
some time to talk. alone.
you, i'll deal with later.

but i swear to myself
then and there
that as far as
mam and i go
there will
never
ever
be
a
later.

Ariel

FORTY-FIVE MINUTES IN GREEN MOUNTAIN'S ROOM feels more like forty-five days. My head hurts, and I'm grateful when a doctor arrives, asking us to leave during his exam.

As we start down the hall toward the elevators, Mom reaches in her handbag, tapping out two Motrin caplets. Before she slides the bottle back, I take it from her, removing a couple for myself. "You too?" Mom asks, tossing me a sympathetic look.

I nod, leading the way toward a water fountain. Swallowing the pills, I think to myself: *I could use an Aunt Lee fix. She always knows just what to say.*

Mom glances at her watch. Reading my mind, she says, "Lee's last class is over in ten minutes. Think we can use your phone to call her?"

I feel in the pocket of my jacket, but my cell's not there. "Damn!" I say, so loud a nurse looks up from her pill cart. "I left the phone in the car."

Mom pats my back. "It's not a big deal, Ariel. I'll walk out with you. The fresh air might do us good."

"Mom, you don't understand." I hurry toward the elevator and push the down button over and over. "I told Shane I'd call him when we got in, and I totally forgot. He's probably been trying to get me."

"Ariel, Shane knows the circumstances, that you might not be available if—"

"He'll be worried!" Again, I poke the down arrow, holding it in place this time.

Finally, the elevator opens. I bolt inside. Push G for the ground floor. Mom steps on behind me. But as the door starts to close she presses Open. My heart's beating so hard I can hear the whoosh of blood in my ears. "What are you doing?"

She motions toward the hall. "The woman with the walker—she signaled for us to wait for her."

"Just *great,*" I mumble.

Walker Woman inches closer. When she reaches the threshold, the rubber tip on one leg catches in the door track. "Oh, dear," she says, "I'm stuck."

Mom bends down, patiently wiggling it loose. Then she takes the old lady's arm, guiding her to the rail. "What floor would you like?" Mom asks her.

"Three, please." She smiles at Mom. Her face fills with a million creases. "That's where my room is. I was visiting a friend on seven."

We slow to a stop on the third floor. Mom offers, "Would you like us to walk you to your room?" Not me. Us.

If the hospital has a psych ward, I might need to check myself in.

Again, the old lady smiles. "My, that would be sweet of you."

The door opens. Walker Woman crosses the threshold, managing not to get stuck this time. Mom signals for me to come along. If I don't follow her, I'll look like the most selfish jerk on the planet.

The minute we arrive in Walker Woman's room, a nurse waltzes in with her meal. As the old lady struggles with its cover Mom asks, "Would you like some help?"

"Look," I lie, "I really need to use the bathroom. I'll get the phone after that."

"All right," Mom says, handing me the car keys. "I'll meet you in the cafeteria. Then we'll call Lee, okay?"

"Okay," I say as I rush out.

When I arrive at the car, I'm cold and out of breath. I grab my fleece jacket and flip my phone open. I have ten missed calls. I press Shane's number and pace beside our car, hugging myself to get warm.

Two girls, around eleven or twelve, walk past laughing. The shorter one reminds me of Olivia in middle school, and the taller one looks a little like me.

Shane doesn't pick up. He's probably giving me a dose of what he felt when I didn't answer.

The girls cross the street toward a strip mall. I study the lineup of fast-food joints, remembering how Olivia always picked Taco Bell, and I always wanted Arby's.

I sit on a nearby bench and check my watch. Liv should be home by now. I punch in the number for her cell.

It takes her forever to pick up. Finally she says, *"Hello?"*

"Liv? It's Ariel."

"Oh my God. I wasn't going to answer. I didn't recognize the number."

"Shane gave me a cell phone. Actually, he got us both one."

"Wow. Great. I'll store the number. How's everything going in Elmira?"

An ambulance speeds toward the ER, siren wailing. The sound rips through my brain. "I've got a headache right now. Can I give you the details a little later?"

"Sure. The dinner party's not until seven, so there's time. I can call you before everyone gets here."

If Shane tries to get me while I'm on the phone with Liv, my voice mail will pick up. *Again.* I try to think of a reason why she shouldn't call me. "Mom's with me most of the time," I explain, "so I don't really have much privacy. Text me instead. Okay?"

"Will you know how to text me back?"

"Liv, come on. It's not rocket science."

"Yeah, but like you've said before, your mom *has* kept you in a state of technological deprivation."

"I'll figure it out," I assure her.

I hear a girl's voice in the background—which wouldn't be a big deal except Olivia's an only child, and there's no other female in her household.

"Got company?" I ask her.

"Um, actually, I'm highlighting someone's hair? This girl in my drama class, Katelyn Carrick, she has the lead in *Evita?* And she asked me if I'd give her some blond streaks after school?" When Olivia's on edge, she turns statements into questions.

"Well," I say, "I should let you go then."

"Yeah, probably. I just started putting on the blue foam junk. And it's supposed to go on all at once so half of your head isn't lighter." Olivia laughs.

I force a laugh too, but mine sounds more like a cough. "Wouldn't want that."

"I'll text you when I'm finished. And Ariel"—she lowers her voice—"I'm really glad you have a phone. Maybe now we can talk for more than just a few minutes before school. I hardly know what you're doing anymore."

Yeah, I want to say. *That makes two of us, Liv.*

* * *

Mom's probably waiting in the cafeteria, wondering where I am, but I have to talk to Shane before I meet her. My hands sweat as I try his number again and again.

Twenty minutes pass. A half hour. Across the street, the two girls leave the Burger King and duck into a pet store. I think of the day Liv and I bought tropical fish at the mall. She picked a golden orange one to match her hair color, and I found a black one (the closest I could get to brown) to match mine. We named our fish after ourselves then traded. Olivia and Ariel lived two years—a long time for fish—and died within a week of each other. Olivia thought that was "cosmic."

On my billionth attempt to get Shane, the ringing stops abruptly, and I hear breathing on the other end. "Oh, Shane," I rush out, "I'm so sorry. I forgot to call when we got in, and then I left the phone in the car when we went inside the hospital. I know you've been trying to call. *Please* forgive me, I—"

"This not Shane," someone says. It's a man's voice. He sounds Asian.

I panic. "W—where is he?"

"He not here. This not his number no more."

"That can't be. This was Shane's number this morning. I—I—talked to him."

"Sorry. No Shane. He say tell you good-bye."

My head is pounding. "How do you know Shane?" I snap.

"How *you* know Shane?" he snaps back.

I feel like I'm trapped inside a *Twilight Zone* rerun. "I'm his girlfriend. He programmed his number into my phone. Shane wouldn't change it and not tell me!"

The voice on the other end is silent.

I pace, circling the bench. If the hospital *does* have a psych ward, I won't have to sign myself in. Anyone watching will come for me. "Look," I say, trying hard to sound reasonable, "if you know Shane, you must know his new number, right?"

"Sorry. I go now."

"Don't hang up!" I plead. But he does anyway.

"No!" I shout. *"No! No! NO!"* Running to the nearest tree, I collapse against its trunk. That's where I lose it. Completely. I cry harder than I've ever cried before. I'm hyperventilating, my nose is running, and I'm inhaling snot just to breathe. But then a sudden sound startles me, and I freeze.

Footsteps crunch across the dried leaves. I assume it's the two girls again, and I don't want them to see me crying, so I walk away. Into the sharp sun, which makes my head throb even more.

The footsteps follow me. *One* set of footsteps, I realize, so it can't be the girls after all.

I feel a hand on my shoulder. It can be only one other person, I tell myself. My mother.

Except, when I turn, it isn't.

Madeline

During sixth-period lunch I sit at a table near the trash cans where no one else ever sits—probably because you can smell what got dumped during fourth period starting to rot.

I peel the wax paper off my lettuce, tomato, Velveeta, and Miracle Whip sandwich, which is actually a half-sandwich now. When I decided I wanted to drop another size, I cut back on my portions. The timing's perfect for eating less since I'm waiting for my period, feeling so bloated I barely have room left for food.

Muralee Blawjen sits three tables over with the cheerleaders. Sharon Ranson's braiding Jeannette Landeau's hair, Jeannette's nibbling a peach, and Nancy Topek, who I never see eat anything, is stroking pink polish on her nails. *Cosmetic rituals,* as they're called in the school handbook, aren't allowed in the lunchroom. But no one would say anything to *them*.

Muralee stands, dumps her garbage into the trash, and carries her tray to the conveyer belt. Except, instead of returning to her table, she stops at mine. It's been a month since Muralee asked me to keep her secret, and she hasn't spoken to me since. But then, why would she? Muralee holds her blue and white cheerleading skirt close to her thighs as she swings one leg over the bench and sits across from me. Her Love's Baby Soft perfume scents the air, drowning out the stench in the trash cans. "Hi," she says. "What's up?"

My last bite catches in my throat. I swallow it down with diet cola. "Um, uh," I stammer, "not much."

Muralee tucks her hair behind her ears. I notice she's wearing Glenn's class ring, which is way too big for her finger. She's wound red yarn around the backside of the band to keep it from slipping off.

A single tear rolls down her pink cheek.

"Are you . . . all right?" I ask, immediately regretting I did. It's a personal question. Something only a friend should ask.

"I'll be fine," she says. "After this weekend."

"This weekend?" I repeat.

"The test you saw me stealing . . ." Muralee whispers, tugging at a string on the ring. "It was positive. Do you know what that means?"

Of course I do. I watch TV. I nod.

Muralee glances over her shoulder at the cheerleaders, who are leaning sideways, watching us. She offers them a halfhearted smile, then turns to face me again. "I've given things a lot of thought. I've decided what I need to do. I'm going to Ithaca on Saturday. I have an appointment. They'll, uh . . . take care of it for me."

"Take care of it?"

"Yeah. You know." She leans in so close I can smell the school spaghetti on her breath. "Get *rid* of it."

Oh my God. I can't believe what I'm hearing.

Muralee studies my face. "What's the matter?"

"Nothing, just, um"—I shake my head—"nothing." I don't know what to say. Finally, I come up with something. "What does your boyfriend think?"

"I haven't told Glenn. He's waiting on a football scholarship to Penn State. He's expecting an answer any day now. I can't ruin his future."

I can't imagine *not* telling Tad if the same thing happened to me. Not that it would. Whenever we have sex together, Tad uses a rubber. Well, except for once at his trailer when his dad wasn't home. But Tad promised me he pulled out in time.

"So, uh . . ." I wring my hands under the table. "You said you're going to Ithaca. Is that where your doctor's office is?"

She rolls her eyes. "Right. My doctor. Who my whole *family* goes to."

"Oh." I hesitate. "So are you going to a clinic?"

"No. The closest one is several hours away. I'd have to miss school, and I'd get home really late. Plus I'm underage, so I'd have to involve my parents." She looks away. "Not an option."

"Who is your appointment with, then?"

She drums her fingers on the table. "An independent agent."

"What does that mean?"

Muralee laughs nervously. "Let's just say you wouldn't find his name in the yellow pages."

Oh, no. I read about back alley abortions in a magazine at the laundromat. The people who perform them aren't clean. Sometimes they take the babies out with coat hangers. Women have died.

Muralee starts to cough. She eyes my soda. "Do you mind?"

I slide the can forward.

To anyone else, this might not seem like a big deal. But, to me, it's colossal. I hold my breath, noticing every detail as Muralee extends her hand toward the can. As her fingers close around the same surface mine just touched. As she lifts the soda to her glossy lips. And sips. From my diet cola.

Jeannette and Sharon and Nancy walk toward us. They pause at the end of the table, addressing Muralee as if I'm not there. Which, to them, I suppose, I'm not.

"Ready?" Jeannette says. "We're leaving."

Muralee sips my soda again. "I'll catch up with you later."

Jeannette rolls her eyes, and Sharon whispers something in her ear. Then Nancy bumps Sharon's hip as they walk away, arm in arm, laughing.

"Thanks for sharing your drink," Muralee says. "I've never tried diet soda before—I'm hooked on Dr. Pepper—but it's not bad."

Staring at the can, I nod.

There's a long, uncomfortable silence.

"So," Muralee says, "you lost a lot of weight, didn't you?"

I feel myself blush. "Yeah. Forty pounds. I've got about ten more to go."

"Wow. That's great. You should be proud of yourself."

The lunch bell rings, signaling the end of sixth period. Kids shuffle past our table. Some stare, probably wondering why Muralee Blawjen, head of the varsity cheerleading team, is sitting with Madeline Fitch, reformed fat girl.

Within minutes, we're the only ones left. The bell for seventh period sounds. I picture Mr. Bennett noticing my empty seat. I've never been late for his class. Or any class. But I'm not moving until Muralee does.

A radio comes on in the distance—in the kitchen, probably—and "Lean on Me" starts to play. The cafeteria ladies appear with their buckets and sponges, wiping the tables around us. They move in unison like synchronized swimmers.

"I love this song," Muralee says. "Who sings it again?"

I think it's funny when people do that—tack the word *again* onto a question when it's really the first time they've asked it. "Bill Withers," I answer.

"Right. And what's that other famous song he had? Something about sunshine."

"'Ain't No Sunshine.'"

"Yes!" She sings the first line and smiles.

The cafeteria ladies work their way toward our table.

"Come with me," Muralee says.

"Where?" I ask, confused.

"To Ithaca on Saturday."

My hands shake below the table. "Um, why me?"

"Because you're the only one who knows. The only one I want to know." Her emerald green eyes lock with mine. "Please, Madeline. I need you."

Muralee Blawjen needs me. *Me.*

What else can I do?

I say yes.

Desiree

when i see mam and larry
leave the apartment,
i hurry inside,
cram jeans, t-shirts,
sweatshirts, sleep clothes,
and loads of socks and underwear
into my navy blue duffel bag.

in the kitchen
i take out the old red shoebox
mam keeps her savings in.
inside is the pink and blue wicker tube
my dad won for her
and a roll of yellowed tickets that say
good for one daily blue plate special.
pushing them aside,
i gather the money,
count the bills.

five hundred and ten bucks.
sweet.
nice going-away present, *mom*.

when i go to put the lid back on the box
i notice something stuck underneath it—
a thin glossy paper about
the size of a bookmark.
i pull it loose,
glance at a strip
of black-and-white photos and
—*shit!*—
drop them like they freaking bit me.

the pictures land at my feet.
staring up at me is
me.
i mean, it's not *really* me,
because i'm with this boy
i've never seen before,
but the she that isn't me
is my twin—
same long, mousy hair,
parted off center,
same wide eyes,
dense eyebrows,
bony cheeks.
same square smile,
full lips,
dimples.

i bend, retrieve the pictures.
mam? i wonder,
then just as quickly
i answer, *no way.*
this girl's too skinny.
too pretty.
too *happy.*
it must be someone else.

next i study the boy—
his light, flyaway hair,
his wire-rim glasses,
the space between
his two front teeth.

shot one:
the boy and girl lean toward
the lens, looking clueless.
shot two: they are serious,
a phony cheek-biting serious
that makes it obvious they're
about to bust up.
which they do
in shot number three.

in shot four,
they are kissing.
kissing like people do in movies,
like their survival depends upon it.
this boy is in love with this girl.
seriously,

completely.
i flip the photos over,
hoping something's
written on the back
that will tell me who they are,
but there is only white space.

so i tuck the photos back in the box,
wedge the money in my pocket,
sling my duffel bag over one shoulder,
and pull the door closed behind me.

* * *

at the 7-eleven
i step into line with
ring dings and a diet coke.
but then i think of the baby
and switch the soda for a milk and
the ring dings for a blueberry muffin.
the muffin's stale,
but i'm so hungry i eat it anyway.

on a bench
at the transit station,
i watch buses burp black smoke
and drive off.

at eight,
i walk to jeremy's house
and knock on his bedroom window.

wearing just jockeys, he opens it.
shivering against the cold,
he exhales a cloud
of morning breath.
i need to talk to you, jeremy.
meet me at the geronimo, okay?
he rubs sleep gunk from his eyes.
okay. gimme ten minutes.

* * *

i sit in an open booth
next to the cigarette machine.
i haven't had a smoke in twelve hours.
i decided to quit for the baby,
just like i decided to stop drinking.
i memorize today's blue plate special,
posted on the chalkboard over the grill—
roasted chicken, noodles, diced carrots.
i mumble it over and over
so my brain won't have
room to roam.

a waitress startles me.
what can i get ya, honey?
her face is pale as oatmeal and
she needs her mustache waxed.
a coke, i say, so she won't
bust me for tying up her table.

i pull a pen from my duffel bag,
print names on a paper napkin.
old-fashioned names.
elizabeth,
sarah,
abigail,
catherine,
sylvia.
except sylvia makes me think of
the poet we studied in english class
—the one who killed herself—
but when i go to cross
her name off the list,
i feel my baby flutter again.

the bell over the door jingles.
jeremy walks in wearing levi's
and his favorite bills sweatshirt.
he looks so much like a little boy
i think i might cry.
except i can't.
i need to be a grown-up now.

the waitress drops off my coke,
and jeremy slides in across from me,
hair still damp from a shower,
smelling of irish spring soap.
reaching for a menu, he asks,
what're ya having?
as if today is like
any other day.

i lean forward. *jeremy,*
do you love me—
i mean really?
he reaches across the table,
weaves his fingers through mine.
yeah, of course i do. why?

i'm shaking.
look, i've gotta go away for a while.
i can't help it—i start to cry.

jeremy moves to my side of the booth
and loops his arm around my shoulder.
he feels so solid. so warm.
dez, what's going on?

when i open my mouth to speak,
it's like turning on a faucet full blast.
my words gush out
in one rapid stream.
i'm pregnant, jeremy, i found out when i went for the pills,
i'm sorry i didn't tell you sooner, but now my mother knows,
and we had a terrible fight, and i'm not going back home
again, ever.
i don't add that
larry's the father.
i'm just not ready.

jeremy stands,
buys a pack of kools,
paces beside our booth, smoking.

when he finishes his second cigarette,
he stamps it out in the ashtray
resting on the edge of the table,
except the tray flips and
topples to the floor.
he stares at the ash
scattered near his feet,
mumbling, *shit, shit, shit.*

should i have an abortion?
i ask him, even though
i really don't want to.
yes, it's larry's baby,
but it's my baby too.
and it's not *her* fault
larry did what he did.
why should she be punished?

but as i wait for jeremy's answer,
i think to myself,
what if he sees something i missed?
what if he tries to change my mind?
and finally,
what if i let him?
could everything go
back to how it was
before?

look, i'm not ready for this—
jeremy waves a hand over my stomach—
but that doesn't mean you can . . .

we can . . .
oh, shit, desiree,
we can't just kill it.
it's ours.

i bite my lip to keep
from blurting out the truth.
what then?

jeremy's forehead wrinkles.
he doesn't look like a little boy anymore.
he looks like he's carrying the whole
freaking world on his shoulders.
he takes a breath,
lets it out.
i'm going with you, that's what.

* * *

i sit on jeremy's bed,
watching as he stuffs clothes
in an army-green knapsack
then fills the pockets with
things i forgot:
toothbrush,
comb,
deodorant,
blow dryer.
his face is expressionless,
his movements precise.

downstairs,
he leaves a note
on the kitchen table:
mom and dad,
i'm going away for a while.
i'll call you when i can.
don't worry. please.
i'll be fine.
jeremy.

his shoulders fold in,
and i hear him crying.
i tell him, *you don't have to do this,*
jeremy. i can go alone.
i'll be okay. really.

but he leans his note against
a bowl of fresh pears
and starts wordlessly
toward the door.

* * *

i've never hitchhiked before,
but there's not much to it.
you hold your thumb out,
someone stops,
you climb in,
pray the driver isn't
another son of sam.

two hippies in an old vw van
who play the same grateful dead tape
over and over
drive us clear through to virginia.

in roanoke
forty bucks gets us a motel room.
jeremy and i sleep together
for the first time.
i don't mean sex,
i mean *sleep*,
as in side by side
the whole night through.

it's strange to wake up
and see him there—
a good strange,
though,
not a bad one.

in the morning,
i pluck my eyebrows thin,
cut my hair chin-length,
scrub off the last of my makeup.
then we buy two bottles of miss clairol
at the revco down the road—
grunge black for jeremy,
barbie-doll blond for me.
we buy sunglasses too—
the kind that reflect everything
instead of showing strangers our eyes.

now if we spot our faces
on a milk carton
we can waltz on by
without worrying.

* * *

we're in florida
by ten the next night,
booking a room at the clover inn.
i have no idea why they call it that—
there isn't a clover in sight.
there isn't even a yard,
just concrete
as far as i see,
an endless ocean of gray.

the man who checks us in
gives us a discount on our room
since the toilet makes gurgling noises.
but me and jeremy don't notice.
we're sound asleep in no time at all.

in the morning,
it's 82 degrees even though
it's almost november.
i leave on the tank top i slept in
and cut the legs off my jeans.
damn, i say, stepping
into the hot, hazy sun,
sure beats the hell out of snow.

next door,
at the clover diner,
there's a paper shamrock
taped to every window.
while i study the breakfast menu,
wondering where we'll wind up next,
jeremy points to a help-wanted sign
posted next to the register.
whaddaya say we apply?
save some money
before we take off again?

outside the window,
a truck pulls in,
gravel popping
underneath its tires.
that's when i notice that
those paper shamrocks
are four-leaf clovers.
feeling their luck rub off on me,
i fake my best southern accent.
y'all got a fine idea there.

Ariel

I WHIRL AROUND SO QUICKLY I FEEL WOOZY. "What the—? How—?"

Shane smiles. "Surprised?"

I blink several times, in case my headache is making me hallucinate. But Shane's still standing there. "H—how did you *find* me?"

"Same way I knew you walked through the Meadows the other day." He holds up his phone. "Tracking device. GPS. As long as you've got your cell with you, I'll *always* know where you are. Cool, right?"

"You mean you drove four hours to see me?"

"Uh huh."

I run to Shane and mash my face into the shoulder of his jacket, inhaling the leather smell, squeezing for all I'm worth. I'm not happy about the spy-phone business, but I really need him to hold me. To provide a link to something familiar.

Eventually, I let go and step back. Actually, I stumble back. The pain in my head is so fierce that now my balance feels off.

"Hey," Shane says. "You okay?"

I glance around for his bike. "I need a break. Take me for a ride, okay?"

Shane changes the subject. "Why didn't you call me, Ariel?"

"I *did* call. Lots of times. You never answered. Then this other person did."

"Really? Who?"

"I have no idea. I didn't ask his name. He was Asian, I think. He said he knows you, and that you don't have your phone number anymore, *he* does."

"That's odd," Shane says, "because I tried and tried to call you too. You never picked up." He shrugs his shoulders, as if to look casual, but the intense expression on his face gives off the opposite vibe.

"I—I'm sorry," I stammer. "I left my cell in the car. Then, when I came out to get it, I couldn't reach you, so I called Olivia. I needed to talk to someone, Shane."

He folds his arms.

"Shane, please. Don't be mad. This has been really stressful for me. I—"

My phone bleeps. I freeze.

"What's that?" Shane asks.

"Probably a text from Olivia."

Shane takes the phone from me. He flips it open and reads, "'Oh my god, Katelyn's streaks are orange. Guess I'll bag the backup career in cosmetology. Laughing out loud.'" He glares at me. "What the hell is *that* supposed to mean?"

"Olivia highlighted Katelyn's hair," I explain.

A sadness fills his eyes. "Ariel, this phone was supposed to be for *us*. You and me. Our connection. Which you've treated like . . . like . . . it means nothing to you."

"No, Shane, that's not true. I love that we can talk anytime.

Really. I just needed to hear Liv's voice. She's my best friend. Can't you understand?"

"No, Ariel, I can't. *Your* voice is the only one *I* need to hear."

My eyes well up. "Oh, Shane—" I step toward him, but my phone bleeps again.

Shane looks down. "Now you've got a picture." He pauses, studying it. "Jesus, who are the faggots?"

I grab the phone from him and check out the photo. Liv's dad and Steve, both wearing suits, are standing beside the table they've set for the party. Irises fill the center. Candles glow. Everything looks so elegant. I wish I were there. "These two *men,*" I answer, speaking slowly to help me stay calm, "are Olivia's father and his partner."

He flashes me his Ms. Delphi smile. "How quaint."

I take several deep breaths. "Shane, look, I think we should forget about the phone and focus on us right now. You're here. We're together. Let's make the most of it, okay?" I reach my arms out to hug him again.

But Shane turns and walks away. I feel partly responsible for his bad mood, so I follow him—behind a tall row of evergreens where his Yamaha is parked. Except there's only one helmet on the seat. Mom would kill me if she knew I planned to ride without one—she doesn't even like me riding *with* one—but I have to get away from this place.

I hurry toward Shane's bike. "Shane, take me for a ride. Please. Just a short one. Five minutes." I'm about to swing my leg over the seat when Shane holds out his hand.

"No!" he says. "Don't!"

I stop.

Shane's eyes lock with mine. They remind me of the obsidian chunks we studied in earth science—dark and glassy and cold.

"Why not?" I ask.

Shane is so motionless he looks like a DVD on Pause.

But in an instant, he's back on Play, breaking up. He laughs so loud and so hard the sound slashes at my temples.

I'm near tears. "Shane, come on. Let's go."

"We—we—can't!" he chokes out.

The pain in my head is so intense, I think I might throw up. "But, *why?*"

Shane straightens, clutching his stomach. "Because. That"—he points at his motorcycle—"that not Shane's bike no more. That *my* bike now."

Oh. My. God. Shane's voice. It's the same as the stranger's. On the phone.

"Oh, Ariel, you were so funny." He flaps his wrist in the air, acting feminine. "Look, I know this is Shane's number. He programmed it into my phone. I'm his *girlfriend.* He wouldn't give up his number and not *tell* me!"

My adrenaline kicks in, sending an enormous surge rushing through me.

I lunge at Shane, knocking him straight to the ground. Then I'm on top of him, arms flailing, swatting him. *Me,* Miss I've-Got-a-Dad-in-Prison-for-Murder-So-I'm-Always-Totally-Rational. I'm worse than the Spandex-clad riffraff on *Jerry Springer.*

My hand connects with Shane's nose. He winces as his head snaps sideways. Blood trickles from his nostril.

In one sudden move, he grabs my wrists and pushes me off him. Then he stands, swiping his nose with the back of his hand. The afternoon sun is over his shoulder, drilling a hole through my brain. "You bitch," he says, staring at the blood on his knuckles. "I can't believe you did this to me."

I can't believe I did it, either.

I roll in the opposite direction, away from Shane, and manage to stand.

Shane's bleeding hard now. I know I should ask him if his nose hurts. I should tell him I'm sorry, offer to go inside and get ice and paper towels from the cafeteria.

I should.

I should.

I should.

But I don't.

Instead, I tell him, "I think I'd like you to leave."

* * *

I breeze past *Frieda: Volunteer* and duck into the first bathroom I come to. A lady balances an infant on the changing table. His diaper is open and the room reeks of baby shit. I barely make it into a stall. Within seconds, I'm puking my guts out.

When I hear the woman leave, I flush the toilet. Wash my hands. Splash cold water on my face. I avoid my image in the mirror, afraid of what I might see—a psycho who's capable of shoving her boyfriend to the ground and giving him a bloody nose.

I reach for a paper towel, drying my hands. Then, I can't help it, I have to look.

When my own reflection stares back at me, I feel grateful. Sure, my eyes are puffy from crying, my pupils are demented from the headache, and my hair is a total mess—but I'm *me.* The same Ariel I was an hour ago. Before Shane showed up.

I get this vague, gut feeling I've been given a second chance on something. Except I have no clue what that *something* is.

I check the cafeteria for Mom, but she's not there. I pause in front of a soda machine, remembering caffeine helps a headache. Except, when I dig through my pockets, all I find is a quarter.

Out of options, I head back upstairs, praying I can count on a Coke.

Green Mountain's sitting up in bed, watching another dumb soap opera. She sees me in the doorway and points the remote at the TV, turning it off.

I lean into the wall across from the empty bed. "Seen my mom?" I ask her.

"Nope. I thought maybe the two of you took off." She shrugs. "Not that I'd blame you. I'm just a mean old woman without tits or tea manners."

"You're not that old—" I start, then kick myself, because it sounds like I'm agreeing with the rest. "What I mean is—"

"Sit," she interrupts.

I pick the chair closest to the door, in case I need to make a getaway. I lower myself onto the cushion—gingerly, like you'd rest an egg on a counter.

Green Mountain stares at me. "What's the matter with you? You look like hell."

"I feel like hell. I've got a really bad headache." I glance at the Coke can she's semiconcealed beside her nightstand, praying she'll offer me one.

"You seeing funny flashes?" she asks, waggling her fingers near her face. "Like spider legs in front of your eyes?"

I nod.

She lifts her Coke, sipping. I'm ready to dive at the can. "Smells bother you?"

"Big time. I got a whiff of a crappy baby diaper in the restroom a few minutes ago and—"

She laughs. "Woofed your socks off, didn't you?"

"How'd you know?" I ask, hoping it's not because my breath smells like barf.

"Classic migraine. They run in families. Does your ma get 'em?"

I shake my head no.

"Lucky her." She motions toward the window. "The light hurt at all?"

"A little."

"Close the blinds then."

I cross the room and twirl the wand. The room grows darker. Cooler. It feels quieter too, even though there's no less sound than there was five seconds ago.

"Grab yourself a Coke," she tells me. "And get my pocketbook while you're there. It's hanging on a hook inside."

Gratefully, I take a soda from the cooler. And I hand her a brown suede bag that looks at least a hundred years old. I think for a minute what I'd do if this were a regular situation—if Green Mountain were really like a grandmother to me, and I was really like a granddaughter to her. I'd make a mental note on my holiday shopping list. Under Grandma, I'd write: *new pocketbook.* But I don't even know if I'll see her at Christmas. Or if she'll still be *alive* at Christmas.

Green Mountain digs through her bag, popping the lid on a bottle of Excedrin. "They say to take two, but you need three for a migraine. Here, hold out your hand."

I do what she says. She taps three caplets in my palm.

I swallow them with Coke and return to my chair, eager for the miracle of pain relief. "Mom always gives me Motrin," I volunteer.

She harrumphs. "Motrin never did diddly for me."

"Me neither," I agree.

"Stick with Excedrin if it does the trick. Doctors'll try to sucker you in with the prescription stuff. That's what mine did. Got me hooked on Percocet. Ever hear of it?"

"Yeah. In health class. It's got Oxycodone in it. A girl in my homeroom OD'd on Oxy. She's in detox now."

"Yeah, well, it turned me into a damn zombie. Your ma could tell you all about that. Wasn't until I got treated for depression—after she left and my husband, well, died—that I realized I was hooked on the stuff. Hillbilly heroin, they call it in NA. She points a finger at me, a finger that obviously means business. "You stay away from the shit, you hear me?"

Her approach is so totally different from Mom's, who trusts me to "make good decisions and do what's right." It's a first, having someone just say no. And mean it.

She squints at me. "What are you grinning about? I asked you a question."

I bite the insides of my cheeks to keep from smiling. "I won't touch the stuff. Promise."

"Okay. Good. Now shut your eyes. I'll show you what my new doctor has me do when I get a migraine. She's trained in all that touchy-feely stuff."

I rest my head back, against the wall. I let my lids drop closed.

"Picture something nice," she tells me. "The ocean or the forest or whatever makes you feel relaxed. Concentrate on it, like you're watching a show on TV."

I don't have to decide what to picture, the memory just comes to me. I'm at Olivia's cottage on Willow Lake the summer after fourth grade. Her dad and Steve said she could invite me along. Normally, their weekends were "family time," but Liv had broken her wrist two days before, and they were worried she'd be bored because she couldn't go in the water with her cast. Anyway, Liv led the way toward this tree, which was right next to where their boat was docked. It had huge pink blossoms that smelled sweeter than anything I'd ever smelled before. As we sat beneath it, I drew on Olivia's cast. She'd sectioned off areas for different people—her cello teacher, her grandpa, her favorite aunt in New Paltz, her babysitter.

And me, of course. My spot was the largest. I filled it with flowers and hearts mostly, and I signed it: *VBFTTWE*—which stood for Very Best Friends Till the World Ends—*Ariel.* Then we lay back on the warm grass, watching the bees buzz through the blossoms, listening to the boat thump the dock.

When I open my eyes, I realize I must have dozed off. My neck is stiff, but my headache is completely gone.

A nurse in a pale yellow uniform stands beside Green Mountain's bed, attaching a blood pressure cuff. She squeezes the rubber ball again and again and the cuff expands, making sounds like small, nervous breaths. The nurse stares at the floor, listening. "Much better," she says. "One-fifty over eighty-four. Now we're getting somewhere." When she rips the Velcro loose, my eyes come to rest on Green Mountain's white, fleshy arm.

Quickly, I turn away.

Then I look back again—the same way you do when you pass a gruesome car wreck and don't want to see it, but at the same time you have this morbid curiosity.

Green Mountain's arm is scarred. Badly. From the cap of her sleeve down to her wrist, her skin is scaly, mottled with patches of raised, off-color skin, clustered in erratic patterns.

The nurse scribbles something on a chart and turns to leave.

Green Mountain slips her arm back into her sweater. She smoothes it in place and glances my way. "Hey," she says, "you're awake. Feel any better?"

"Yeah, I do. Thanks."

"Good." She tries to sit up. Stops. Winces.

"Are you okay?" I ask. Which is stupid. How could anyone in her situation be okay?

Creases line her forehead. "Drainage tubes're hurting. I think I'll close my eyes for a few minutes. You mind?"

I stand quickly, worried I've stayed too long. "No," I rush out, "that's fine."

But when I start toward the door, she calls, "Wait!"

I look back at her. I mean, *really* look. Her eyes are blue, like mine. Her hair, streaked with gray, is the same shade of brown as Mom's. And even though her face is very round, her features are small, almost delicate."Yeah?"

"I didn't mean you have to leave. I've got magazines if you like to read."

"That's okay." I tip my chin toward the hall. "I should try to find Mom."

"Oh, sure." She nods, but I can tell she's disappointed.

Suddenly I feel responsible for her. "Do you, um, need anything before I go?"

She lifts her chin toward an old transistor radio on the windowsill. "Put on some music for me. It's too damn quiet in here."

"What station?" I ask.

"Should be set already. Ninety-two FM. Only station I listen to. My bingo buddy, Thelma, goes for that toe-tappin' country-western crap, but I like the seventies stuff."

So does my dad, I think but don't say. Bringing him up wouldn't go over well.

The reception on the radio is fuzzy, so I move the antenna around. An instrumental song comes on, one I've never heard before.

"That's from *Jonathan Livingston Seagull,*" Green Mountain says. "Ever see the movie?"

I shake my head no.

"It's about a seagull named Jonathan who doesn't fit with the crowd." Her face softens and she sighs. "I felt a lot like that lonely seagull when I was your age. Thought my dreams would save me. Anyway"—she forces a smile—"rent it sometime."

"I will." I wait until her eyes drift closed before starting quietly toward the door.

* * *

Outside, I press Liv's number. She answers on the second ring. She must be in her room. I hear Coldplay in the background.

"Hey, Liv."

"Hey, Ariel."

"My condolences to Katelyn. Is she still there?"

"No. She had a rehearsal to go to."

I'm secretly happy to hear that. I was worried Liv might invite her to stay for the dinner party.

"How's your headache?" Liv asks.

"Better. My . . ." I hesitate. "My grandmother gave me some Excedrin and a Coke, then she had me do a visualization."

"Wow. She sounds awesome." Liv would say that. Her dad uses guided imagery with his clients. "What did she have you visualize?"

"She told me to pick something that makes me feel calm. The first thing that popped into my head was the weekend at Willow Lake, after you broke your wrist."

"Really?"

"Yeah. Why do you sound surprised?"

"I thought you'd visualize something you did with Shane."

I try to pinpoint what I'm hearing in Olivia's voice. Is it jealousy? A by-product of feeling squeezed out of the picture? Does she think my Liv memories are history now?

Stepping back, taking a look at the situation, I realize—that's how *I'd* feel if the tables were turned.

Suddenly I want to give her something. I need to give her something. Something a friend would give another friend. The truth.

"Liv," I start, "I probably thought of Willow Lake because"—I force the words out—"I don't exactly feel calm with Shane."

"You . . . *don't?*"

"No. I feel on edge. A lot."

"Wow. Ariel. I had no idea. Not that I've seen you two interact much—Shane seems to want you all to himself—but, well, I got the impression you were happy."

A door busts open inside me. A door to a room I haven't dared enter. Until now.

"I don't know *what* I am," I tell Liv. "Confused, I guess. I'm always so busy trying to keep Shane from getting hurt or disappointed or mad that I sometimes feel like there isn't a place for my feelings anymore. I can barely find myself. And when I do"—I picture Shane's nosebleed—"I don't always like who I see."

Liv sighs. "Oh, Ariel, this relationship doesn't sound healthy for you."

She's channeling her dad again. But she's right.

After a long pause, Liv asks, "Do you think Shane had an ulterior motive for giving you a phone?"

I panic. The phone. Oh my God. If Shane has a tracking device on it, could it be tapped, too? Could he be listening to my conversation right now? "Liv," I say, changing the subject, "I really want to have a long talk with you when I get home. I know I've been a terrible friend lately and I've hardly given you any time. But I want that to change. I miss hanging out with you and going shopping and being silly and laughing and doing all the things we used to do."

"Wellll," she says, "next Friday I'm performing a solo at the holiday concert. Dad and Steve are taking me out to dinner first. Maybe you can come too?"

Tears prick my eyes. I'm filled with a rush of feelings I don't have words for yet.

But then reality hits. Friday is date night.

"You don't have to answer now," Liv says. "We'll talk about it when you get home."

"Okay, Liv. Thanks."

There's a long silence, then she says, "I have no clue whatsoever why I just thought of this. But remember in fifth grade when we went to see *Holes,* and you got a major crush on Zigzag?" I can hear the smile in her voice.

For a split second, I slip back into fifth-grade me. "God, Liv, I miss you."

Madeline

Muralee offers to pick me up on Saturday morning, but I don't want her seeing where I live, so I suggest we meet at Franklin's Five and Dime.

I arrive first, dressed in a pair of size ten bell bottoms (with a sanitary napkin pinned to my underwear, in case I get my period, which is a week late) and a turtleneck sweater—emerald green, like Muralee's eyes. Over that I'm wearing a brown corduroy jacket I found at a rummage sale. I think Muralee will like my outfit—it reminds me of something she'd pick out.

Remembering Muralee's favorite soda, I buy a bottle of Dr. Pepper. It's not diet, so I won't drink much, but I hope she'll be interested in sharing it.

I sit on the bench outside Franklin's waiting.

Muralee's late. By ten minutes. Twenty.

An excruciating half hour passes. I'm worried Muralee's decided to ask Jeannette or Sharon or Nancy to go with her instead of me. But then a bright red Chevy Impala slows to the curb beside me. A window opens and Muralee sticks her head out, calling, "Hop in."

I slide in and fasten my seat belt.

Muralee's wearing powder blue slacks with an off-white cardigan sweater. Her dark sunglasses rest low on her nose like Audrey Hepburn's in *Breakfast at Tiffany's.*

Clutching a cigarette, her hand shakes as she inhales.

"I didn't know you smoked," I say.

"I don't," she breathes out. "My dad keeps a pack in the glove compartment. He'll never notice if a few are missing. Want one?"

I've never tried smoking before. But I'd probably drink arsenic if Muralee Blawjen suggested it. "Sure. Why not?"

Muralee lights a cigarette for me, handing it across the stick shift. I notice her lipstick print on the filter and place my lips exactly where hers were. I draw smoke into my lungs, just like I've seen Tad and my mother do.

Then I cough my brains out. I'm so embarrassed, I contemplate opening the door and rolling into oncoming traffic. But Muralee says, "God, don't you hate that? You're trying to look cool, and your body has the nerve to *betray* you."

I'm thinking how profound the thought is, and how nice it was of her to express it, when Muralee starts to coughs too. Longer and harder than I did. She reaches her hand toward me, wiggling her fingers, trying to tell me something.

"Soda?" I guess.

She nods, choking.

I hand her the bottle and she drinks. Then we laugh until we're both near tears.

* * *

Muralee parks in front of a tall brick building. Scorch marks left by a fire blacken the blood red stone. A third story window's boarded up.

"Is this the place?" I ask, hoping she'll tell me it's not.

But Muralee nods her head yes.

We're silent for several minutes. Then Muralee reaches beneath the neck of her sweater and holds out a silver medallion. "I wore my Saint Christopher necklace. Do you think it'll help protect me?"

Mom never took me to church, so I'm not sure how these things work. But there's only one right answer. "Of course," I answer. "And I'll pray for you the whole time you're gone." I don't know where that last part came from. I've never said a prayer in my life. But for Muralee, I'll figure out how.

"Do you, um"—she hesitates, glancing at the building—"do you think that when I die, I'll go to hell for doing this?"

I have no idea what they teach in church about hell. I have to protect Muralee, though. So I tell her, "No, I think God will remember you as a good person."

She reaches for my hand, squeezing it. "Thanks, Madeline."

When she says my name, my skin prickles.

"This is for the best," she continues. "Glenn, he"—her voice catches—"a baby would ruin everything for him. College. His football scholarship. Daddy would make him marry me. Glenn would probably end up resenting me and the baby, and then—"

"But what about *you?*" I ask. "How do you feel?"

"I'm starting at the University of Florida in the fall. It's Daddy's alma mater and he's already worked it out so I'll stay with my grandparents in Gainesville." She swallows hard, and it's obvious she's fighting back tears. "Look, Glenn and I both want children someday. When we're ready. But right now, well, it's too soon. The timing isn't right."

Muralee opens the door and steps out. I watch her walk toward the ugly, red building. I imagine the smell of burned curtains, the sight of coat hangers, men with dirty hands. I can't let her go through this alone. I open my door and start to follow her.

Muralee turns. "Please," she whispers. "Wait in the car. I'll probably need you to drive. You have your license, right?"

"Yeah, but—"

She holds her hand up, stopping me. Then she hurries toward the wooden door, swings it open, dissolves into the darkness on the other side.

I return to the car, watching the clock on the dashboard, blinking only when I have to. And I pray, asking God to keep Muralee safe. At first I feel stupid, talking to someone who's invisible. But eventually, I find the words comforting.

A half hour passes. Forty minutes. Fifty.

An hour later, the brown door opens. Muralee clings to the railing, starting slowly down the stairs. When she reaches the car, she leans against the passenger side door. "Slide over," she whispers.

I straddle the stick shift and drop into the driver's seat.

Muralee eases in carefully, like every movement hurts. "That cost me two hundred fucking dollars," she says. It's the first time I've ever heard her swear.

She lifts the flap on her purse and hands me the car keys.

I start the car. I'm about to shift into first when I glance at Muralee, curled down low in her seat. There's blood on the thighs of her slacks. "You're, um . . ."

"Bleeding. I know. He couldn't stop it. I've got a *dishrag* between my legs." She leans sideways, collapsing against me. Her head is on my shoulder and she's crying.

I wish I could be Muralee's friend. A *real* friend like Jeannette or Sharon or Nancy—someone Muralee would choose. But I know that will never happen. We've only been thrown together by circumstance. But, for now, I'm all she has so I rest my hand on Muralee's reddish-brown hair. Stroking her long locks, I whisper, "Shhhh. It'll be okay." Over and over until, finally, she stops crying.

* * *

Back in Elmira, I park in the lot behind Franklin's. Muralee's asked me to buy her a box of Kotex napkins and a sanitary belt for her bleeding. Before I leave, I give her my corduroy jacket to cover her lap, in case anyone walks past the car. I feel proud of myself for guessing what Muralee might need.

Inside, I head straight for the feminine products aisle, pausing at the pregnancy tests. I glance at the pharmacy window, where Mr. Franklin's busy filling a prescription, then reach for a box identical to the one Muralee stole. I stuff it inside my handbag, gather Muralee's supplies, and start for the register.

When I return to the car, Muralee's crouched down lower still. "I think the bleeding's worse," she says. "But I'm scared to look. Check for me?"

I lift the corner of my blazer. She's right. It's worse. "I think I should take you to the hospital," I tell her.

Muralee grabs my wrist. "No, please! No one can know about this. You have to promise me you'll never tell anyone. *Ever.*"

I nod. Smoothing the jacket back, I ask, "Then what?"

"Take me somewhere to clean up. A bath might help stop the bleeding." She hugs herself like she's cold. "Your place. Let's go there."

It's too big a risk to take her to our apartment. Mom could be there, having sex with a stranger, or passed out in her own puke. Still, I have to think of something.

I check the clock on the dashboard. It's almost three thirty. My brain scrambles to remember what Tad told me earlier—that after he finishes work, he's buying new brakes for his truck. A friend who owns a garage in Corning is letting him use the lift after the shop closes. And since it's Saturday, Tad's dad is on the four-to-midnight shift.

My heart races. "I know where we can go."

Muralee closes her eyes while I drive. Fifteen minutes later, we're at the turnoff for the trailer park. As I veer down the bumpy dirt road, dust clouds billow up around us.

When I swerve to avoid a pothole, Muralee's eyes fly open and she grabs the door handle to brace herself. "Where are you taking me?"

"Somewhere you can wash up," I answer, pulling beside a rusty barrel propped on concrete blocks. There's a foul smell in the air, like someone's been burning rubber tires.

Hurrying to Muralee's side, I help her out of the car. I hold her arm, steadying her along the walkway, then up the narrow metal steps. At the top, I reach inside an old work boot, lifting out the spare key Tad showed me the time we had the place to ourselves.

I unlock the door and lead the way into the kitchen. There's a mound of dirty dishes in the sink. A fly circles a saucepan.

Muralee grimaces. "No offense, but you don't live here, do you?"

Ignoring her question, I flip a light switch and start toward the bathroom. "This way," I tell her. I dig through a tiny closet and manage to find towels but no washcloths.

When I pull the shower curtain back, exposing the tub, its insides are stained a mossy brown. "I'll scrub it for you," I offer. "There has to be some Ajax somewhere."

Muralee reaches behind the mildewy curtain, turning the water spigots on full blast. "Don't bother," she says. "I'm just going to make it dirtier."

* * *

I'm in the kitchen sucking an ice cube when Muralee returns, a bath towel wrapped around her. Her arms and legs are pink from the hot water, and her wet hair's a deep bronzy color. I'd love to be as beautiful as she is.

"Where should I put these?" she asks, holding out her blood-stained clothes. She sounds about ten, her voice is so small.

I jump up and take them from her. Then I search below the sink for a bag, stuff the garments inside, and set the bag next to the door. "How's the bleeding?" I ask her.

"Better. It's let up." She pulls out a chair, wincing as she lowers herself into it.

Once, I saw a TV show about healers who can take away other people's pain. I wish I'd paid more attention so I could do that for Muralee now.

I sit across from her, staring at the centerpiece of fake fruit. I bite my ice cube, shattering it in one quick chomp.

Muralee pokes a plastic grape. "You shouldn't do that."

"Do what?"

"Chew ice."

I poke a grape, too. "Why?"

"It means you're sexually frustrated."

I laugh. "You made that up."

Muralee leans her elbows on the table. "I didn't. I read it in a magazine."

When I don't say anything back, Muralee says, "I'm sorry. I didn't mean anything by that. I was just making conversation."

I consider telling her the truth—that I'm not only having sex, I'm a week late for my period. Instead, I say, "I'm not sexually frustrated. I have a boyfriend."

Muralee grins. "The guy I saw you with at McDonald's?"

I feel my cheeks redden. "Yeah."

"How come he's never in school?"

"He graduated," I lie.

"Oh, an older man." She says it with such authority. "Where does he live?"

I'm getting nervous with all the questions. But I'd never do anything to make Muralee not like me, so I lie again. "Out of the area. Owego."

She smiles. "Nice town."

I smile too, glad she approves. Then we both sit back, quiet.

The clock ticks.

The faucet drips.

The refrigerator moans and groans.

Muralee clears her throat. "Um, I don't want you to get the wrong impression of me. You know, because I had an abortion. I really do want kids someday—when Glenn and I are finished with college and our lives are more copasetic."

Copasetic, I repeat to myself. I've never heard the word before. It reminds me of Chloraseptic, the sore throat spray. I'm not sure what to say back, so I nod, pick a dried ketchup blob off the salt shaker, flick it to the floor. I notice the linoleum is covered with dried, muddy footprints. I'd like to spend a day here, cleaning.

"So," Muralee asks, "does this place have a washing machine?"

"No. Why?"

She tips her chin toward the bag beside the door. "My clothes, remember? I don't have anything to wear."

I consider offering to drive to the laundromat and wash them, but that would take too much time. Tad might be home by then. "What size are you?" I ask her.

"Ten."

“Hang on. I have an idea.” I head for Tad’s room and rifle through his dresser drawers. I slip off my clothes and fold them neatly in a pile.

Tad’s jeans are big on me, but with a belt, they work. I put on an Impeach Nixon T-shirt and tuck it in. Over that, I slip on a long-sleeved flannel shirt. It’s loose and baggy, so I tie the tails together at my waist. Then I button the sleeves at the wrists so my lizard arm is completely covered. I check myself in the mirror. There’s a girl in my English class, Lydia Marcotte, who dresses like I’m dressed now. Rumor has it, she’s a lesbian. I can see why she prefers clothes like these. They’re comfortable.

Back in the kitchen, I hold my outfit out to Muralee. “Here, try these.”

She just stares at me.

“What’s wrong?” I ask, worried I’ve offended her somehow.

She stands. Steps toward me. “Aren’t you afraid to wear those?” she asks, giving the flannel sleeve on my right arm a firm tug.

Everything happens in slow motion. The sleeve slips off my shoulder. Glides down the length of my arm. Gathers at my wrist. Stops.

Hesitantly, I look down. There they are. My scars. In plain sight.

Muralee blinks several times before politely turning away.

I hike the sleeve back into place and smooth the fabric flat. Again and again, like this might erase what Muralee has seen.

“What happened?” she asks me.

“It was, um, an accident. When I was ten I got burned.”

“So that’s why you wear long sleeves all the time, even during a heat wave.” It’s not a question, it’s a statement.

I stare at the floor. Nod.

“Oh, Madeline”—she sounds genuinely sad —“I—I’m sorry you

had to go through that. Life is so unfair sometimes." She surprises me with a sudden hug.

Aside from Tad holding me in his arms after sex, it's the first hug anyone's ever given me.

When Muralee lets go, I blink back tears and hand her my clothes.

Desiree

ned—the same man
who booked our room—
schedules an interview
with jeremy and me.
the diner closes at eleven,
he says. *charlotte and*
me'll talk to you then.

we show up at 10:30
pick a booth in the corner,
share a banana split,
passing time.
at eleven ten
the last customer files out.

ned hits the outside lights,
flips the *open* sign to *closed*,
drops a coin in the jukebox,

sits down across from us.
his black beard is laced with silver
and his fingernails are chewed to the quick.
as an old elvis presley song plays
a lady slides in beside him,
her red hair gray at the roots.
she lights a cigarette, inhales.
so you two kids want a job?
she asks,
her words
encased in smoke.

jeremy and i nod.
yes, ma'am, i add,
folding my hands
on my belly bulge.

hoarsely, she laughs.
you don't have to call me
ma'am—i'm charlotte.
when are you due?
my heart speeds up.
larry got me pregnant in early june,
but i didn't have sex with jeremy
till the start of july.
i do the math. shrug.
february or march, i guess.

another husky laugh.
hell, i didn't start
losing track till my third kid.

how long the two of you been married?
um, well . . . i start.

pfff! she smiles.
relax, honey.
ned and me got four kids together
and we ain't never tied the knot.
she rolls her eyes.
he calls me his significant other.

ned's fingers drum the table.
the openings are for a waitress
and a dishwasher.
you two got experience?

washing dishes,
we blurt out together.
how about waitressing?
charlotte asks.
i'm a fast learner, i tell her.
she motions toward my belly.
you better be!

there's a long moment of silence.
elvis croons *only you.*
even though it's not my
kind of music,
it's getting under my skin.

the lady draws on her cigarette again.
when could the two of you start?

i mean, if we hire you.
knocking knees with jeremy,
i answer, *right away.*

ned nods,
finds a hangnail to nibble.
the jobs are under the table.
either of you have
a problem with that?

not knowing what
he means
i tip sideways,
glancing beneath our booth.

charlotte elbows ned's side.
girl's got a sense of humor,
ned, i like that.
whaddaya say we
put these kids to work?

* * *

my first day on the job
i cut my finger slicing lemons and
toss a kid's retainer case in the trash.
for my encore,
i drop a plate.
breath held, i wait
to see if anyone jumps,
screams,
has a coronary.

but no one does.
broom in hand,
charlotte appears,
sliding the shiny white shards
into a dingy, gray dustpan,
saying, *relax, honey, it's only a plate.*

* * *

waitressing is harder than it looks,
especially remembering
who ordered what.
the last thing i want is for
a table full of people to
play musical plates after
i've dropped off their food.
that's a sure way to nix a tip,
and jeremy and i need the money.

after several days, i get an idea.
i make notes on each slip before
clipping them on the line for ned.
hey, desiree, he calls from the grill,
what the heck's a sem cap turk club?
rushing past, i answer,
the guy in the seminoles hat
ordered a turkey club sandwich.
when he shakes his head,
charlotte says,
the girl's got a system,
ned, deal with it!

* * *

charlotte gives me plenty of advice—
what foods to eat for my baby,
what kind of vitamins to buy,
which types of shoes to wear,
so i won't get varicose veins.
she even drives me into town
to sign up for medicaid
so i can see a baby doctor.
some folks might call
her overbearing,
but i don't mind.
i like having someone care.

* * *

every night now
i get up several times to pee—
probably on account of the baby,
since i used to sleep straight through.
i try to move slowly, carefully,
so the mattress won't squeak
and bother jeremy.

except sometimes
i wish he would stir.
like if i forget where i am
and expect to hear mam snoring.
or when i wake from a school dream—
wandering the halls alone,

searching for carol ann,
about to miss a test
i didn't study for.
fragmented moments,
evidence of the life
i left behind.

sometimes,
i'm disappointed
i was only dreaming.

* * *

ned cuts us a deal on
a bigger, better room,
complete with a kitchenette,
and charlotte gives me
her old maternity clothes.

at the diner,
i pick up her slang—
bossy in a bowl for beef stew,
shivering liz for jell-o,
sweep the kitchen for hash.

after two weeks,
she puts me in charge
of deciding the daily
blue plate special.
so i do what i've seen

her do many times—
stand before the open fridge,
hip cocked, inhaling refrigerated air,
waiting for the leftovers to speak to me.
hey, charlotte, i call,
we've got three big tubs
of mashed murphy and
hockey pucks climbing the walls.
how's shepherd's pie sound to you?

charlotte breezes past,
hauling a bag of trash
to the dumpster.
you're a natural!

* * *

one humid wednesday,
our day off,
jeremy and i
take a bus to cedar key
then walk to the nearest beach.
the bluest water i've ever seen
reflects a cloudless sky.
seagulls caw overhead.
excited, i turn to jeremy.
i love the smell here. don't you?

he wrinkles his nose.
smells like dead fish to me.

i swat his arm,
kick off my flip-flops,
hurry across the hot sand.
as warm, wet fingers
tickle my feet
a bumpy white shell
with pink insides
bumps up against my big toe.
when i reach to pick it up,
my baby kicks up a storm.

sometimes it freaks me out
knowing there's
this living,
breathing thing inside me,
growing bigger every day.
overwhelmed, i start to cry.

jeremy pulls me close,
our stomachs touch,
then he feels the baby kick too.
surprised, he jumps back. *whoa!*
that dude's got some strong-ass legs.

laughing now,
i wipe tears away.
it's not a dude,
it's a dudette.

that so?

i nod. *definitely.*
jeremy rests both hands on my belly.
did i ever tell you my dad played
soccer at buffalo state?
i roll my eyes.
only a zillion times.
well—jeremy smiles—
maybe our little dudette
is gonna take after her grandpa.

hours later,
when the sun's gone down,
my pretty shell sits on the dresser
and jeremy snores beside me.
i lay awake,
taunted by the memory of his smile.
how will i ever tell him the truth?

in the middle of the night
my everyday fears become monsters
that threaten to swallow me whole.

* * *

a week before christmas
jeremy and i take a bus
to the kmart in ocala.
we buy a tiny fake tree,
pine-scented candles,
and a can of artificial snow.

on christmas eve,
the diner closes early
and jeremy and i
order takeout
to eat in our room.
holiday music plays on our radio,
candlelight flickers on the walls,
fake snow lines the sill.
i slide jeremy's present
out from under our bed.

he peels back the paper,
beams. *wow, a vcr!*
now i can tape the simpsons.

my gift's in a tiny box.
inside is a ring with
a thin, shiny band
and a tag that says
genuine gold plated.
jeremy slips it on my finger.
since we're gonna have a baby together,
i'd say it's time we got engaged.

i push the truth aside,
bury my face in jeremy's neck,
and hug him as hard as i can.

* * *

by the time
the new year rolls around
i have the regulars pegged.
stew, the one-eyed meter reader
who always orders steak and eggs.
joe hobbs, who manages the feed store,
a grits-and-pancakes man.
sally haas, the town librarian,
who drifts in just before the lunch crowd,
ordering the blue plate special
without even asking what it is.
there are a dozen more like them—
folks whose habits give them away,
predictable as the daily noon whistle.

but one afternoon,
in the lull before the dinner rush,
when business slows to a crawl
and charlotte's busy in the kitchen
setting up the next day's salads and
watching *oprah* on her tiny tv,
an unfamiliar lady breezes in.

she has auburn chin-length hair
and a beige suit with matching pumps.
she's probably mam's age,
only thinner, prettier.

her heels click toward
a two-top in the corner.

she opens her briefcase on the table,
unloads a black leather binder,
clicks a fancy silver pen,
writes across a smooth, new page.

i mosey over. i got that from charlotte—
she's always moseying here
and moseying there.
not looking up, the lady says,
i'd like a cup of earl grey tea with lemon,
a chef salad with extra swiss, no salami,
and italian dressing on the side, please.
i can tell from the flat, twangless
slap of her syllables
she's a northerner, like me.

after bringing her order,
i study the northern lady
from the register.
she removes a single pit
from her lemon wedge,
holds it over her steaming mug, squeezing.
then she dunks her tea bag in the cup,
flattens it against her spoon,
places it gently on the saucer.

when i refill her cup with hot water
and leave her a brand-new bag,
she looks up, finally.
she has pretty eyes—

green as the shamrocks
taped to the windows—
and a small, delicate face.
tucking her hair behind one ear
she glances at my belly and smiles,
saying something about a bud being snug,
and a sprat—whatever *that* is—
doing something inside a pickle jug.
i haven't got the slightest idea
what she's talking about.
i just stand there,
dumb as dust.

the northern lady smiles.
i'm sorry, that's a line
from a poem called you're.
i was imagining that's how
your baby must be feeling,
tucked in that cozy space.

i nod, relax.
where'd that poem come from?

she reaches in her briefcase,
removes a small, thin book.
i glance at the cover and
recognize the poet's name—
she's the one who offed herself.
here, keep this. it's an extra.
i bought it at the airport this morning.

i forgot my copy at home.
i'm not an organized traveler.

ariel, i say, touching the cover.
ariel *by sylvia plath.*
my baby kicks and kicks
like she's running
the new york marathon.

* * *

that night i drink black decaf tea,
something charlotte got me to try,
and read *ariel,* cover to cover.
some lines i can't figure out,
but i like the way the words connect,
the sounds they make inside my head.

when i'm finished,
i feel melancholy.
the *daddy* poem especially
filled me with so many thoughts—
of my own daddy,
who i wish i could've met,
of jeremy,
about to become a daddy
to a baby who isn't even his.

i turn to look at him,
parked in front of a football game,
sipping a coors.

except he seems
a million miles away.
jeremy, is everything okay?
he steadies the remote
and lowers the volume.
i was remembering when
i turned thirteen and my dad
got us tickets to see a bills game.
man, was he psyched.
i swallow hard. *you miss him?*

he nods, pauses.
but i miss my mom even more.
she, like, takes all this shit for anxiety,
and i worry i'm making her more nuts
than she already is on account
of not knowing where i am.

a long, hulking silence follows.
it slithers and crawls through
our room, belly down,
sucking up the last bit of air.

finally, jeremy continues.
maybe after the baby's born
we can go back for a visit.
i know this is important to him
because the bills score a touchdown
and he watches me, not the screen.
whaddaya think?

my life is here now,
but i can't break
his little-boy heart.
i pick up *ariel,*
a connection to the new life i have,
deciding i'll read it once more.
sure, we'll go.

* * *

the next day,
the northern lady's back,
same time, same table.
as i walk toward her
carrying a spot with a twist
(diner-speak for tea with lemon),
she looks up, quoting a poem from *ariel*—
the one where kindness carries tea
and steam circles it like a wreath.
that's from—she starts and
i finish, *from the poem* kindness.
she smiles. *so you've read* ariel?
i smile back. *yeah—i mean yes. twice.*

after she finishes eating,
she folds her napkin on her plate,
leaves me a generous tip,
stands and pushes in her chair—
something no one ever thinks to do.
as she glides through the door
a wind whips across the parking lot,

lifting the rusty vacancy sign
that hangs from a pole outside.
screech, screech, screech,
it claps against a cloudless sky.

that lady is just like the breeze,
appearing straight out of nowhere.

Ariel

There's no sign of Mom in the cafeteria, which irks me. I know this visit is rough on her, but leaving me to fend for myself is kind of thoughtless. She's not the only one affected here.

Not knowing what else to do, I wander outside again. The sky's a brilliant blue and the foliage is brighter than fire. Olivia calls autumn colors hyper-hues. She says they look like they're cranked up on Jolt cola.

I glance around, making sure Shane's bike isn't parked in the shrubs. That he's not lurking somewhere, waiting to push my buttons so I can turn into a head case again. When I'm convinced I'm alone, I return to the bench I sat on earlier.

A bird chirps in a nearby tree, and a familiar ache crowds my heart. My Missing Dad ache, which shows up in moments like these—when talking with Mom isn't an option. Hearing what happened with Shane this afternoon would put her over the edge. But Dad might understand. Or at least not completely freak out.

My eyes land on the spot where I tackled Shane. And there, shaded by a nearby shrub, is my phone. Which I'm obviously developing some serious issues with.

I glare at it, wishing it weren't mine. Hesitantly, I stand to pick it up.

I flip it open. 8 MISSED CALLS.

ShaneShaneShaneShaneShaneShaneShaneShane.

I power it off and stick the phone in my pocket, telling myself that—since I forgot to pack the charger—it's wise to save on the battery.

* * *

When I return to Green Mountain's room, I expect to find Mom there, asking me where I've been. But she's not. There's a person in the second bed, though. I catch a glimpse of her through the small space where her privacy curtain doesn't close. She's old with wild, wiry white hair.

"Find your ma?" Green Mountain asks.

"No," I answer, sitting down.

She tips her head toward her new neighbor. "Colon cancer. She's going into surgery tomorrow."

The curtain ripples as Wild Hair smacks it. "Mind your own damn business!"

We both stifle a laugh.

"Why don't you tell me about yourself," Green Mountain says. "What grade are you in?"

"I'm a junior."

"You a good student?"

I shrug. "I guess. My schedule's hard this year. I'm taking three AP classes."

"AP?" she repeats.

"Advanced Placement. If I pass the exams, I might get college credit for the classes."

"That so? Where do you wanna go?"

"Brown's my first choice. Smith is my second. If I don't get accepted, I'll probably go to Hudson Hills University. That's where Mom got her bachelor's."

She looks shocked. "Your ma went to college? How'd she swing that?"

"Mom works at HHU. With her employee discount, tuition was super cheap."

"I wanted to go to college," she tells me. "Never got to, though. I got pregnant with your ma during my senior year of high school."

"What would you have majored in?" I ask her.

"Nursing." She glances out the window then back at me. "How about you? What'll you study in college?"

"Probably psychology. Mom and Aunt Lee both think I'd make a good therapist because I'm intuitive and I read people well."

Her eyes narrow. "How'd you wind up with an aunt? Your ma and her boyfriend were only children."

"Oh, Aunt Lee's the woman Mom works for at the university. She's not really my aunt, that's just what I call her. We couldn't be any closer if we were related."

She nods. "You got a boyfriend?" she asks me next. Then quickly, she adds, "Or a girlfriend? Sorry, I don't mean to assume. My bingo buddy, Thelma, the one who smuggled in the you-know-what?"—she points to the closet—"she's a lesbian. Came out of the closet two years ago on her forty-seventh birthday. She says us straights make too many assumptions. So I'm cool with the whole gay thing. Just in case."

"Thanks." I smile. "I've got a boyfriend, actually. Shane."

My left eye starts to quiver. I rub it until it stops. But as soon as I take my hand away, the twitching starts up again.

"What's the matter?" she asks me.

"Oh. It's just this weird thing my eye does sometimes when—"

"That's not what I mean. When you said your boyfriend's name, your face went all funny."

I rub my eye again. "We had a fight a little while ago."

I hadn't planned to tell her that. The words just fell out. Immediately, I feel a surge of paranoia. I glance under Green Mountain's bed—like I'm afraid Shane's hiding there, weighing every word.

"Did Shane come along with you and your ma?"

There's no way I can admit what happened—that Shane put a tracking device on my phone and followed me here. It'll sound like he's stalking me or something. "Um, no"—I dig in my pocket and hold up my cell—"we had a fight on the phone."

I suck at lying. I probably look guilty as hell.

Her eyebrows knit together, and I get a feeling she knows there's more I'm not telling her. When she changes the subject, I'm relieved. "I had a boyfriend in high school, your ma's father. I lost over fifty pounds for him." She pats her large, round stomach. "Unfortunately, I found 'em again."

"Where'd you guys go on dates?" I ask her.

"Movies. The Drive-in. The arcade."

"Did you have proms?" As soon as I ask, I want to kick myself. It sounds like I'm saying she's ancient.

"Sure. Except we rented dinosaurs instead of limos."

I laugh. I can't help it.

Green Mountain laughs too, guffawing so hard she snorts.

"Quiet down over there!" Wild Hair shouts.

Green Mountain sticks her tongue out at the curtain. Then she reaches into the drawer on her nightstand, holding out a small cylindrical tube. It's five or six inches long, made of woven pink and blue wicker, with an open hole on each end. “My boyfriend won this for me playing Skee Roll. Ever see one?”

“No.” I lean in, interested. “What is it?”

“Chinese handcuffs.” She slides her finger into one hole, directing the opposite end toward me. “Here.”

I copy her, slipping a finger inside. “Now what?”

She tugs her end backward. The pink and blue strands clamp down on my knuckle. “Gotcha!” she says, triumphant.

I attempt to pull my finger out. But I can’t. I try a second time. A third. I’m stuck.

My mouth is suddenly dry. I lick my lips. Swallow. Try a fourth time. A fifth. Harder. I can’t get free. “Let me go!” I blurt out.

But she doesn’t. She just watches me, grinning.

My heart kicks into overdrive. My pulse pounds in my ears. “I mean it—let me go! Now!”

She finally gets it. That I’m freaking out. “Lean in,” she tells me, and I do. The tube loosens its grip. My finger slides out effortlessly.

Collapsing back in my chair, I stare up at the ceiling squares.

I feel Green Mountain watching me. “You okay?”

When I smooth my hair back, my scalp is damp with sweat. “I’m fine. Why?”

“Well, you’re shaking, for one thing. And your face is white as these bedsheets. Something tripped your switch, big time.”

Suddenly, I feel exposed. I picture Mom’s closed door the night of the Phone Call, wishing I had my own to duck behind. But since I don’t, I put the vibe out instead: Do not enter. I slide my chair away from the bed. When it comes into contact with the wall, I focus on the hallway. The nurse’s station. The bright florescent lights that flood the long ivory corridor.

Changing the subject, Green Mountain asks me, “Did your ma

ever tell you how her father died?"

"In a car accident," I answer, still staring into the hall.

She reaches into her drawer again. I turn to look as she removes a strip of black-and-white photos. There are four of them, printed vertically on a paper the size of a bookmark. "Well, since we're strolling down memory lane together"—she holds them out for me—"this is him and me in high school. Only picture I have of us."

I take the pictures from her and study the images, shocked that Green Mountain was so, well, skinny. She looks more like I imagine Mom might have looked as a teenager.

"Only time in my life I was thin," she says, reading my mind. "I'd always gotten picked on for my size and, well, other things . . ." She tugs on her sweater sleeve. "But when I met him"—she smiles down at the boy's face—"for the first time ever, it mattered to me how I looked. Then, after he died . . ." Her voice trails off.

"You stopped caring again?"

She looks away. Nods. "Uh-huh."

I study the boy. He's got wire-rimmed glasses and spazzed-out hair and needs braces, but obviously none of that matters. Because it's clear the skinny girl who is my grandmother and the boy who is my grandfather are in love. Majorly.

"We were supposed to go out on a date the night he died. I'd planned to tell him I was pregnant. Never got to, though. Driver ran a red light"—she claps her hands together, and I jump—"barreled straight into him."

I hand the photos back. "That's terrible."

"I wish I could go back in time," she continues. "Keep him on the phone a little longer. Or tell him I had homework and couldn't go out. Anything to keep him from crossing that intersection when he did."

When I glance toward the hall again, Mom's standing in the doorway. "Where have you been?" I ask her.

She crosses the room and leans against the arm on my chair. Her coat smells like the outdoors with a hint of something else mixed in. Coffee beans, maybe. "When I couldn't find you," she says, "I went for a walk. I got a tea at Starbucks down the block and planned to bring it back here, but then I ran into a friend from high school, Carol Ann. Her husband, Dan, has a job here selling insurance. They just had their *fifth* kid."

Mom goes on and on. When she comes up for air, I whisper, "TMI."

"Oh." She glances at her mother, who's glancing back at her. Their eyes connect. Quickly Mom turns away, staring out the window at the sky, which has turned a silvery gray. "So," she asks her mother, "how long will they keep you here?" Her words sound stiff, like she's imitating an automated phone voice.

"Not much longer, now that my blood pressure's back to normal. Or as normal as it gets with me." Green Mountain squints at Mom. "How's *your* blood pressure?"

"Actually it runs a little low."

"Good." Green Mountain says.

"How did the exam with your doctor go?" Mom asks her.

She shrugs. "Okay, I guess. He put me on Tamoxifen. And he wants to start me on chemo, in case the cancer's anywhere else."

A silence spreads over the room. It's loaded with an electrical charge, reminding me of the static before a storm that always makes my arm hairs prickle. Minutes pass, feeling like hours.

Green Mountain smoothes her sweater sleeves.

I wipe dust off the toes of my Mocs.

Mom glances at her watch. "Ariel, I never got to call your aunt Lee. I'm sure she's home by now. Could I borrow your cell phone?"

"Mom . . ." I say, talking quietly out of the side of my mouth. ". . . You just got back. Don't you think you should visit for a while first?"

"Well, whaddaya know?" Green Mountain says, louder than necessary. "I'm missing *General Hospital.* You two don't mind, do you?" As she points the clicker at the TV I know exactly what she's doing. She's beating Mom to the punch—putting her second to a soap opera before Mom can put her second to a phone call.

As the sound from the television fills the room Wild Hair swats the curtain again. "Turn that thing down!" she snaps. "I'm trying to sleep over here!"

* * *

Mom and I trek outside. She collapses on a bench, and I flip my phone open. Power it on. Hand it to her.

Nibbling her lip, Mom presses Aunt Lee's number. Then she waits.

"Oh, Lee," she breathes out, "I'm so glad to hear your voice."

Mom listens intently, nodding. "Not all that well. It's very stressful. Yes, she's my mother, but we've been strangers for sixteen years. I hardly know what to say."

A breeze whistles through the trees, and a leaf lands in Mom's hair. I reach over, picking it free.

After several minutes, Mom says, "Ariel? Sure, she's right here." Mom passes me the cell. "Aunt Lee wants to talk to you."

I take the phone from her. "Hi, Aunt Lee."

"Hi, sweetie. How are you holding up?" I hear papers shuffling.

I've seen Aunt Lee in action. She can never just sit and talk.

"Okay, I guess. I had a really bad headache, but she, um—my grandmother—she gave me some Excedrin, and it helped."

"Good. A headache's the *last* thing you need at a time like this. What's your grandmother like?"

Mom taps my knee, pointing toward the parking lot. "I need to get something from the car," she whispers.

I nod, watching as Mom walks away. "She's all right. I know she was a terrible mother when Mom was growing up, but, well, she hasn't exactly had an easy life."

More paper shuffling. "Really? What has she told you?"

"Like how she lost all this weight in high school for her boyfriend. But then he was killed in a car accident before she could tell him she was pregnant."

There's silence on the other end, and I'm thinking maybe I've lost her. But when I check the face of my phone it's lit, and I have plenty of bars. "Aunt Lee?"

She clears her throat. "Sorry, Ariel. I'm here."

"Aunt Lee, my grandmother, she, um . . . she has these horrible scars."

"Well, sweetie, she couldn't very well have a mastectomy without them. She'll probably want to consider reconstructive surgery."

"No. That's not what I mean. When the nurse was taking her blood pressure, my grandmother's sleeve was pushed up, and I saw her arm. It looked like she might have gotten burned or something."

More silence.

Finally, Aunt Lee says, "What's your grandmother's name, Ariel?"

"It says M. Murdock on her door."

"That couldn't be her, then," she mumbles, like she's thinking out loud. "Unless, of course, she married someone else after her boyfriend died. . . ." In her regular voice, she asks me, "What does the M in M. Murdock stand for?"

"I don't know." I glance across the parking lot at Mom, who's rummaging through our trunk for something. "Aunt Lee? Are you there?"

"Yes." She clears her throat. "I'm here."

"You sound funny."

Her desk chair screeches back and forth several times. "I feel funny."

"Aunt Lee, you're scaring me. What's wrong?"

"Ariel, do you remember the Kurt Vonnegut book I gave you last summer?"

"Sure. *Cat's Cradle.* I loved it."

"Then you remember the concept of the karass, and how we're unknowingly bound to certain people?"

"Of course," I say, surprised she has to ask. She and I talked about the concept for, like, hours. We agreed she and Mom and I are all part of the same karass.

"A karass is propelled forward by conflict," she continues.

"Aunt Lee, *please,* why are you telling me this?"

"Because, it's possible our karass just got a lot more complicated. Ariel, you need to find out your grandmother's name. If it's Madeline—Madeline Fitch would be her maiden name—I know her. Madeline and I went to the same high school. There in Elmira. In the fall of our senior year, we were thrown together by, well, circumstances."

"What kind of circumstances?"

"Let's just say that Madeline—she helped me through a very difficult situation."

A can top pops. I picture Aunt Lee at her desk with a Dr. Pepper. I wish she were drinking it here instead.

"Around Thanksgiving," she continues, "Madeline's boyfriend

died in a car accident. Madeline started working at Grand Union after school. She and I didn't travel in the same circles—not that Madeline really had a circle, all she had was her boyfriend—but sometimes I'd stop by, to see how she was managing. She wouldn't talk to me after he died, though. She'd stare right through me like she'd constructed a fortress around herself no one would penetrate again."

Aunt Lee pauses, sipping soda. "By spring—I remember it was close to Easter because I was at Grand Union buying chocolate eggs—I noticed Madeline had gained back the weight she'd lost, but there was something different about her. By the time the school year ended, it was obvious she was pregnant."

"So what happened?" I ask.

"I never found out. I gave Madeline a gift at graduation—something I hoped would help her—but I never saw her after that. I always wondered if she put her baby up for adoption, or if she decided to raise it herself. Though, I have to admit, I couldn't imagine her caring for a child. After Tad died she seemed so withdrawn, so depressed."

Aunt Lee exhales a slow breath. "Oh, Ariel, this is too bizarre. If your grandmother is Madeline Fitch, the baby she was pregnant with could be your mother."

I'm totally numb. I can't even think, I'm so stunned.

"Ariel," Aunt Lee says, "are you all right? Say something."

"I don't know what to say. I'm just . . . trying to take it all in."

"Yes, I know what you mean." After a long pause, Aunt Lee adds, "Ariel, maybe I shouldn't say this, but I have to. From what I've gathered the few times Desiree has mentioned her mother, I'm guessing she was a terribly neglectful parent. And please don't take this the wrong way because I'm not trying to defend her actions, but, well, if her mother is Madeline Fitch, the woman's had a very tragic life."

"What are you saying, Aunt Lee?"

"Perhaps, if your mom can see past her own hurt"—she pauses—"then maybe she can forgive her mother."

Mom reappears, starting up the walk toward me. It feels like she's been gone light-years. "Aunt Lee," I say, "Mom's coming back now. What should I do?"

"Find out your grandmother's name. And go from there."

"If Madeline Fitch *is* my grandmother, do you want me to give her a message? Should I tell her Lee Stemple said hello?"

"That name won't mean a thing to her," she answers. "I used my full name in high school, and I wasn't married to Glenn yet. But yes, you can tell her Muralee Blawjen sends her best."

Madeline

When I get home, Mom's in her room, door closed, singing along to her radio.

As I'm breaking lettuce in a bowl for a salad the phone rings. Answering it, I smell Mom's boozy breath on the receiver.

"Hi," Tad says, "where've you been? I've been trying to get you since I got back."

I glance at Mom's closed door, praying she didn't hear the phone ring. That she didn't pick up and talk to Tad. "Sorry," I say. "I had to help a friend with something."

"Really? You never mentioned having a friend."

His saying that makes me sound so pathetic. I'm kind of irritated he pointed it out. "Yeah, well, I do."

"What's your friend's name?"

I reach for a cuke and a tomato, start dicing them into neat squares. "Muralee."

"What'd she need help with?"

"It's private. I promised her I wouldn't tell anyone."

"Oh."

I steer the conversation back to him. "What are you doing?"

"Fixing a roof leak. Wanna see a movie when I'm done?" He drops his voice and adds, "At the drive-in?"

My period still hasn't shown up, so the coast is clear. "Sure. What time?"

"I'll pick you up around six."

I glance at the kitchen clock, wondering how I'll be ready that soon. I have to change out of Tad's clothes. And shower. And redo my makeup. And style my hair. "Okay," I say, "I'll see you out front."

"Madeline, um, maybe you could invite me in for a few minutes this time. Since you met my dad, well, I thought maybe I could meet your mom."

My heart leaps into my throat. I stare at Mom's closed door again. "No, I—"

"Look, Madeline, if you're embarrassed about your place, don't be. Remember, we live in a trailer park."

When I don't answer, Tad says, "I love you, Madeline. I mean what I told you—I want to know everything about you."

My eyes fill, and my heart settles back in my chest. "Everything?" I whisper.

"Everything," he repeats.

Mom's bedroom door groans open. She starts toward the kitchen, coughing her raspy cigarette cough.

"I've gotta go," I blurt out, and hang up. Fast.

Mom crosses the kitchen, drops two empty beer bottles in the trash, and reaches in the fridge for another. When she sees me standing there, pouring dressing on my salad, she jumps. "I didn't hear you come in," she half-says, half-slurs.

I poke my salad. Tomato innards ooze around the tines of my fork. "Yeah, well, I'm here."

She steps closer. "Remember the man I told you about? The one with the vanilla pipe tobacco? Guess what?"

"He switched to black cherry and now you don't like him anymore?"

"No." She slaps my arm, giggles, takes several swallows of beer. "He gave me his phone number, so I called him. He asked me out for a drink."

Poor, stupid Pipe Man. He has no idea what fate awaits him. No one asks Leona Fitch out for a drink. She could drain his savings account before the night's over. But, hey, maybe it'll be worth it. Maybe she'll give him something to remember her by, like she did with my father. Whoever *that* sucker might be.

My mother sidles up next to me. "Oh, honey, I think he might actually be the one. You know how you just get that feeling sometimes?"

I nod. "Actually, I do."

Of course, she doesn't ask me *how* I know. I've been dating Tad for months and I'm out almost every night, but still she hasn't caught on.

"Anyway"—she gulps more beer—"Dusty and I are—"

"Dusty?" I laugh. "What kind of a name is that?"

"He was named after Dusty Cooke, the Yankees player."

I roll my eyes and take another bite of my salad. "Since when are you interested in baseball?"

"I'm not, silly. I'm interested in Dusty." She slaps her knee and cracks up, like she said something incredibly funny. Then she gets all serious. "Oh, Maddie, wait'll you meet him. You'll see what I mean. This one's husband material. Maybe me and you are finally done with those cemetery trips. Wouldn't that be nice? If we never had to go back to Cherry Hill?"

It's hard to imagine not having to perch on the rock beside Sophie DeSalvo's concrete angel or shiver from the mist of the nearby fountain. Not having to listen as Mom's slurred words hang like tarnished stars from the flat, black sky while she mourns another loser.

Mom reaches in the junk drawer for a piece of gum. When she opens the wrapper, the stick breaks into stale, brittle shards. She shovels them in her mouth anyway. "Dusty and me have so much in common," she continues, talking and chewing. Gum chips cling to her teeth. I look away, disgusted.

"Like what?" I ask, more curious than interested.

"Tons of things. We both love John Lennon."

"Everyone loves John Lennon," I snap. I glance down at Tad's Impeach Nixon T-shirt. "It's not like you both love Richard Nixon or think he shouldn't have been impeached. Now *that* would prove you're soul mates."

She ignores me. "Dusty and I both cried when we heard Elvis Presley died. Can you believe it? A man who cries and admits it?"

"Terrific," I say flatly. "Where's he taking you for a drink?"

"Well, he not exactly taking me."

"But you just got done saying—"

"Dusty doesn't have a car." She checks the kitchen clock and brushes past me. "So I'm driving."

I follow her and yell, "No way! They revoked your license, remember? If you get caught driving drunk again, you could go to jail."

"I don't *plan* to get caught. I *plan* to be careful." She opens the coat closet and holds up a blue jacket I bought at the thrift store. It has a warm lining, and I thought it would be perfect for the drive-in since it's the end of the season and the nights are chilly. "Is this *yours?"* she asks, like it's impossible I'd own anything that nice. Or that small.

"Yeah, it is. Put it back."

She slips one arm in a sleeve.

I glare at her, this pathetic excuse for a mother who takes and takes and takes. The woman Tad wants to meet. Yeah, right. I can't wait to graduate, start my own life, and get the hell away from her. "Put it back," I demand. "*I'm* wearing that tonight."

Her other arm glides in. She buttons the front, admiring herself in the mirror. "But it looks so nice on me. And it's Dusty's favorite color."

I reach for the sleeve and whirl her around. "I don't care that it's Dusty's favorite color"—I grab her shoulders, shaking her—"I *said*, put it back!"

The phone rings, startling me.

Mom stares down at my hands. "Better get that," she says, lifting her chin toward the kitchen.

I hurry toward the phone, in case it's Tad. Except the person on the other end just breathes, so it's probably an obscene caller. Or Dusty the Dustball, warming up for a big night.

By the time I hang up, Mom's already making her escape. Keys jangle as she grabs the ring off the hook at the bottom of the stairs.

For the first time ever, I don't chase after her, hollering, "Come back!" I don't attempt to wrestle the keys from her hand. I'm so damn sick of worrying about *her* all the time. I've got a life of my own now, one completely unrelated to Leona Fitch.

Walking to the window, I watch Mom climb in her Charger and rev the gas. She backs out without checking behind her, cutting off a van with peace signs spray-painted along its sides. The van blasts its horn, screeching to a stop to avoid her while Mom, oblivious, keeps driving.

I stare at the empty driveway, at the dark puddle that means Mom's car is leaking fluids again. Seeing the stain makes me think of Muralee's bleeding, and the pads I bought for her at the drugstore. And that makes me think of the package I stole.

Reaching inside my handbag, I pull out the home pregnancy test, open the flap, and study the directions inside. All I have to do is mix my pee with the chemicals—except they don't say pee, they say *urine*—then wait for the results.

I lock the deadbolt, breathe deep, and start for the bathroom.

Desiree

at eight months pregnant
i'm as big as a barn,
my back hurts like hell,
and it's hard to sleep.
i lie in bed, belly up,
playing connect-the-dots
with the ceiling stains.
last night i found a butterfly,
the night before that a flower.
but tonight there's nothing.
the dots just won't connect.

outside the window,
the clover inn lights buzz and blink.
rigs thunder by on the highway.
jeremy mutters something in his sleep
and his arm goes thump across my chest.

in the darkness
i squeeze his hand,
until the ceiling dots
don't matter anymore—
only jeremy and me and the baby,
the family i never had
but will now.

* * *

two weeks later,
on valentine's day,
jeremy gives me a rose
and a card that plays
you are my sunshine.
after work
we order catfish takeout and
i balance my plate on my belly as
we watch *wayne's world* on the vcr.
i'm sure jeremy would rather
be doing something romantic,
but i can barely move i'm so huge.

when jeremy gets up for another beer,
i put the video on pause,
swallow hard, ask him,
are you ever scared?
he reaches in the fridge. *scared?*

yeah. about taking care of a baby.
she could be here soon.

he taps his fingers, counting.
but it's only been seven months.
my heart races. *yeah, well,*
s—sometimes babies come early.
especially, um, when they're big.
as if i'm offering proof,
i wave my hand over my giant middle.

the catfish churns in my stomach.
you know, jeremy, if you want out
it's still not too late to—

look, dez. i know this is going
to be hard for both of us—
he pops the tab on a beer,
staring down at the can
—but i'm not bailing on you.
that wouldn't be right.
we'll find a way to deal with this.
we'll save our money and
get an apartment. he laughs.
everyone'll want to come visit us
when they get tired of shoveling snow.

i picture carol ann and eric
sitting next to us
in lawn chairs in a *real* yard,
sipping drinks and eating munchies
while the baby splashes in a kiddie pool.

jeremy loops his arm
around my shoulder.
it'll be okay, dez.
we'll make it work.
i love you and i know
i'll love our baby too.
there's that word again.
our. the three letters
i keep avoiding.

* * *

a week after valentine's day,
i start with the contractions
charlotte warned me i'd have
right before the baby comes.
they're like really bad
time-of-the-month cramps,
she'd told me.
bull.
shit.
they're a million times worse.
the pain is un-fucking-believable.

i take my poetry book to work
so if there are any slow moments
i can *try* to keep my brain occupied,
but it's busier than usual and
ariel sits on the counter
untouched.

as i'm writing up a breakfast order
for a couple with a smart-ass kid
who can't keep his finger
out of his nose,
a wetness oozes out of me,
dribbling down both legs.
charlotte looks up from
the spuds she's mashing,
hurries to my side,
grabs my tablet.
your water broke, sweetie.
i gotcha covered.
she tosses ned
his key ring and hollers,
get 'em to the hospital fast!
jeremy ushers me toward the door,
looking every bit as scared as i am.

inside ned's truck
pain rips through my middle.
i grip the dashboard.
fuuuuuuuuuuuuccckkkk!
jeremy clutches my hand.
ned guns the gas pedal hard.

* * *

six hours later
the pain is a nightmare
i've already begun to forget.

in my hospital room
i hold her.
my baby.
a girl, just like i predicted.

jeremy stands beside my bed,
studying us like we're
another species.
a nurse comes in,
smiles at him.
would daddy like to hold her next?
an assumption.
fine with me.

jeremy's arms bend at odd angles.
he looks so worried he'll drop her.
soon he relaxes,
kisses her forehead.
hey, pretty girl.

that's one lucky baby,
getting what i never had—
a daddy's arms encircling her.
not that jeremy's *really* her daddy.
but he sure is acting the part.

he glances from the baby to me.
s*he's got your nose, dez.*
back at her.
and your cheeks.

at me.
and your dark hair.
he walks to the mirror,
studies himself,
then the baby again.
who'd she get the blue eyes from?

my heart hammers my ribs.
i—uh—well—

the nurse reappears.
most babies are born with blue eyes.
they'll turn later—
she looks at jeremy then me—
especially with brown-eyed parents.
talk about perfect timing.

* * *

as we come through the diner door
charlotte claps flour off her hands
and rushes toward us.
oh, ain't she beautiful?
what'd you name her?

i notice my poetry book
sitting right where i left it,
a sign i chose
the right name.
ariel.

well, ariel—
charlotte tickles my baby's tummy—
welcome to the sunshine state!

* * *

charlotte loans us the crib
from her baby-raising days,
which jeremy sets up next to our bed.
i unpack charlotte's present—a nylon bag
stuffed with diapers,
wipes,
onesies.
in our kitchenette
she makes jeremy a kmart list.
shaking his head, he reads it.
diaper-rash cream,
petroleum jelly,
baby oil.
where the hell do i find this stuff?

she takes his shoulders,
directing him toward the door.
just ask a friendly sales associate.
now hightail it.
ariel has a workin' mama,
so we've got formula to make.

i watch as charlotte
lines baby bottles across
the counter in our kitchenette.

you got a mama somewhere, desiree?
her shadow,
i copy every move.
yeah, in new york,
but it's complicated.
she doesn't even know
she has a granddaughter.
mumbling, i add,
she barely knew she had a daughter.

charlotte puts a saucepan of water on to boil.
i never got along with my ma either.
damn shame, ain't it?
it's like having a hole
in your heart that never heals.
i nod, agreeing with her.

together
we mix formula,
divide the formula into the bottles,
load the bottles in the fridge.
when we're through
i'm tired as hell,
hoping i can
squeeze in a nap.

charlotte starts toward the door,
gotta run, honey.
a league of bowlers
made a reservation for noon.
they're bossy as hell.

must be those big balls.
from her crib,
my baby starts to cry.
life before ariel is over.
gone. for good.
her tears trump mine now.

in the doorway
charlotte turns and winks.
time to try out that formula.

* * *

i don't know how
people with babies
manage to function.
ariel wakes us several times a night.
i check her diaper then hold her
while jeremy nukes the formula
if it's time for her to eat again.

one night i wear the floor out
walking ariel from one end
of our room to the other—
back and forth,
back and forth,
rubbing her back
in small, patient circles.
shhhh, shhhh, shhhh.

but after an hour
she's still crying.
i walk to the window,
staring out at the parking lot.
biting my lip, i start to cry too.
but then i feel jeremy behind me,
see his arms spread wide like wings,
closing around us,
making us one.

* * *

charlotte's sister, shirley,
agrees to watch ariel
for fifty bucks a week
which—on a busy weekend—
i can cover in a single night's tips.

at the end of my first day back
i nab an empty jar
from the recycling,
take it to our room,
drop six quarters inside.
jeremy lifts it off the dresser.
what are the quarters for?

three damns,
two shits,
and an asshole.

he screws his face up. *huh?*

i want to clean up my act for ariel,
i explain. *every time i swear,*
i have to feed a quarter to the jar.

he strips off his work shirt.
shoot, how'll we pay for diapers?
i swat him—*you little shit!*—
and drop another quarter in the jar.

* * *

each morning i check ariel's eyes,
praying they've turned brown
while we slept.
but always, always,
they're bluer than the day before.
i imagine telling jeremy the truth,
that ariel isn't really his daughter.
i wrap my tongue around the words:
there's something i have to tell you . . .
but then he'll bend to kiss ariel's nose
or plant a raspberry on her belly
and i'll say *i love you* instead.

* * *

the northern lady returns,
wearing a charcoal gray suit,
and takes a booth near a window.

a girl with pimples
and long, mud-colored hair
sits across from her.
when i walk over,
the lady smiles up at me.
you had your baby!
what were you blessed with?
embarrassed by the attention,
i feel my face go red. *a girl.*

the lady looks from pimple-face to me.
i'm sorry. i'd introduce you two,
but i don't even know your name.

desiree, i tell her.
desiree, she repeats.
from desiderata.
latin for wanted child.
yeah, right, i think but don't say.
desiree, northern lady goes on,
this is emily merrick.
she's in tenth grade
at gainseville high.

i force a smile.
we exchange hellos.
i'm interviewing emily
for my next book,
the lady explains.

my mouth falls open.

you mean you already wrote one?
pimple-face flashes her tinsel teeth.
three of them. her most famous is called
watch your back, *and it's about*
how cruel girls are to one another.
it won, like, a zillion awards.
already, i hate emily merrick,
who gets to go to high school and
have lunch with northern lady
while i sling hash and wait tables
for two bucks and twenty cents an hour.
what's your name? i ask northern lady,
hoping emily merrick
won't answer that question too.

dr. stemple.
she reaches in her binder,
hands me a business card.
i study the raised print.
wow. i'm from new york too.
johnson city, outside binghamton.
you probably never heard of it.

oh, yes, i have! she answers.
i graduated from high school in elmira,
about an hour from there.
i teach college in poughkeepsie now,
but went to the university of florida
so i come back often for research.
pointing to the card, she tells me,
call if you're ever in the area.

i smile, say, *i will,*
and tuck the card in my apron.

* * *

outside our room
i sit next to jeremy,
feeding ariel,
while he calls
his parents on the pay phone.

i hear his mom answer.
hello? hello? who's this?
jeremy just breathes.
i'm worried she'll think
he's a perv and hang up.
instead she yells—so loud
ariel's eyelids blink open—
jeremy, honey, is that you?
shaking, he hangs up fast.
i stand, take his hand,
lead him back to our room.
after putting ariel in her crib
i lie next to him on our bed.
he's my baby now too,
so i rock him back and forth,
rubbing his head, saying, *there, there,*
until his crying slows, then stops.

* * *

the next afternoon,
just before a storm blows through,
dr. stemple arrives for lunch again,
except she orders a dr. pepper
instead of hot tea with lemon
and a sandwich instead of salad.
her clothes are different too—
slacks and a dark silk blouse.
classes start again next week,
she tells me. *i'm flying back*
to poughkeepsie tonight.
i was hoping we could talk.
can you spare a few minutes?

aside from a trucker,
finishing his liver and onions,
the place is dead.
when i drop down across from her,
dr. stemple sets a gift bag in front of me.
a blush creeps across my face. *for me?*
she nods so i plow through the tissue,
lift out three books by
three lady authors.
adrienne rich,
anne sexton,
nikki giovanni.
i flip through the pages.
they're books of poetry.

dr. stemple smiles.
you seemed to enjoy sylvia plath,

so i thought you might
like to sample more.
i'm stunned speechless.
i feel my eyes well up.
desiree, you're a courageous
and ambitious young woman.
when i was your age,
a woman either worked
or she became a mother.
rarely did she attempt both.
she sighs.
i wrestled with that myself.

i quit high school, i blurt out.
my mother, she—i freeze.
why am i telling her this?

let me guess.
she didn't deal well
with your pregnancy?

i nod.

that's her loss, desiree.
there are plenty of women who would
consider themselves blessed
to have a daughter like you.
and a granddaughter.
she smiles a sad smile.

i glance at the poetry books,
wondering how my life
would be different if i'd had
a mother to learn things from,
a mother who believed in me
and told me i mattered.
a mother like dr. stemple.

she glances at the clock and stands.
unfortunately, i need to go.
i still have packing to do.
but call me if you're in new york.
i mean that, desiree.
i want to know how you're doing.
in the meantime, let's stay in touch.
you have my e-mail address.

i've heard of e-mail
but ned and charlotte
use an antique cash register,
so i doubt they even own a computer.
still, i say, *i want to stay in touch, too.*

* * *

that night after ariel wakes us
and jeremy's waiting for
her formula to warm,
he mumbles, *recessive genes.*
i freeze. *huh?*

we learned about 'em in biology.
that's how two brown-eyed people
can have a blue-eyed baby.
i nod. *oh yeah. i heard that too.*

later, as we lie in bed,
jeremy takes my hand
and brings it to his lips,
kissing my fingers one by one,
and i remember the day joan kissed
pete's finger while they smoked pot
on carol ann's porch.

i have what they have now,
but i'm so scared to trust it,
scared the truth will ruin it all.

Ariel

The elevator door opens on the seventh floor, and Mom and I step out. She pauses beside a window, looking out at the lot we're parked in. I wait, watching a black SUV pull into a handicapped spot. A door opens and a woman sprints toward the entrance. I hate it when able-bodied people park in designated areas. I want to tell them off.

I turn to face Mom. "Are you okay?"

She looks numb. "I have no idea. I'm on overload trying to process what you told me. I mean, I can't believe my mother went to high school with Lee. And that Lee feels all this . . . this . . . sympathy for her." Mom's eyes fill. "Damn it, Lee's supposed to be there for *me*. She's *my* ally."

"She still will be," I say, patting her arm to reassure her.

Mom breathes a heavy sigh. "Let's go," she says, starting down the hall.

A nurse is just leaving Green Mountain's room. "We gave Mrs. Murdock something to help with her pain, so she'll probably be a bit groggy."

"Déjà vu," Mom mumbles.

"Huh?"

"When I was a teenager, she was high on pain pills most of the time. She could sleep through anything. And *did.*"

Mom pauses beside the privacy curtain that divides the room. It's parted now, and Wild Hair's bed is empty.

The heat in the room is stifling. A window is open slightly, so Green Mountain must be warm too. Except she still has her sweater on.

The chair I sat in earlier has been moved next to Green Mountain's bed. I feel funny sitting that close, but Mom motions me toward it, taking the more distant one for herself. I sit, telling Green Mountain, "Someone said to say hi."

"Oh, really?" Her tongue sounds thick, like it's too big for her mouth. "An' who would that be?"

"The woman we talked about before. Aunt Lee. She says she knew you in high school."

Her eyes narrow into slits. "I never met anyone named Lee."

Mom looks so fragile I wish I didn't have to keep going. But Aunt Lee will ask what happened. "Lee is short for Muralee," I tell her. "Muralee Blawjen."

Green Mountain's eyes widen. "You're pulling my leg, right?"

"No, I'm not. We just talked."

"Holy shit." She doesn't sound drugged anymore. "How do you know Muralee?"

"I told you, Mom works for her."

Green Mountain shakes her head, confused.

"I met Lee in Florida," Mom explains. "She used to have lunch at the diner I waitressed at when I was pregnant with Ariel. Lee was interviewing girls at the local high school, doing research for her book. When we came back to New York and I got my GED, she hired me."

Green Mountain stares at Mom, unblinking. "Muralee wrote a book?"

"Seven of them," Mom answers proudly. "She's working on her eighth now."

"Can't say I'm surprised," Green Mountain says. "Muralee was a smart cookie."

For a long time, we're all silent. Then I ask, "What was she like as a teenager?"

"Pretty. Popular. Thin." Green Mountain exhales a slow breath. "Everything I wasn't." She turns to my mother. "Remember when you were your daughter's age and I told you about the cheerleader I used to wish I could be?"

Mom squints. "Vaguely. Why?"

"That cheerleader was Muralee Blawjen."

"Aunt Lee could *not* have been a cheerleader," I blurt out. "She's a feminist!"

Green Mountain laughs. "Everybody's capable of surprises." Turning back to Mom again, she asks, "She end up marrying her boyfriend, Glenn?"

Mom nods. "Married and divorced him, unfortunately."

"Damn shame. Must be hard on the kids."

Mom and I exchange glances.

"What's wrong?" Green Mountain asks.

"Aunt Lee doesn't have kids," I tell her.

"Why not? She said she wanted 'em after college."

"She and Glenn tried for years," Mom tells her. "Lee couldn't get pregnant."

"*Sure* she could. Why, she was—" Green Mountain stops herself. "Shit!"

I sit forward. "What were you going to say?"

Green Mountain looks away. "Nothing. A promise is a promise."

Mom's eyes narrow. "You promised Lee something in high school?"

"Sorry"—Green Mountain holds a hand up—"end of discussion."

To use an SAT prep word, the tension in the air is palpable. "Aunt Lee would've made a great mother," I say, trying to smooth over the moment. Then, I'm not sure why, but I add, "She says Mom and I are like family."

"That so?" Green Mountain's face pales.

Immediately, I regret tossing in that last part. As if agreeing with me, the sky starts to darken.

A beep sounds in the next room. Someone sneezes in the hallway. A person wearing slippers scuffs past.

Then, silence. Except for the ticking of a clock, the room is quiet. Too quiet.

"You know," Mom says, covering a yawn, "I'm feeling pretty tired from the trip. Maybe we should let . . ." She turns to her mother, and I'm guessing she's wondering what to call her. ". . . Maybe we should all get some rest." She stands, like we've voted and decided that's the plan.

I watch Mom cross the room. Probably because there's nothing else to watch. Or because Mom, in her own feeble way, is the one steering the ship. Not that a ship is a good metaphor for our visit. A bike with flat tires is more like it.

In the threshold, Mom turns. "We'll see you tomorrow then. Rest up."

Rest up is so lame. Resting up won't make Green Mountain's breasts grow back or cure her cancer. Or fix the rift between Mom and her.

Still, I don't have much choice. I follow her.

"Hold your horses," Green Mountain barks. "There's something I need to say!"

Mom stops. "Can't it wait until morning?"

"No, it can't. I'm tired of putting things off. Someday we're gonna run out of mornings."

Mom returns, lowering herself into the chair.

"I'll wait in the cafeteria," I mumble.

"Not so fast!" her mother snaps. "I want you here too, Ariel."

This is the first time she's called me by my name. The impact is kind of major—startling, and, well, comforting. I lean against the wall by Mom's chair, positioning myself so I can see both of their faces.

Green Mountain reaches for her Coke, taking several long swallows. She burps, excuses herself, and says, "You're a lucky woman, Desiree."

Mom snorts. *"Lucky?"*

"Damn straight. Lucky you found your knack for mothering. Lucky you had one to find. Lucky you get to go to sleep at night without being haunted by all the mistakes you made. Lucky that, when you're my age, God willing, you won't be lying in a hospital bed beating on yourself for all the times you fucked up."

I stifle a gasp. Not that I'm an expert on grandmothers, but I've never heard anyone else's use the F-word before.

"Bottom line," she continues. "As mothers go, I sucked."

Mom opens her mouth. Then, just as quickly, she closes it.

Green Mountain nods. "Good. At least we agree on something."

Mom laughs nervously.

"I'm not making excuses for my behavior, but I was somebody's daughter once, too. You aren't the only one who got handed crap in the mothering department, Desiree."

"What are you saying?" Mom asks her.

"Your father didn't die in any ordinary car accident. He was killed. By a drunk driver who took away the only person who'd ever cared about me."

Mom sits forward. "But what does that have to do with your mother?"

Green Mountain pushes a button and her bed groans, lifting her mattress so she's sitting upright. She looks straight at Mom and says, "The driver was Leona Fitch."

Mom's jaw drops. "Your mother?"

Green Mountain nods.

"Oh my God," Mom and I mumble in unison.

"After Tad died"—Green Mountain swallows, a hard, dry swallow—"they hauled my ma off to jail, and I got a job so I could pay the rent. Fortunately, I turned eighteen before social services caught up with me. Every day, I dragged myself off to school, then work, then home around midnight, tired, pregnant, and hungry. Food was my only comfort. Before long, I'd gained back all the weight I'd lost, and then some. Apparently Muralee Blawjen took pity on me. She gave me a present after we finished our senior year."

I think back to what Aunt Lee said about giving Madeline Fitch a gift. "What kind of present?"

"An envelope with five hundred dollars in it. I didn't want to take it from her, but Muralee said a rich aunt had given her a thousand dollars when she graduated. She insisted I split it with her. That was a tidy sum back in the 1970s. Muralee said, 'Make a new start for yourself, Madeline.' So I did. I bought a Binghamton newspaper, found myself an apartment in Johnson City, and got the hell out of Elmira." She glances at Mom. "You were born there three weeks later. Except I didn't know the first thing about being a mother." She pauses, reaches to sip her water. "And I ran out of money, of course, so I was on welfare till you started kindergarten. That's when I finally went to a doctor for my headaches. He put me on pain pills and, let me tell you, it was like a miracle. I even got a job, working at Kmart, but boy, did I get hooked on those little babies. By the time you were a teenager, we were quite a pair."

Green Mountain forces a smile. "I was stoned all the time, and you had the rudest, most foul mouth I'd ever—"

"I was a *teenager,*" Mom interrupts.

"I was a teenager once too," Green Mountain counters, "but I never talked to my mother the way you—"

"And your mother didn't have a boyfriend who *raped* you!"

A gray-haired nurse appears in the doorway. "Everything all right in here?" she asks. Her arms are loaded with linens, and the bleach smell permeates the room.

Mom and Green Mountain glare at each other.

"We're fine," I tell the nurse. "We just got a little loud. Sorry."

Hesitantly, she walks away. Outside the window, a delivery truck drives in reverse across the parking lot, sounding his backing-up beep. If only people gave off signals like that; we'd know what they were planning next.

For several minutes, no one speaks. Then Green Mountain turns to Mom, talking to her like I'm not there. "So Ariel knows about Larry?"

"Of course," Mom answers. "I've been very up-front about everything. The last thing I want is for Ariel to have to Google the truth."

"And Jeremy?" Green Mountain asks.

"Wow," Mom says, "you got his name right. Yes, Ariel knows that Jeremy's not her biological—"

"He's the only father I've ever known," I interrupt. "And could the two of you please stop talking about me like I'm not here?"

Sorry, Mom mouths.

Green Mountain grins at me. "You've got a backbone. I like that."

"Jeremy has another parole hearing next year," Mom adds.

"So"—Green Mountain peers at Mom's hand—"I see you're wearing a wedding ring. When did you two tie the knot?"

"As soon as we were both eighteen," Mom answers. "Prison weddings aren't the most romantic, but we didn't have any other options."

"Guess not," Green Mountain says. Then after a long silence she adds, "I never should've married Larry Murdock. After he died, I didn't miss *him* so much as I missed having another person around. You know, for company. To make me feel like I was sharing something with somebody. Most of the time I wasn't that fond of him."

Mom stares at her incredulously. "Then why did you have a *relationship* with him?"

She shrugs. "He paid attention to me."

"That's *it?*" Mom asks.

"Oh, Desiree, you have no idea." Green Mountain struggles to sit forward. "You've always been thin and pretty and had friends. But it wasn't that way with me. You wouldn't think somebody as big as I am could feel invisible, but that's exactly how I felt. Like no one saw me." She turns to glance out the window. "The day Larry Murdock came through my express lane with a tub of Turtle Wax, a box of toothpicks, and a Bic lighter, and asked me out to a movie—why, he was the first man since your father to look my way. Desiree, I would've said yes to anything. To anyone. That's the problem with being desperate for attention. You never ask who the other person is—he could be a serial killer, for all you know—you're too busy feeling grateful he picked *you* to notice."

Her words hit a raw nerve. My stomach clenches and I think of Shane. I know so little about his past—he never wants to talk about it; he claims it doesn't matter. A relationship is about two people, he says, and everything else is irrelevant. And I've never pressed the issue, because Shane paid attention to me. He said he wanted to take care of me. He told me I was pretty and sexy even though I know I'm very ordinary. He made me believe he could never get enough of me. And, I have to admit, it's a *high* having that effect on someone.

When I shiver, Green Mountain notices. She tips her head toward the window and I stand to close it, shutting out the hum of life outside. I notice the delivery truck is gone. I envy the driver—unloading his cargo, moving on.

Sitting again, I feel exhausted. And confused, because I realize I've missed a chunk of conversation. When I tune back in, Green Mountain's glaring at Mom. "I saw how Larry looked at you," she tells her. "Like the boys in high school used to gawk at the cheerleaders in those skimpy uniforms they paraded around in. It killed me, seeing Larry give you the attention I wanted all to myself. And *you*—you never had the modesty to cover up in front of him." She sits forward. Coughs. Grimaces. "But none of that matters now. The day you told me what Larry'd done to you, I messed up in a big way. I got mad at the wrong person and let you go—my own flesh and blood—instead of showing that bastard the door like any decent mother would've done. And I got just what I deserved. I wound up losing you both."

Green Mountain's cheeks are streaked with tears. "I've been living in the dark, Desiree—with food and pills and grief and plain old stupidity—but I can't go on like that. I've gotta flip a few lights on before it's too late. Some of what I see'll scare the hell out of me, no doubt, but I'd like to think I'll find a reason to go on, too. That's why I wanted you here." The corners of her lips start to quiver. "I can't change the past, Desiree. But if I beat this cancer, if I'm lucky enough to wake up on the right side of the grass for a few more years, I'd like to have a chance to get to know you"—she turns to face me—"and my granddaughter."

Granddaughter. The word sounds strange and familiar at the same time.

Mom opens her mouth, but no words come out.

"Think about your answer," Green Mountain tells her. "Just don't hate me if you can help it. I hated my mother for years and the only person it hurt was me. Hate poisons you. It makes you bitter."

"I don't hate you," Mom says. "Maybe I did, once, but now . . . well, I'm still figuring out how I feel. I need time."

"Sounds fair." Green Mountain reaches in her drawer, pulling out the black-and-white photos she showed me earlier.

She holds them out for Mom, who looks at them like she's seen a ghost. "Oh my God, I—I saw these before. A long time ago."

Green Mountain forces a smile. "I know. There was a lot more room for 'em in my shoebox after you took off."

I have no idea what she means. I watch Mom's face for a clue, but there isn't one.

"When I was a teenager," Mom says, "I looked just like this girl. Who—?"

"God, Mom," I say, "don't be so dramatic, it's—"

"She's *me,*" Green Mountain interrupts.

Mom's head jerks up. "You?"

"Yes. Me. With your father. I was young once too."

"I know, but—"

"When you were a teenager, Desiree, it was painful to look at you. Every time I did"—her voice cracks and she clears her throat to cover it—"I'd see myself. The person I used to be. The person I'd never have a shot at being again." The lines in her face soften. "I saw everything I'd lost."

Mom's voice is barely a whisper. "We *both* lost a lot."

Green Mountain nods. "Yes, I suppose we did."

When Mom reaches out to hand back the photos, Green Mountain holds up her hand. "Keep them, Desiree."

"But you said they're the only pictures you have of you and my father."

"I have an idea," I offer. "My friend Olivia has a scanner and a really nice photo printer. I can get her to print a copy for Mom and me then mail the original back to you."

Green Mountain smiles. "I'd like that, Ariel. Thank you."

Outside, the overhead lights in the parking lot blink on.

A cart clatters down the hall, stopping near Green Mountain's door. I smell pasta and my mouth waters.

"That'll be my dinner," she explains. Reaching in the drawer again, she removes a strip of yellowed tickets. She separates two, handing one to Mom and one to me. Below a picture of a wagon wheel, in grayed print, it says:

The Second Chance Diner
12 River Road
Elmira, NY

And on the back: GOOD FOR ONE DAILY BLUE PLATE SPECIAL. Whatever *that* is.

"Tad gave those to me on one of our dates. But I could never go back to the diner after he died." She tips her chin toward the window. "It's just a few blocks from here. Have supper there, why don't you? Maybe they'll still accept the tickets."

Madeline

I PACE FROM THE FRONT HALL to the living room to the kitchen then back, over and over again, repeating Tad's exact words. *I care about you, Madeline. I want to know everything about you. Everything.*

"Tad," I practice, "I have something to tell you . . ." But I can't seem to force out the end of the sentence, the part that goes: "I'm pregnant."

When the phone rings, I dive at it. *"Tad?"*

"Hi, Madeline. Sorry I'm running late. You sound funny. Are you okay?"

I stare down at what I'm wearing—a sea foam green turtleneck, Jordache jeans, and a pair of Frye boots. I put a dent in my shoebox savings for this outfit—which I bought brand-new at Sears and Roebuck instead of the thrift store—but it doesn't matter. I don't need college anymore. I'm not going to be a nurse, I'm going to be a mother. And a wife, I hope. Mrs. Thaddeus Leary. And after we have the baby I'm carrying, we'll have more. Tons of kids. Because that's what Tad wants.

"Don't worry about being late," I tell him. "I'm fine." Then I toss in a lie to make him feel better. "I haven't even done my hair yet." I glance in the mirror at my perfectly formed curls, the pale blue shadow lining my lids, my pink tinted lips. The cosmetics were a present from Muralee for going with her to Ithaca. It's the nicest gift I've gotten in years. Okay, it's the *only* gift I've gotten in years. Unless you count the Chinese handcuffs Tad won for me

Studying my reflection, I realize I'm as thin as Muralee now. Except I won't stay that way for long. I grip the phone between my chin and shoulder and slide both hands beneath my sweater. Palms out, I stretch the fabric to fake a baby swell. Staring at the green hill, I say, "Tad, I have something important to tell you."

"What is it, baby?"

Baby. Tad said the word. It's a sign.

"I, um, I want to tell you in person."

"Okay." Tad hesitates. "Is it *good* news, I hope?"

I imagine living with Tad and his dad in their trailer until we can get a place of our own. Tad's room is the biggest, thank goodness. I'll paint his brown paneling yellow, Tad's favorite color, and we'll cuddle close in his twin bed. We can clean out his dad's junk room and maybe turn it into a nursery. I saw a used crib in the classifieds for ten dollars. "Yeah. It's good news."

"Great. Look, I'm gonna jump in the shower. I'll see you in a little while, okay?"

"Um, Tad, wait." I swallow hard. "Did you mean what you said earlier? About wanting to know everything about me?"

"Everything," he answers again.

* * *

It's been dark for a while now. Tad and I have never gone to the drive-in this late. The first feature has probably ended.

I walk to the window, staring out at our empty driveway. An

ambulance hurries past, darting through the red light at the corner. Its siren slices the stillness, dicing the night into bite-size pieces. I imagine what the pieces might taste like. Baker's Chocolate, I decide. Bittersweet.

Next, a fire truck rushes past. Then the night is quiet again, returned to its unbroken blackness.

I walk to the kitchen and glare at the phone, willing it to ring. But it doesn't.

The clock over the stove ticks and ticks. A baby cries in the apartment next door.

I pace again. From the front door to the living room to the kitchen. From the kitchen to the living room to the front door. Twenty-two steps each way. Times ten trips is two hundred and twenty steps. Times twenty trips is four hundred and forty steps.

The baby is still crying. I press my hot cheek against the cool wall, slap the wall hard, and yell, "Pick up your baby, damn it!"

My stomach groans, waking the Beast. I swing the fridge door open and glare at the contents. A box of AYDS candy, a head of lettuce, two cucumbers, a lone radish, a quart of skim milk, two cans of Tab. Diet food. I could kill for a package of Ring Dings.

Closing the door, I check the clock again. It's almost nine thirty. If only my mother hadn't taken the car, I could drive to Tad's and see for myself why he's so late. Nervously, I walk to the phone. I dial Tad's number, which rings and rings.

Finally, someone picks up. Tad's dad. His voice is groggy. "Yeah? Who's this?"

"I—I'm sorry," I stammer. "I didn't mean to wake you, b—but—"

"Madeline?"

"Yes, sir. I'm calling because Tad was supposed to pick me up and, well, he hasn't shown up yet. I was wondering, um, if he's still there."

"Hell, no," he answers gruffly. "He left a long time ago."

"Oh," I say, and hang up.

I walk down the stairs that lead to our apartment, flick on the porch light, and step outside. The air is chilly. My breath hangs in small puffs in front of me. A boy and a girl walk past, holding hands. The street lamp bathes them in light. "Tad," I whisper, "where *are* you?"

As I turn to go back inside, a police car slows to the curb. An officer steps out, then opens the door to the backseat. He leans in, tugging on a woman's arm. A woman who's dressed in a blue jacket, just like the one I bought, except hers has a huge rip in one arm.

The policeman guides the woman up our sidewalk, toward our apartment. Our porch. Me.

When they reach the top step, she shakes his hand away.

The policeman asks me, "Is this woman your mother?"

She squints at me, attempting to focus on my face. She looks pathetic. But I'm sick of feeling sorry for her. Tired of her needs always winning over mine. For the first time in my life, I admit to myself: I really, truly can't stand her.

"Mad'line, honey," she slurs, "please, tellthenicepoliceman-whoIam."

Turning to the cop, I say, "She's the person who's made my life a living hell."

Desiree

every wednesday, my day off,
i write a letter to dr. stemple.
my words flow easily,
like water pouring
straight from the tap.
when she writes back,
dr. stemple says kind things,
like how lucky ariel is to have me
and how lucky i am to have her.

once, i ask her if she has kids,
and what she tells me is sad—
that her and her ex-husband
tried really hard to have them
but her doctor said she
couldn't get pregnant.
that night i cry for her,
hugging my baby girl tight.

* * *

in may
when jeremy turns sixteen
and gets his license,
we start saving
to buy a used car.
after three months
we're proud owners
of an '82 chevette that
reminds me of a giant green cricket.

on the day jeremy picks up the plates—
just before labor day weekend—
he phones his parents
from the pay phone
outside our room.
i'm inside
folding laundry while ariel naps.
all seems right with the world
until

i hear sudden pounding
and rush outside.
clutching the receiver,
jeremy's slumped to the ground
slamming his head
against the wall,
crying, *no, no, no.*

jeremy—i reach my hand out
to stop him—*what's wrong?*
he falls forward,
collapsing into my arms.
my ma, he chokes out. *she—*
she's in the goddamn psych ward!

* * *

ned offers us a week off with pay—
pretty generous since we've only
worked for him nine months—
and charlotte gives us
a long-distance phone card
with 240 prepaid minutes
so we can call whenever we want.

the morning
after jeremy phones home,
he feeds ariel strained peaches
and i make sandwiches for the trip.
as i pack our bags in the hatchback
i notice the *c* on the clover inn sign's
burned out. *lover inn.*
tears sting my eyes.
we haven't even left yet and
already i can't wait to come back.

the sun's rising
as jeremy carries ariel to the car,

perched on his sunburned shoulders.
his hair is the longest i've ever seen it,
held back with a twisted red bandanna.
his grunge-black color's grown out
and my barbie-doll blond has too,
so we look like our old selves again.

dah! ariel blurts,
slapping jeremy's head. *dah!*

jeremy's mouth opens in a wide o.
shit! dez! d'you hear that?
she called me da-da. oh, man!
my heart crowds with
so much feeling
i think it might break in two.

as i reach for my disposable camera
jeremy flashes the first smile
i've seen since the phone call,
and ariel clutches his red bandanna,
laughing and calling, *dah! dah! dah!*

* * *

twenty-two hours later,
we cross the border into new york
and park at a roadside rest area.
i step out, stiff as hell,
squinting into the morning sun,

which seems dimmer than
the sun we left in ocala.
we're almost home,
jeremy says, stretching.
maybe you're home,
i mumble to myself,
but i'm a thousand miles from mine.

* * *

when we pass our old high school,
i realize my junior year
is starting without me.

i glance at my watch. 8:12.
almost time for first period.

i picture carol ann fluffing
her hair in the bathroom mirror,
no clue where i've gone,
who i've become.

remembered smells haunt me:
old books,
fresh sweat,
chalk dust.
the bell sounds.
lockers clang closed,
lip-locks end,
kids hurry toward classrooms—
places i thought were unimportant.

i wish i had a regular
school day to do over.
i'd try harder,
study for tests,
hand in homework.
i see what i didn't see then—
the teachers weren't
evil brain-sucking tyrants
getting their rocks off
by busting our asses.
they were trying to grow our minds
so we'd turn into people like dr. stemple,
reading poetry and writing books,
instead of becoming losers like mam,
like me.

* * *

an hour later
i'm in jeremy's old living room
holding ariel while he paces,
mumbling, *it's all my fault,*
it's all my fucking fault.

his father doesn't argue with him.
his stare scorches me, saying,
it's your fault too, you little bitch.

he signals jeremy into a room
i've never seen before.
i catch a glimpse as the door opens—

dark, knotty pine paneling,
stuffed pheasants lining the shelves,
a wooden desk shaped like a coffin,
photographs trapped behind glass.
a man's room.
the door closes,
a hungry mouth that
swallows them both.

i stand, step close, listen.
are you sure that kid is yours, son?
she doesn't look a damn bit like you.

dad, of course she's—

because there's something
about that girl i don't trust, jeremy.

look, dad, i love her, okay?
and i love my daughter.
now can we talk about something else?
like mom. what happened?
how's she doing?

silence.
footsteps.
a drawer opens.
a lighter flicks.
cigar smoke reaches my nose.
your mother overdosed, jeremy.

that's why they're keeping her there,
to be sure she's not a threat to herself.

ariel whimpers
and i step back from the door,
shrinking farther and farther away
from the sound of jeremy's sobs.

upstairs
i lay ariel on jeremy's old bed
and prop her between two pillows.
i reach in my backpack,
pull out dr. stemple's card,
dial her number on jeremy's phone.

an answering machine picks up.
hello, you have reached lee stemple.
i'm not available to take your call
so leave a message after the tone.

beep!
i panic,
hang up.

i lie next to ariel,
imagine jeremy and me
watching *the simpsons,*
imagine jeremy imitating homer,
making me worry i'll pee my pants laughing.
the real jeremy appears in the doorway,

jerking me back to reality.
his eyes are puffy and red.
you and ariel stay in here, he says.
i'll make up the pullout in the den.

jeremy, we freaking live together.
why can't we both stay in here?
not answering, he turns.
i'm going to visit my mom.
you can come along if you want.

* * *

the elevator stops
at the behavioral sciences unit.
jeremy empties his pockets
into a clear container and
a silver-haired nurse buzzes
him through a metal door
that closes behind him
with a deafening clang
i feel echo in the space
between my ribs.

i sit in the waiting room
next to the pill station
in the second of six ugly chairs,
joined at the hip like siamese sextuplets.

i tuck ariel's face in the
hollow below my chin

so she won't have to see
what i see—the man in the
dirty green bathrobe pulling
patches of hair from his scalp,
the lady with slippers on the wrong feet,
chanting the same seven words over and over:
faze-days-blaze-mayonnaise-craze-polonaise-gaze,
faze-days-blaze-mayonnaise-craze-polonaise-gaze.

at a minute past five,
the metal door buzzes open.
jeremy stops at the counter,
refills his pockets,
flashes a leather wristband.
it's from my mom.
she made it for me
in crafts hour.

the letters that form his name are
punched in the thick tawny hide.
the spacing's uneven,
the *m* is up too high,
and the band is huge
for his wrist.
it's nice, i lie,
because i know jeremy.
he'll keep that stupid thing forever.

* * *

the next morning,
i phone charlotte.
take your time, she says.
family comes first.
your jobs'll be waiting for you
whenever you're ready to come back.
i don't tell her
that i'm ready to come back *now,*
and i miss florida and the clover inn
like i've never missed anything before.

* * *

that afternoon
ariel pulls on her ear, crying.
by the time jeremy leaves
to pick up hoagies for dinner,
her forehead is burning.
he drops me off at wal-mart
so i can buy ear drops
and baby aspirin.

ariel's strapped in her carrier,
riding in my shopping cart,
tugging her ear again, whimpering.
i get what i came for and step into line.
a woman with dark squiggly hair who
reminds me of scary from the spice girls
totals and bags my order.
as she hands me my change
i hear, *jesus, dez, is that you?*

i recognize the voice.
shaking, i turn.
and a few feet
behind me
there
she
is.
there *they* are—
mam in a striped shirt and shorts,
looking fatter than ever,
and larry with a stupid john deere hat,
a toothpick clenched between his teeth.
their fingers sport matching gold bands.

glancing from mam to larry,
ariel sucks in a sudden, sharp breath
and lets out an earsplitting scream.
her face goes red
as she bunches
her tiny white fists,
punching the air around her.
good instincts, i whisper,
stroking her small, damp head.

mam steps toward me. *dez,*
where the hell've you been?
i was worried about you.
i back toward the exit.
get away from me
or i'll scream.

she winces,
but i don't care.

ariel tugs at her ear again.
i pull a bottle from my bag
and she takes it,
blubbering softly.
larry looks straight at me,
rolling that goddamn toothpick
from one side of his mouth to the other.
pretty little girl you got there, desiree.
bet she'll be fighting off the boys,
just like her mama.
then he winks.
he fucking winks at me.

i'm not sure what i throw first.
something i yank off a display
in the center aisle—a tonka
truck, i think—then i grab
whatever's beside it.
a war tank. a model car.
i whip them in larry's direction,
but he manages to sidestep every one,
laughing like it's so freaking funny,
which pisses me off even more.

ariel drops her bottle and cries.
mam reaches forward.
stay away from her! i holler.
you're not allowed to touch my daughter!

as i pick ariel up
two guys in suits race toward us.
they look like the blues brothers,
minus the shades.
i read their badges: *security.*

jeremy appears out of nowhere,
stepping between them and me.
it's okay, he tells them.
we're leaving.
he slips an arm around my shoulder,
guides us toward the exit, fast.
i collapse on a bench outside.
i'm shaking and my hair's wet with sweat.
jeremy pushes my bangs back.
what the hell happened in there?

do you think your dad
will watch ariel?
i ask jeremy.
we've gotta go
somewhere and talk,
just you and me.
there's something
i really need to tell you.

Mom books us a room at the Riverview Inn, just down the street from the hospital. Outside our window the Chemung River churns past, choppy and gray. Mom decides to shower before dinner—"to wash the day away," as she puts it—so I check my phone while I'm waiting for her.

There are twelve missed calls. All from Shane, of course. Plus I have a text from Liv.

Glancing toward the closed bathroom door, realizing this may be my only private moment, I enter the command to retrieve my voice mail. Shane's first message is calm. He sounds genuinely apologetic. He's sorry about playing the phone joke on me. He knows it was really insensitive and he should have learned his lesson before.

The second message is a lot like the first. He repeats almost everything verbatim.

On the third, there's an edge to his voice. Like he's inspecting every word before giving it runway clearance. And he reminds me he's already said he's sorry. Twice.

Shane's irritation surfaces during the fourth message. He's almost home and he wants to know why I haven't called back to accept his apology.

In his fifth message, he tells me I'm being too sensitive. That his joke wasn't all that bad, and the average person would have laughed it off by now. Because, as jokes go, it *was* pretty funny.

In his sixth message, Shane informs me his nose is bleeding again. He includes a few choice expletives.

I've listened to all that I can. Before I chicken out, I hit Delete, erasing all twelve messages. Then I read Liv's text.

can't w8 2 talk when u get home! :-)

The shower stops running. Quickly, I hit Reply and type,

me 2. lots 2 tell u about my grandmother

—my thumbs hover over the keys, hesitating—

and shane.

Quickly, I press Send, then Power Off.

Mom appears, wrapped in an oversized bath towel. "Hey," she says, touching my arm. "Are you okay?"

"Yeah." I nod, clapping my phone closed. "I am."

* * *

As we cross the parking lot, a band of magenta stains the sky beyond the roof of the diner. It's so brilliant and awe-inspiring, I actually have to catch my breath.

Mom holds the door open for me. "Imagine" by John Lennon fills the air. Glancing around the inside, I immediately love the place. Dad would too, because the decorating is totally retro—seventies wall colors like avocado and orange, lava lamps on the sills, framed record covers I recognize from his collection. Janis

Joplin. Steppenwolf. Nazareth. The only thing reminding me it's the Obama era is the neon sign blinking *FREE WI-FI!* in a window facing the parking lot.

As we start down the aisle between two rows of booths, I wonder where my grandmother and grandfather sat when they ate here. It's weird having all these new thoughts whirling through my brain—like connect-the-dots, waiting for me to link them.

"Wow," Mom says, "has this place changed. It used to have ugly dark paneling and a funky Wild West decor."

"You mean you've been here before?"

We drop down in a booth near the kitchen. "A long time ago," she answers. "Your dad and I and Carol Ann—the one I ran into at Starbucks—and her boyfriend-at-the-time, Eric, came here after the Harvest Dance in tenth grade."

A waitress hurries past, dropping off two menus and two ice waters. Then, tapping a bell near the grill, she calls, "Order in. Gimme a hockey puck, keep off the grass, and put out the lights and cry."

Mom smiles. "Wow, does *that* bring back memories."

I glance at the waitress, then back at Mom. "You *understood* what she said?"

"She asked for a burger, well-done, without lettuce, and a plate of liver and onions."

"Wow. I'm impressed."

"Diner lingo is a language all its own," Mom says, waxing poetic.

"You liked waitressing, didn't you?"

"It's not that I liked *waitressing,* per se—it was hard work. But I wanted to look responsible and grown-up. I was so excited the day Charlotte put me in charge of deciding the Blue Plate Special."

"Wait. Where did I just see that? Oh, yeah"—I reach in my pocket for the ticket Green Mountain gave me—"here it is. Good for one Blue Plate Special. What *is* that?"

"You seriously don't know?" Mom asks.

"No clue."

"Okay"—Mom laughs—"*I* feel old." She sips her ice water. "I doubt many places still have them, but diners like the Geronimo, where I grew up, used to have a daily deal they pushed. Nothing Bobby Flay, just your ordinary meat-and-potatoes-with-all-the-fixings kind of meal. At the Clover Diner, Charlotte tried to use left-overs to make the specials so they wouldn't pile up and go to waste. Extra pork roast and carrots were a good start for stew. Corn could be turned into chowder. Anyway"—Mom opens her menu—"I felt creative coming up with that every day."

I flip mine open too. "I don't see a Blue Plate Special listed here."

"I'm not surprised. A lot of old-fashioned trends fall by the wayside."

I look down, running my finger over the ticket. "So I can't use this?"

"Probably not."

I stick the ticket back in my pocket. "That's good, actually."

Mom looks up. "Why?"

"Well, when we get home I thought maybe I'd start a little keepsake box for her things. You know, the photos and the ticket. And I can add to it."

Mom studies me. "You like her, don't you?"

I shrug. "Yeah, I guess."

"I'm curious"—Mom leans her elbows on the table—"do you like her because you like her? Or because you feel sorry for her?"

Before I can answer, Mom adds, "Because, as shocked as I am to hear myself say it, I like her a little bit too. Mostly I like how she is with *you*. It's as if she's able to give you something she wasn't equipped to give me. But, still"—her forehead creases—"I don't want to confuse affection with sympathy."

"What do you mean?"

"Oh, God. Do I have to spell it out?"

"Sorry."

"I don't want to like her because she could be dying."

That last word wallops me in the gut. This person I didn't even *know* yesterday suddenly matters to me. "Then don't," I say. "Like her because you're ready to. Because things are different now that you're an adult."

Mom shakes her head. "It can't be that simple."

"Why not?"

"Because things never are between mothers and daughters. It's against the laws of nature." Mom pauses, deep in thought. "She's right about one thing, though . . ."

"What's that?"

"Mothers *do* make mistakes with their daughters. I'm sure I've made my share."

"Mom, what are you talking about? You're, like, the best—"

"For instance," she interrupts, "what if you told me *you* were pregnant? I certainly wouldn't turn my back on you like my mother did me, but I couldn't hide my disappointment, either. What if I wasn't the person you needed me to be?"

I lower my voice so no one can hear. "Mom, I'm not going to get pregnant. Not in the near future, anyway. I remember everything you told me about birth control and—"

"Ariel, preventing pregnancy and HIV is important, but a condom doesn't make you ready for sex."

I sit back. Fold my arms. "Translation, please?"

She lowers her voice. "When I had sex with your dad—with *Jeremy*—I cared about him, yes, but I also, well, I *used* him. I allowed him to believe you were his daughter. Your dad wouldn't be where he is right now if I'd—"

"Mom, cut yourself some slack. You were a teenager. You'd been *raped.*"

"All I'm saying"—Mom twirls the pepper shaker on its base—"is that sex has consequences. There's a lot more to it than knowing where the condoms are kept. The choices we make can stay with us a very long time."

Her words hang in the air between us. Sometimes her monologues are pure Mom Rants, but this one sticks. I think back on Shane sneaking into my room and pressuring me to have sex. And how I almost agreed to it because he looked so sad and broken after I said no. But if I'd hooked up with him then, it would have been for the wrong reasons—to keep him from getting angry or hurt or sad or whatever. It wouldn't have been for me because, like I tried to tell Shane, I'm not ready yet. And it's totally *okay* that I'm not.

I glance at Mom, swallow hard. "I haven't had sex yet," I whisper. I'm not sure why I volunteer this. I just do.

As the waitress arrives to take our order, Mom pats my hand. "I won't pretend I'm not happy to hear that."

* * *

"Good morning," a cheerful voice coos.

I roll over, rubbing sleep from my eyes, forgetting for a moment where I am.

Mom's standing at the foot of my bed, sipping tea from a Styrofoam cup. She must be desperate for caffeine. Normally she won't even look at Styrofoam, let alone get close enough to touch it.

After we've showered and packed and checked out of our room—all before the obscenely early hour of ten—we have breakfast and head to the hospital.

When we arrive, Green Mountain's dressed in regular clothes, not a hospital gown. She's sitting on the edge of her bed, her battered pocketbook beside her. And she's got a visitor. A woman with gray, close-cropped hair wearing jeans and a Syracuse Orangemen sweatshirt.

"Hey," Green Mountain says, waving Mom and me in. "Meet my good friend, Thelma. Thelma, this is my daughter, Desiree, and my granddaughter, Ariel."

After everyone says hi, Mom asks, "Where are you going?"

Green Mountain smiles. A wide, toothy smile that makes her top lip recede, revealing her gum line. The same thing happens to Mom in the middle of a laughing fit. "I'm checking out," she tells us.

Mom looks concerned. "But you just had surgery three days ago."

"Hell, they wouldn't have kept me *this* long if weren't for my blood pressure jumping off the charts."

"That's right," Thelma agrees. "My sister, Louise, had a breast removed. Got sent home the same day, howling with pain. Drive-through mastectomies, they call them."

Mom grimaces. "That's horrible. How's your sister now?"

I tense up. Instinct tells me there's a lot riding on her answer.

Thelma raps the closet door with her knuckle. "Four years cancer-free, knock on wood."

"Good." Mom sighs. "I'm relieved to hear that."

I am too.

Thelma takes Green Mountain's suitcase, and the cooler that held the Coke she smuggled in. Then she reaches for a key ring hanging from a clip on her belt. "I'll bring the car around front," she says. "Pleasure meeting you both."

We wave and Thelma leaves. A silence falls across the room.

Not a bad silence, though. More like the hush after it snows, making everything seem tranquil and new.

"What's next?" Mom asks her mother. "With your treatment, I mean."

"Thelma's driving me to my first chemo appointment on Thursday. I'll have one every week for six weeks, then the doctor'll check me again to see if I've got any more cancer in me." She fishes inside her handbag, drawing out a small folded paper. Handing it to Mom, she says, "Here's my address and phone number, in case you ever feel like stopping in."

Mom studies the paper. "You moved?"

"Yep. Too many memories in that old apartment after you left and Larry died. Anyway, call first and make sure I'm around. I keep pretty busy. Thelma and I play bingo two nights a week, I've got my NA meetings—"

"NA?" Mom cuts in.

"Narcotic Anonymous," I volunteer.

"Oh . . ." Mom stuffs the paper in her pocket.

"Plus, I promised my doctor"—Green Mountain turns to me-"you know, the touchy-feely one? I promised her I'd start going to Weight Watchers meetings."

A tiny, blond nurse brushes past, stacking clean linens on the now-empty bed near the window.

"Well," Green Mountain says, reaching in the closet for her coat, "guess I'd better get out of here before they charge me for another day."

The nurse overhears her and says, "You'll need to wait for a wheelchair, Mrs. Murdock. Hospital policy."

Green Mountain harrumphs. When I notice her struggling with her sleeve, I step closer to help. Easing her arm through the opening, knowing we'll leave her soon, a heaviness fills my heart. I have to see my grandmother again. We need to talk. Really talk. Maybe I'll work up the nerve to ask her about her scars.

"Well," she says, starting toward the door, "I appreciate the two of you coming."

An aide walks by wheeling a cart piled high with lunches. The smell makes me think of what Mom told me at the diner—about the challenge of creating a meal from leftovers. I mean, we *all* inherit someone else's leftovers, don't we? There's nothing I can do about the fact that my dad is in prison for murder. Or that the man who *was* my biological father attacked my mother and married my grandmother, who turned her back on Mom. That is so seriously messed up. But it's what was heaped on my plate the day I came into this world. That's what I have to work with. I can sit there and stare at it hopelessly, or I can—

"Wait!" I hurry toward Green Mountain, surprising even myself.

She turns. Studies my arm on her sleeve. "Something wrong?"

This woman is your grandmother. She's a part of your Blue Plate Special. A part of you. "Um, you never told me what to call you."

"Whatever suits you." She laughs. "Thelma calls me the Old Fart."

"I was thinking of something, well, maybe . . . you know . . . more . . ." My throat catches. I don't have time to spare so I step forward, drawing my arms around Green Mountain's waist, resting my chin on her shoulder.

She just stands there, motionless. Still, I don't let go. I inhale the smells on her coat, attempting to identify each one. There's a hint of cigarette smoke. A cologne I remember catching a whiff of at Target. And something sweet. Life Savers, maybe.

In a raspy whisper, she says, "Gram's okay. So's Nana. But I'll have none of that *Granny* crap, you hear me? People'll think I'm a hundred friggin' years old."

Even through the layers of clothing, I can feel her heart's steady beat. "I think I like Gram," I tell her.

Finally, her arms lift and land, tightening around my shoulders.

My grandmother hugs me back.

Madeline

"LOOK," THE POLICE OFFICER SAYS, "this woman says she's Leona Fitch, but she doesn't have any ID. She claims you're her daughter and you can verify that she lives here at fourteen and a half Center Street."

People gather below the streetlight.

"What are you staring at?" I yell. It feels good to get angry. Freeing. Like something knotted tight inside me has loosened.

I check my watch—it's close to ten—and turn to my mother. "I need to go someplace. Where's the car?"

She doesn't answer.

I glare at her—at the dry cracks in her lips, the uneven pencil lines drawn above her eyelids, the mascara chunks perched on her lashes. "I asked you something. Where's the goddamn car?"

"Mad'line"—she pouts—"that's notta nice way to talk to yer mother."

"Too bad. I'm through with nice. Nice is for people who don't mind getting walked on. Nice is for losers who take seventeen friggin' years to see what's right in front of them. You don't care about me. Why should I care about you?"

The policeman folds his arms. "Miss, please. We haven't got all night. Are you this woman's daughter? Are you Madeline Fitch?"

The people under the streetlamp crowd closer.

My rage eats a hole through my stomach. I turn to my mother and holler, "You can screw up your own life all you want, but you're done screwing with mine. Do you understand?" I grab her arm. Roughly. "Now, listen to me. I have to go somewhere. To check on someone. Someone who matters to me. So tell me, where's the fucking car?"

"Look," the cop says, "you're not gonna be driving anywhere in the car this woman was operating. There's been an accident. Your mother—if we can determine that's who she is—was at fault. She ran a red light and hit a pickup truck broadside. Totaled both vehicles. Now we need your cooperation."

Horrified, I shrink back. "Was anyone . . . *hurt?*"

He clears his throat, lowers his voice. "A young man—the other driver—was rushed to the hospital."

"Will he be okay?" I ask.

"I can't release any information about his condition at this time."

More people gather to gawk at us. There must be twenty of them now.

"Go home and watch *The Love Boat!*" I shout, waving my hands in the air.

They step back, afraid. I feel powerful.

But then the cop reaches out, as if he might restrain me. He probably thinks I'm a nutcase like my mother. So I act normal. I tell him what he needs to know. "Her name is Leona Fitch," I say calmly. "She's not supposed to drive because of her DWIs. That's why she didn't have a license with her. It was revoked."

I glare at my mother, penetrating her cloudy gaze. I hate those eyes. I hate all they don't see. All they've *never* seen. Like me. The person she gave birth to. Her daughter.

The cop tugs my mother's arm, directing her back down the steps toward the cruiser. He holds the door open and motions her in. After closing it, he turns to me. "Miss, your mother will be spending the night in jail. Will you be all right here alone?"

I want to tell him, *I've been alone my whole life.* But I don't. I've behaved badly enough. "I'm fine. My boyfriend's on his way here to pick me up."

"Well, give him some extra time," the officer says. "Traffic's tied up for miles on account of the accident."

I swallow hard. "It's that bad?"

He nods. "'Fraid so."

My mother watches me through the window. She's crying, and her mascara's running. *I'm sorry,* she mouths, over and over.

Except I don't care that she's sorry. And I don't care that she's crying. I hope they keep her in jail so long she rots. Dissolves to dust. Disappears. Because my mother doesn't matter anymore. What matters is telling Tad I'm pregnant so he can ask me to marry him. He'll be a wonderful daddy and I'll learn to be a mom. That part scares the hell out of me, but with Tad's help I'll figure it out.

As I walk toward the apartment, a song pops into my head—"Desiree," by Neil Diamond. It played on the radio the night Tad and I made love at his trailer while his dad was working—the one time he didn't use a rubber. The time I must've gotten pregnant. I decide that's what I'll name my baby if it's a girl. I place my hands on my stomach. "Desiree," I whisper, "your daddy will love you, just like he loves me. He'll make sure we're happy."

An owl hoots in a nearby tree. I've never heard a real owl before, only a TV owl. I tell myself it's a sign.

Inside, I lock the door to our apartment, glancing outside the window one more time. The sidewalks are empty now. The night is glued together again. Solid and dark. Life will finally work out. Because Tad loves me and he wants a family. I plan to give him everything he wants. Everything will be fine.

Just as soon as he arrives.

Desiree

after we leave ariel
with jeremy's dad,
we drive to a bar in vestal
that doesn't card.
jeremy has a shot of tequila
and follows it up with a beer.
i order a glass of white wine.

we find a table in the corner,
next to a pac-man machine.
when i lean my elbow
on the table, it wobbles,
so jeremy props
a book of matches
underneath one of its legs.

that's jeremy in a nutshell—
the one who makes the wobbling stop.
i pray he can make it stop now,

in this moment we teeter on the edge of,
and the one that will come after that,
because what i am about to tell him
could change our whole life as we know it.

i take a deep breath,
pull my chair closer to his
and lean into his shoulder.
you're shaking, he says,
looping an arm around me.

i sip my wine.
actually, i gulp it—
three big swallows
that warm me up and
make my mouth feel loose
enough to say what it has to.
jeremy, i have to tell you something.
i know i should've told you sooner,
but that guy in wal-mart,
the one with my mother,
her boyfriend,
he—
he—
i can't say it.

jeremy lights himself a cigarette,
then he lights a second one for me.
i haven't smoked since the day
i told him i was pregnant.
i'm tempted,

but i shake my head no.
he what? jeremy asks.

something happened, i whisper
the day I got a ride from him,
and again,
after the harvest dance.
he—he forced me to have sex.
i tried to stop him,
but i couldn't.
jeremy—i start to cry—
he got me pregnant.

jeremy presses his hands
together like he's praying.
he balances his chin on his fingers.
staring into space, his eyes fill.
is he ariel's father?

i reach for his hand, but he pulls away.
jeremy, you're the only father
ariel has ever known.
you'll always be her daddy.
that will never change.

sadness vanishes,
replaced by rage.
i mean biologically, desiree.
is that asshole her biological father?

my bones rattle.
if i were a building,
i'd implode.
i blink back tears.
yes.
jeremy swallows hard.
his adam's apple
leaps up then plummets,
making a dry, scraping sound in his throat.
why didn't you tell me before?

i wanted to, jeremy.
i kept hoping there'd be a right time,
but there never was.
then today,
when i saw them,
when i saw him—

jeremy walks to the bar,
orders two more shots,
slams the empties down so hard
i'm shocked the glass doesn't shatter.
when he returns to our table,
the wobbling starts up again.
what's his name?

larry murdock.

where's he live?

i remember their matching gold bands.
at my mother's, probably.
they're married now.

sick fuck, jeremy mumbles.
he stands, so i stand too.
i'm going alone—he reaches for
the car keys—*wait here.*

as he starts toward the door
i follow him anyway.
he whips around,
jaw clenched.
with fire in his eyes
and fire in his voice, he yells,
i said wait here!
then he's out the door fast.

i watch through the window
as jeremy sprints toward our car,
watch as our green cricket kicks up gravel
as jeremy peels across the lot.

i find a booth in a back corner,
drink another white wine.
when someone drops a glass
i think of the plate
i broke my first day
working at the diner,
recall charlotte's words,
as she shoveled shards into the trash:

relax, honey, it's only a plate.
she was right, i should have relaxed
because look what's broken now—
something that can't be swept up and tossed.
my life.
jeremy's
my baby girl's.
shattered.
i stand,
shovel change
into a vending machine,
punch the buttons for an almond joy,
the first i've paid for.

when i reach to put
my wallet in my pocket
i see dr. stemple's card again.
call me if you're in new york.
i mean that, desiree.
i want to know how you're doing.

glancing at the pay phone,
i tell myself,
you can't call her now,
it's too late.
but my feet move me toward it.
i pull out our long-distance card,
punch in numbers.

four rings.
then silence.

throat clearing.
hello?
my hands shake.
dr. stemple?

yes? who's there?

um, it's desiree.
you know, from the
clover diner in florida?
i'm sorry for calling so late.
you're probably sleeping.
i—i— i start to cry.

desiree,
what's going on?
where are you?

i wrap the phone cord around my finger,
pull until the tip turns blue.
in new york. vestal.
we—we had to come back
because jeremy's mom's
in the hospital and—and—
i'm drowning in a deluge of tears.

is she okay?
dr. stemple asks.

i don't know.
i mean, that's not why i'm upset.

i—i saw someone today.
someone i knew from
before we left new york.
i never wanted to see him again.
but i did.
and everything's changed.
i'm so freaking scared.

desiree,
who are you talking about?

larry.
my mother's boyfriend.
excepts he's her husband now.

desiree, i'm not following you.
what does he have to do
with why you're upset?

i turn my back to the bar,
whisper hoarsely,
before we moved to florida,
he—larry—he raped me.

the syllables scald my tongue.
i taste ash,
swallow hard,
bury the fire in my gut.

oh, desiree,
sweetie, i'm so sorry.

the words hurt to hear—
they're the ones
i wish mam would have offered.
larry got me pregnant, i continue.
except i never told jeremy.
not till tonight.
he just found out that ariel—
that she—

isn't his baby?
she finishes.

yeah.
i feel like i'm going to die.

no, you're not, desiree.
you're going to be okay.
not in the next ten minutes,
but eventually.
please trust that. trust me.
your daughter is counting on you.
now, is jeremy there?
can i talk to him?

no. he took off.
i think he went to look for larry.
he's been gone a long time.

where's ariel?

at jeremy's parents' house.

good.
long pause.
here's what we're going to do.
you and i will stay on the phone
until jeremy gets back.
you shouldn't be alone.

i nod. *okay.*

what are you thinking?

that i screwed everything up.
i should have put ariel up for adoption,
given her a shot at a decent life.
she'd be better off without—

no, desiree!
you and ariel belong together.
no one will ever give her what you can.
she hesitates.
you'd regret losing her
for the rest of your life.

i grip the phone.
what are you saying?

desiree, i was pregnant in high school.
except i didn't keep my baby.
i had my mind made up:
glenn and i would wait until
after college to have children.

but we were never given
the opportunity again.
she sniffs.

i'm sorry i upset you.
i shouldn't have—

desiree,
she interrupts.
don't gamble with things
you might never have a second chance on.

the jukebox cuts off.
the bartender yells, *last call!*
the overhead lights flicker on
and the room goes white
as a bleached sheet.
i wince at the sudden brightness.
the place i'm at is closing now.
i have to go.

do you have somewhere to wait
until jeremy gets back?
i glance outside at a bus cage.
there's a bench inside.
yeah. i mean, yes.

desiree, promise me you'll call
as soon as you know something.

i promise, dr. stemple.

please. lee.

lee.
okay.
thanks.
bye.

i head outside,
duck inside the bus cage,
and wait.
i wait and wait and wait.

* * *

at two a.m. jeremy pulls to the curb.
he leans across the front seat,
pushing open the door on my side.
the dome light blinks on.
ariel's in the back,
asleep in her car carrier,
eyelids pink as seashells.
our suitcases are beside her on the seat.
jeremy says, *get in! fast!*
so i do.

i close my door
and the dome light cuts off,
a moon blackened from the sky.
what's going on? i ask him.
why is ariel with you?
jeremy doesn't answer.

instead he checks his mirrors
before pulling away from the curb.
anyone following me?

i glance around. *no.*
that's when i notice
the blood on his shirt.
jeremy—i touch his sleeve—
what is—how did—?

he pushes my hand away.
i'll tell you when we
get on the highway.

ariel starts to stir,
then cry. i reach for her
and hold her close to me, saying,
mama's baby girl, mama's baby girl,
over and over and over.

* * *

jeremy drives the speed limit,
something he never does.
where are we going? i beg.
can't you at least tell me that?
jeremy check his mirrors again.
home.

home as in florida?

when he nods,
i'm so relieved
i almost forget
about the blood.

* * *

we drive without talking.
we're a mile from the
pennsylvania border
when a police car speeds
to catch up with us—
siren screeching,
red lights slashing gashes
in the black fabric of the night.

shit, jeremy,
what the hell does he want?

jeremy flips on his signal,
pulls to the side of the road.
his head drops against
the steering wheel
and the horn blows.
when he sits upright,
the sound stops.
the silence is deafening.

jeremy feels for my hand,
closing it inside his own.

he stares ahead,
at the exit we should have taken.
remember, dez, i love you.
i'll always love you. and ariel too.
don't let her forget that, okay?
she's my little girl now. all mine.
she'll never have to look at
that fucking bastard again.
and neither will you.
he'll never have
another chance to hurt you.

i choke on my sobs.
j—jeremy, w—what the hell
are you t—talking about?

the cop raps on the window
and jeremy opens his door.
he hands me the car keys,
forces a smile, and says,
drive carefully.
then he steps out
slowly,
lifting
his
arms
in
the
air.

Ariel

It's raining when we leave for home—large, plump drops that look like they'll turn into snow any second—so Mom drives even slower than usual.

Not that I mind. I'm really unsettled about the whole going-home thing. My life feels like a room that's been redone, with new items brought in and old ones removed, and I need time to learn where everything is kept now.

I open the Snapple I bought at the mini-mart where Mom filled Marge's gas tank.

"So . . ." Mom says, not taking her eyes off the road.

Mentally, I prepare myself. Sentences beginning with "So . . ." usually turn out to be questions, ones often related to Shane.

"Shane hasn't called in a while," she goes on. "Is everything okay with you two?"

A slow pain burns in my chest. I stare straight ahead and sip my Snapple. "I've had my phone off," I tell her. "I haven't been in the mood for conversation."

My instincts warn me to glance around. To make sure Shane's not crouched in the backseat, listening. Or driving one of the vehicles speeding past us, reading my lips.

God. When did I become so paranoid?

"Anything you feel like talking about it?" Mom asks.

"Not really. But thanks."

Mom nods and lets it go.

Except I'm wishing she wouldn't this time. I'm wishing she'd ask the typical Mom questions you don't want your mother to ask, but you secretly need her to ask.

I sigh, staring vacantly into space. My eyes come to rest on the wristband fastened like a giant O around Mom's key ring. My dad's name, *Jeremy,* is stamped on the old brown leather, except the spacing is off and the *m* is up too high. Once I asked Mom why she kept the band with her keys, and she said, "Because your dad wanted something of his to be with me wherever I went." Which I thought was really romantic.

Noticing Mom's key ring makes me think of the spare to our house that I forgot to find a new hiding place for. Panicking, I think: What if Shane's let himself in? What if he's sitting on the futon when we get home, drinking Aunt Lee's Dr. Pepper, watching our widescreen TV? Or reading my e-mail, or sprawled out on my bed, plotting his next practical joke?

At that moment, I face the inevitable: that I *will* have to level with Mom. Like, soon. As in, before we get home. Because finding a new hiding place for the key won't do at this point. Too much time has passed. Shane could have made himself a copy by now. Mom'll want to call a locksmith right away.

I'm attempting to decide my best strategy for transitioning into the dreaded topic when Mom flips her turn signal on.

I glance at the clock on the dash. We've only been on the highway forty-five minutes. The trip from Poughkeepsie to Elmira is a pretty straight shot. We stay on Route 17 until we reach the Liberty exit, which is still over an hour away.

Then the obvious occurs to me. "Gotta go, gotta go?" I ask, imitating the bladder control commercial.

Mom shakes her head no and veers onto the exit ramp for Johnson City. Clearly, she's not in a laughing mood.

"Where are you taking us?" I ask.

Mom doesn't answer me. She passes through several lights, then turns down a long, narrow street lined with grungy duplex apartments. She stops in front of a mustard-colored unit that's seriously in need of a paint job. An old olive green sofa sits on the front porch. A rusty pickup truck is parked in the driveway.

"That's where we used to live," she says. "My mother and I."

A confederate flag hangs in the front window. I'm about to say, *You're kidding, right?* But something tells me she's not.

Mom points to a door off the porch. "The stairs were just inside. Our apartment was on the second floor." She smiles. "It was on the other side of that very door that I felt you move for the first time. Actually, you kind of *fluttered.* That's the night I knew you were a girl."

Mom's smile fades. She grimaces, like a kid whose hair has been pulled.

"Mom, what?"

"Nothing. Never mind."

"Come on, tell me."

Mom blinks back tears. "Do you remember that night, Ariel? It was right after the Harvest Dance. Jeremy walked me to the door, then he left. When I was inside, in the foyer—well, something bad happened. And I've always wondered if you recall anything about it, but I've been so afraid to ask you because—"

"Mom, stop!" I laugh uncomfortably. "How could I remember something the night of your dance? I wasn't even *born* yet."

"Yes," she says, sounding relieved. "Yes, of course, you're right." Then she shifts Marge into drive.

Except she doesn't retrace her tracks, back onto Route 17.

"Where now?" I ask.

"To the cemetery," she says, gripping the steering wheel. "I need to see Larry Murdock's grave. I need to know where he's buried."

* * *

Ten minutes later, we pass a deserted-looking school called Cherry Hill Academy. Just past that, Mom takes a left into Cherry Hill Cemetery. God, I can't imagine going to a high school that shares a name with a graveyard.

We pass through a gated entrance and park beside a building marked Office. Inside the office, a man sits at a desk. His dark eyes are sunken, and he reminds me of Uncle Fester on *The Addams Family*. Mom tells him who we're looking for.

"*The* Larry Murdock?" he asks. "The fella killed by that high-school boy?"

Mom nods.

The man rifles through a stack of papers. "Kid's still in prison, I hear. 'Cept he wouldn't be a kid anymore. He'd have to be—oh, close to thirty, I'd say."

"Thirty-two," Mom corrects him.

"That so?" The man wheels his chair across the room, stopping in front of a computer. His monitor is one of those old-fashioned, putty-colored things, the size of a microwave oven. He pokes several keys and a paper appears in the printer tray. Handing it to Mom, he says, "Section C-12. Straight up the hill. Take your third left. This map'll help you find your way."

Mom thanks him and we turn to leave.

"Say," the man calls, "are you by any chance related to that Murdock fella? 'Cause you"—he narrows his Uncle Fester eyes at me—"you look a little like them pictures of him they ran in the newspaper."

Mom ignores him, hurrying us both through the door.

* * *

Mom navigates the narrow lanes, and I watch the map.

"Just ahead," I say, and she parks beside an old rusty water pump.

Our shoes crunch across the grass, still green beneath a layer of frost. I shiver from a sudden chill. Except it's an okay chill, more like a tickle of energy than something cold or foreboding.

Here and there, flags poke out of the soil. For Veterans Day, I'm assuming. The idea seems really odd—decorating graves for the dead when only the living can see them.

As we weave in and out through the markers, Mom reads names off the stones. "Arnold . . . Koslowski . . . Sherman . . . Bellavance . . . Hillman . . ."

It's hard to believe that every one of these graves represents someone who used to be alive, *above* the earth like Mom and me, and now they're *below* it, decomposing. I decide when I die I'll be cremated. That way no one will walk on me, muttering my name, while they search for someone else.

In the distance, I hear water bubbling. At the top of a hill just ahead, I find the source. "Mom, look. A fountain." I start toward the large marble structure, which is almost as tall as I am. Water cascades down the sides, spilling into a basin below. Just beyond it is a giant, white concrete angel, spreading her massive wings, which are dotted with spray.

I sit on a low flat stone and brush leaves away from the inscription. I feel sad when I realize the angel's for a really young girl named Sophie DeSalvo. She was only two when she died.

When I stand again, I notice a rose-colored headstone—two rows over from Sophie's. "Mom," I say softly, "I found it."

Mom follows me. "My God," she says, staring at the stone.

There are two names, separated by a column of ivy, meticulously etched down the center. The left-hand side reads:

LAWRENCE JAMES MURDOCK

APRIL 3, 1958–AUGUST 15, 1994

The second name, the name beside his, is my grandmother's, Madeline Fitch Murdock, except only the birth date is filled in. As I study it, I think to myself: *Next month, she'll turn fifty. If she survives.*

Suddenly I get this feeling. And like Mom said she knew—long before I was born—that I'd be a girl, I know my grandmother will live. Maybe not until she's ninety but long enough for me to get to know her.

Mom loops her arm through mine. "Sometimes I wonder how my life would be different if my mother hadn't met Larry Murdock. I wouldn't have gone through what I did, and your dad wouldn't be serving time." She turns, touching my cheek. "But I wouldn't have you, either. And you're the best thing that's ever happened to me."

I hug her and we turn to leave, weaving around the same stones we passed.

Hillman. Bellavance. Sherman. Koslowski. Arnold.

Off to my right, I notice a freshly dug hole, obviously waiting for an occupant. There's a bench beside the gaping black rectangle.

"Hey, Mom?" I call.

Several steps ahead, she turns. "Yes?"

"I, um, I just need a minute alone. I'll meet you at the car, okay?"

"Are you all right?" she asks me.

"Yeah," I answer, "I'm fine." Which is the truth. I feel strangely solid here.

Mom waves, ambling back toward Marge.

I sit on the bench, reach in my jacket for my cell, and power it on. 17 MISSED CALLS.

I have to talk to Shane before I leave this place. I don't know why. It's just a hunch. A very strong hunch. But before I can enter a command, "Only U" by Ashanti plays.

I stare at the name on the screen. *Shane.* Who else.

My mouth is dry. I search my pocket for a mint or a piece of gum. Anything. But I come up empty. I push Answer and hold the phone to my ear. "Hello?"

"Jesus fucking Christ, Ariel! Where the hell have you been?"

My heart pounds in my throat. I feel the same way I did in my grandmother's room when my finger was stuck in the Chinese handcuffs. Cornered. Trapped.

I hold the phone away from my ear. Calmly, I say, "Don't yell."

"I've been worried out of my fucking mind about—"

"Don't yell!" I repeat. Louder.

I connect with a sudden strength, and I have no clue where it's coming from. Maybe from Sophie DeSalvo's angel. Or from my grandmother. Or—how bizarre to even think this—from Larry Murdock, offering me courage as a redeeming gesture.

"Look," Shane says, quietly now, "it's been driving me crazy, not being able to get a hold of you, babe, I—"

"My grandmother's going home today," I interrupt.

"Huh?"

"I *said,* 'My grandmother's going home today.' Since you forgot to ask how she's doing, I thought you'd want me to tell you."

"Oh, yeah. Sure."

"She's starting chemo Thursday." I take a deep breath and let it out. "I think she's going to be okay. No one's said that officially. But something tells me she will be."

"Hey, that's great. Congrats. So, um, when can I see you?"

"Shane, have you heard a word I've said?"

"Sure. Family crap. Whatever. But I—"

Impulsively, I snap the phone closed. I've never done anything like that before. Not to Shane or anyone.

Seconds later, "Only U" plays.

And at that precise moment, I get it. The Big IT, as Liv would say. I know why Shane picked that song for our ringtones. Because everything in Shane's world *is* only me, and everything in my world is supposed to be all about *him.* Completely. There's no room for anyone else in this claustrophobic universe he envisions for us. Not Liv. Not my mom. Not my grandmother. No one.

I push Talk. Wait.

"Ariel? What happened?"

"I've gotta go, Shane. My mom's waiting in the car for me."

"Hang on. Where are you?"

I remember the tracking device on my cell. Shane's been treating me like a pet on a leash. "Why don't you just check your spy phone?" I snap.

"Hey, Ariel, chill." Shane laughs. A laugh that I suddenly recognize for what it is. Condescending. "I'm just making conversation."

"No, Shane. It's not called conversation. It's called control. You always have to know where I am. Who I talk to. Who I spend my time with. When I'm—"

"That's ridiculous! I let you go away this weekend, didn't I?"

"You *let* me go away? Excuse me?"

"You're stressed, babe. It's all the family crap that's—"

"Stop calling it family crap! We're talking about people's lives here! People who are related to me!"

"Look, call me when you get home, okay? I'll pick you up and we can—"

"No!" I blurt out, dangerously close to crying. But I refuse to break down. I swallow hard and talk slowly, carefully, like annunciating each word might help me fend off tears. "I don't want to go anywhere tonight, Shane. I'm tired. I want to stay home and take a hot bath and call my best friend, Olivia, then crash in front of the TV with a pint of Cherry Garcia."

There's a long silence.

"That's it?" Shane yells. "I haven't seen you since Thursday, and calling your fucking friend with the fucking faggot fathers is more important than *me*?"

I glance back at the parking lot, where Mom's waiting, then down at the dark, open grave. I think of the Chinese handcuffs again. And how I couldn't escape by pulling away. Resistance did nothing. I had to stop struggling and relax. I got free by giving up the fight.

Lean in, my grandmother tells me.

Firmly but gently, I say, "I'm going to hang up now, Shane." Then I clap the phone closed.

Lean in, she tells me again.

I lift my arm. Stretch it out. Across the dark, open grave.

Lean in, lean in, lean in. She won't let up until I listen.

I stop struggling.

Relax.

Give up the fight.

Let go.

I.

Let.

Go.

I watch my phone drop in slow motion.

When it hits bottom, seconds or minutes or hours later, I kick a clump of dirt over the top.

The battery will probably die out soon. Mom and I will be home by then. My grandmother will be too. Wherever *her* home is. Someday soon, I'll find out.

The phone rings, muffled by the rich, brown earth. As "Only U" plays to the specks of new-falling snow, I turn and walk toward our car.

When I slide in the front seat, Mom's studying the strip of arcade photos my grandmother gave me.

"She really *was* young once," Mom says without looking up.

I roll my eyes. "You're just now figuring that out?"

Mom tucks the photos in the side pocket of my backpack. Then she smiles and shifts into gear. "Yeah. Maybe I am."

Author's Note

If you are a victim of sexual crime, you are not alone and help is available. The National Sexual Assault Hotline, at 1-800-656-HOPE, provides free, confidential help 24 hours a day, 7 days a week. Services for adolescents are also available online on the RAINN (Rape, Abuse, and Incest National Network) Web site. Visit them at www.rainn.org and click on 24/7 Online Hotline.

Acknowledgments

Heartfelt thanks to everyone at Chronicle Books—especially my editor, Julie Romeis—for believing in *Blue Plate Special* and honoring it as Chronicle's first young adult novel. Thanks to Peg Davol for repeated readings and helpful critiques as the novel grew and changed; Steve Blenus for behind-the-scenes support with technological snafus so I could focus on the business of writing; my Tuesday Night Group for insightful suggestions for several chapters; and Barbara Burrows, my rock, for being there from square one and offering encouraging words, iced coffee, and sandwiches, and whatever else the moment called for. *Sei uno spettacolo!*